SAVING KINGS

Martin J. Roddini

DEDICATION

This book is dedicated to the memory of Grace and Martin, the pillars in my life, and to my wife, Lisa, without whose loving support this book would not exist, and to my three children: Donna, Marty and Bobby.

Chapter One

Payback's a Bitch

From a somewhat slanted viewpoint, a cold, snowy November Saturday could only bring delight to two types of individuals: skiers and thieves. There wasn't too much room to ski on Kings Bay Boulevard and Kings Highway, but there were plenty of purses to snatch and stores to steal from inside the Shopping Mall. At the Three Kings Shopping Mall, three kings because the Mall was in Kings County, in the Kings Bay area of Brooklyn and adjacent to Kings Highway, Christmas shopping had already begun as many people were trying to get an early start on the holiday rush. At 10:30

am, the inside parking lot was already full, and the outside lot was quickly reaching capacity. The flow of shoppers was so great that the newly installed electronic doors seemed to remain in the "open" position for most of the time. Already, one had to wait in line at any one of the fast-food places before he or she could sit down and enjoy a quick breakfast of a buttered roll and a cup of coffee. However, hustle and bustle just seemed to add to the air of excitement as Christmas quickly approached. Having waited approximately thirty minutes for a seat at the bunnery, Tony and Marty were just starting on their buttered rolls and coffee when the public address system blared the announcement that "maintenance ninety-nine" was wanted. This was a prearranged code for any police officers in the Mall to immediately contact the security office. Since Tony needed his morning coffee to actually start the rhythmic beating of his heart, Marty left for the "dial-in." He walked past the center island of the Mall and entered a door that read: "Employees Only." The door led to the delivery entrances of the individual retail stores. The major anchor stores have their own trucking ports. Once through the door, on the adjacent wall, Marty found the Mall intercom phone. He dialed the security office number, and a male voice answered

"Hello, this is the Security Office. Can I help you?"

"Yeah, hello this is Detective Iniddor responding to the code ninety-nine signal." Bob Baxter, the Security Director, answered: "Marty, this is Bob. It seems that we have two suspicious males looking over Best Jewelry Store on the lower level. I already sent two security guards into the area, but I'd like you to know what's going on, just in case." The store owners were ordinarily nervous, but the holidays amplified their paranoia. It became obvious that the jitters had also penetrated the flow of operations in the Mall security office, and so, Marty reluctantly responded: "Okay, Bob. Give me the descriptions and we'll take a look."

"They are two males, one is black, approximately six feet, wearing a tan overcoat; and one male white, approximately five foot ten, wearing a black leather jacket. They are both about thirty-five to forty years old, and they have been there for a good twenty minutes." Marty heard the alarm in Bob's voice and answered: "Okay, Bob. We're on the way." Marty knew from past experience that Bob Baxter would be sitting on pins and needles until he heard an "all clear" from the detectives. Security Director Bob Baxter is a retired New York City Police Department Sergeant, who is just as nervous now as he was then. Probably even more so now since his job was totally dependent upon his performance evaluation.

The jewelry store was at the other end of the Mall, and it would take about five minutes to get there. Marty could just imagine what Tony's reaction was going to be: "That nervous son-of-a-bitch is worse than a dog in heat. I can see what kind of a day this is going to be already; I can't even enjoy a cup of coffee. We'll go over there now, take care of business, and then stop in the Security Office and tell Baxter that he has to buy us a real breakfast." Anyone who knows Tony can tell you that he does not like to be disturbed whenever he is eating or fucking – and probably in that order. You couldn't tell by looking at him, but Tony had an enormous appetite which he continuously attempted to satisfy. So, you could imagine his chagrin at having been interrupted during breakfast, or at least the start of breakfast.

Weaving through the morning holiday shopping crowds is an art in and of itself, but the two detectives were able to negotiate turns and detours arriving in time to observe the two "suspicious" males who were now standing just to the right of the entrance to Best Jewelry. One of the males, the black one, looking over his shoulder, caught Marty and Tony looking. He nodded his observation to the two detectives, and Marty and Tony just kept on walking. Detectives Barry and Goosman from Central Robbery were apparently on a stake-out, and Marty and Tony were not going to be the ones to blow it. That's a major problem with the Police Department, no one knows what anyone else is doing. There was no contact with the Brooklyn South

Detective Squad to notify them that a central unit was working in the Mall. Unfortunately, this occurred much too often and was looked at as a common practice.

Tony Ossur and Marty Iniddor maneuvered their way back to Baxter's office where they informed him that the two suspicious males were good guys, and that there was no need for further worry. Bob Baxter lashed out: "Why wasn't I informed that Robbery Detectives were working the Mall? How come I didn't know about it?" Tony didn't take to Baxter's tone or query: "Because we don't have to check with you on any and all police actions taken in the Mall." Tony didn't want to admit to Baxter that they weren't even informed about the stake-out, and it was in their area. Marty tried to smooth things over: "We do it mostly as a professional courtesy letting you know whenever we can. These guys are from Central Robbery, and sometimes they don't even talk to us." Tony Interrupted: "Let's go to breakfast, Bob, and I'll try to explain things that you should already know or have already forgotten." Little did Security Director Bob Baxter realize that Tony's invitation meant that Bob would be paying. Tony seemed to revel in the satisfaction of sticking it to Baxter. Tony felt that retired Sergeant Robert Baxter owed him a few comebacks from his time on the job.

Bob Baxter had been the supervisor of the plainclothes unit assigned to public morals offenses in

Manhattan South. Tony Ossur was the senior detective in the unit when Baxter took over command of the unit. They didn't hit it off from the get-go. It was either Baxter wanting to leave no doubt who was the boss, or Tony letting him know that he, the senior detective, was the one who unofficially ran the office or both. No matter the situation, it was obvious that there was a clash of personalities. Unfortunately for Tony, Bob Baxter would have the last say since he had passed a civil service examination that promoted him to the rank of "Sergeant."

It was a hot August night, and the unit had gotten a squeal on a new sex joint at East 28th Street between Lexington and Park Avenues. They were going to "take" the house and get on the sheet for the month. This one police action would take care of the necessary activity for the entire office for the month of August. Their activity sheet would be full. At 0100 hours (1:00 am), ten detectives listened to the instructions from newly appointed supervisor, Sergeant Bob Baxter, on the dangers and pitfalls of "taking down" a house of prostitution. All of Tony's inserted well-intentioned suggestions were immediately rejected and, in fact, the final preparatory outline was probably in direct opposition to Detective Ossur's recommendations and his way of thinking. Just for the mere sake of Tony's success record, the unit had come to respect and follow Detective Ossur's police strategies. He had been doing this type of work for a long time and had shown a great deal of street savvy when it came to vice. Also, for the most part, Tony was a likable guy and deemed a "team player."

However, newly appointed, and insecure Sergeant Baxter assumed that a power play was taking place. So, he took the opportunity to make sure that no doubt remained in the mind of anyone in the office that there was only one boss, Bob Baxter. He emphasized to the group that his orders and guidelines were to be followed to the letter. To the Sergeant's credit, the raid went down surprisingly well, without much of a hitch. A problem arose, however, when one of the females who was being arrested, pleaded to Detective Ossur that she was not on the scene but was just speaking to another person in the rear yard vicinity of the building. In court, this particular arrest might be thrown out, and it became apparent to those listening that Tony had previously known this woman from other times and other places. The woman was apparently attempting to broker a deal where she would supply future information if things were to go easy on her tonight. Anyone who knows the street and had documented plainclothes police arrest experience, would probably take her up on the proposed deal and cultivate a "confidential informant," especially since she was not technically involved in the "house."

Tony seized the opportunity and informed the woman that she now owed him. However, Sergeant Baxter, who was within earshot of the informal understanding between Detective Ossur and the unidentified subject, immediately intervened and nixed the whole idea. Bob Baxter had spent all of his nine years in the Department with the Communications Unit and was definitely demonstrating his unfamiliarity with the street, and especially vice. He viewed this tete-et-tete as an infraction of the rules and a total disregard of ethics on the part of one of his officers. A heated argument ensued. Tony had already solidified the agreement and to back down now would only serve for Tony to lose face in the street. Experience showed that you cannot work the street, especially in a unit like this, if you cannot be taken at your word. Tony had given his!

Tony's potential "confidential informant" was arrested and on the report of Sergeant Baxter, Tony had to appear before the Chief of Detectives to justify what was deemed "unauthorized actions." As a result of the meeting and the direct influence of Bob Baxter, Detective Tony Ossur was bounced out of the Manhattan South Public Morals Unit and transferred to routine detective duty in the Brooklyn South Detective Squad. If it wasn't for Tony's long-standing successes, unblemished record, and most importantly, a phone call from a legislator whom Tony once saved from a potentially embarrassing situation, he most likely would have gotten official "specifications and charges." These would certainly have come with more stringent disciplinary punishment.

It was, therefore, a pleasure for Tony to have breakfast on Baxter. In any small way that Tony could fuck his former supervisor would be a moment of enjoyment. However, Tony really wanted more, and he knew that the time would come when the tables would be turned. As far as Tony was concerned, they always did. There would be a time when Detective Tony Ossur's actions or lack thereof, would control the fate of former Sergeant Bob Baxter. What Tony did not know is that the time was right around the corner.

One could only imagine how thrilled Tony was when he originally heard that his former supervisor had retired and landed the security position at Three Kings Shopping Mall - the same shopping mall that falls into the jurisdiction of the Brooklyn South Detective Squad — Tony's squad. It had become a lot less difficult to meter out what Tony perceived as justified revenge.

Chapter Two

The Crew

The 65th Precinct housed a number of specialized units including Mounted Unit A. It was nauseatingly obvious that every workday introduced you to the pungent and sickening aroma of horseshit. Though the entire building shared in this aromatic wealth, the office of the Brooklyn South Detectives was located on the second floor directly above the stables. The squad, therefore, had the cream of the crap at their immediate sniffing levels. In the beginning, it acts as a great asset for those who are trying to shed pounds and stick to a disciplined diet. However, after a while one even gets used to smelling one substance and enjoying another, necessity becoming the mother of invention. In fact, this strategic location might have been the "stable" influence that allowed for a minimum number of visits by outside bosses. That notwithstanding, it is correct to assume that the Brooklyn South Office was most efficiently run. As long as the ratings had nothing to do with class, the Brooklyn South Detectives were on top of the list for productivity and results.

In no small way was this due to the efforts of the boss, Sergeant Mario Dello. Sergeant Del, as most of the guys referred to him, is a man who never aged, but who has the experience of approximately thirty years of police work. There wasn't too much that he hadn't seen. He also had the ability to maintain a calming air when things seemed to be heading toward a climactic uproar in the office. With news reporters hounding for specifics on a particular case, and bosses wanting immediate results, Sergeant Del kept a cool level track and held the reins on the rest of the office. Nothing really riled him. Ironically, it might have been this lack of flamboyance and flair that retarded his career growth in the Department. One must make a name for himself even if it includes hurting and stepping-on fellow workers. It is the standout who receives political appointments on the job. The position of Supervisor of the Brooklyn South Squad was not the most sought-after job in the detective ranks; but in spite of that, Mario Dello remained a nice guy. When things needed to be done, the hierarchy would not hesitate in asking Del and his squad to perform. So even though the Sarge and the Squad were not considered the classiest act in the Detective Division, they demanded a certain amount of respect.

Brooklyn South covered thirteen precincts and extended from Eastern Parkway, south to the Queens line, and from Bensonhurst and Red Hook east to East New York. If it was going to happen, it would happen in Brooklyn South. The make-up of the office was just about as reflective of the ethnic make-up of the areas served.

Jim Jones and Frank Austin made up the black contingent bringing both narcotics background and street savvy with them. Jones had 15 years on the job and Austin was completing his 13th. They knew the job and had good communication with the street. In fact, because of the ease with which Jimmy could call a squeal and get immediate results - facts that would take anyone else days to uncover - he earned the nickname of the "operator." Always breaking Jimmy's balls about getting off the phone was Detective Juan Medina who seemed to have more broads than the local pimp. Juan came from Vice and probably carried over some of the "important" numbers with him. He spent six years in Public Morals, two in sex crimes and three in uniform. Juan's bi-lingual abilities in Spanish and English proved to be an asset to both him and the entire office. Angel Torres and Ralph Clemengas learned a lot from Juan, while Juan got a certain amount of pleasure and enjoyment in being able to teach the ropes to two other Spanish Cops.

Torres was born in Puerto Rico and stayed there until he was a teenager. He came here to live with his aunt and uncle who promised to help him find work. What he found was a town that did not like Puerto Ricans who could only speak Spanish, and a community that was not flourishing in the wealth of America as he had been told. He took the police test because there was nothing better to do, and it paid more money than most other jobs available. He still carried a strong Hispanic accent and a prejudice against those Ricans who would rather sell drugs, do crimes, and collect welfare than work. For the past twelve years, he committed himself to bettering the Spanish Community through dedicated police work.

Ralph Clemengas was Angel's nemesis. He was an opportunist who would do the least amount and try to get the most out of it. To say that the two of them did not see eye-to-eye would be an understatement. It was not the caliber or quality of his work that kept Clemengas in the unit, but rather a genetic inheritance. He spoke fluent street Spanish, was born in New York, and his coloring allowed him to also work as a Black undercover. He could be used in a variety of situations. He was quite aware of his value and played it to the hilt whenever he could. He milked as many cases as possible and always carried the lowest caseload. Clemengas was lazy and had been getting away with it for ten years. Because of his street familiarity and knowledge of youth gangs, he was taken right out of the academy, as a rookie, and put into an undercover role which lasted for about a year. Clemengas' work ultimately entitled him to the Detective Gold Shield and the assignment to Brooklyn South. He has been resting on his laurels for the last seven years. According to Juan, however, Clemengas could be a damned good cop, if he tried.

Ira Jacobs spent nine years of his past seventeen on "tit" jobs. His assignments spanned the gamut, from driving and delivering the mail, to transferring vehicles from the Quarter master, to individual precincts. He even clocked some time working in the Chaplain's Office. Then, whether he needed more money or just became bored with what he was doing, he made a phone call to one of his well-connected "rabbis," and was transferred as a police officer to the Detective Division. After approximately one year and his "rabbis" still pushing for him, Ira was officially promoted to and received his gold shield with the accompanying pay raise.

While in uniform, Ira had met Police Officer Gary Glasser, and for a short time was his patrol partner. They became good friends and kept in touch even after Ira got his transfer. Shortly after Jacobs' arrival in Brooklyn South, Gary was transferred to a detective unit in Queens. It was not long after that, that Ira made another phone call, and Gary was added to the roster of those detectives assigned to Brooklyn South. In contrast to Ira, however, Gary was glad to be where he was and wanted to earn his place in the squad.

It was Gary who intervened between Ira and Nick one night when it seemed that there would definitely be bloodshed. Detective Nick Possidos was a loner who sacrificed efficiency for the sake of speed. He hardly ever spoke. Even subjects like family, baseball, or even food did not wet his verbal appetite. He only spoke about the job, and that was on a need-to-know basis. At times, because of his rather inefficient investigative report writing, Sergeant Mario Dello, the Squad Supervisor of the unit, would assign another member of the squad to tie together the loose ends of Nick's cases. This particular night, Ira, Gary and Nick were alone working in the office. Ira had been given another one of Nick's cases to "clean-up." Being in an annoyed mood, Ira decided to badger the Greek about it. The office learned that night that Nick had a very bad temper. He jumped over the desk and started swinging at Ira who was about five inches shorter than the Greek. If Gary hadn't jumped in, Nick would have added a few swollen inches to Ira's already Jewish nose.

Maybe because of the fact that they were seasoned cops (another term for "old timers"), or maybe because they tried to avoid the obvious politics of the office, Tony and Marty were often called upon to unofficially settle differences, especially when personalities conflicted. They worked well together. In relationships, especially of the heart, it is said that opposites attract. In this particular case, having nothing to do with the pangs of the heart, the adage could not ring truer. Rather than to enumerate all those opposing likes and dislikes, let it suffice to say that Detectives Tony Ossur and Marty Iniddor agreed on three specific items: they both needed more money than they were paid, they were both looking forward to retirement, and for reasons known to them alone, they shortened their surnames. In addition to whatever reasoning they personally had, the names "Ossurighetti" and "Iniddoriglio" had trouble fitting on the standard police department forms. So, the decision to "shorten" turned out to be a good one.

As Tony was being transferred out of Manhattan South Public Morals to the Brooklyn South Detective Squad, Marty was returning from a six-month temporary special assignment working with the city colleges to implement a more realistic Criminal Justice curriculum for future police candidates. Sergeant Dello, always just referred to as Del, had been asked by the Chief to submit a name from the squad as a possible choice to work with the Police Academy and the Board of Higher Education. Since Del knew that Marty had earned a Master's Degree and enjoyed a good intellectual challenge, the Sergeant submitted Detective Iniddor's name.

Although it had originally been a welcomed change, the assignment became frustrating, annoying, arduous, and confusing. However, the assignment was successfully completed, and the new curriculum was well on its way. It made the Chief, Sergeant Del and Detective Iniddor look exceptionally good when evaluation time came around.

While Marty had been on the special assignment, his former partner was promoted to Sergeant, and following the customary procedure, was transferred out of the squad. So, when Detective Iniddor returned, he was the odd man out not having a steady partner. When Tony arrived, therefore, it was a natural fit to partner Marty up with the newly arrived transfer. They clicked and came to know each other pretty well as time went on. They depended on that knowledge out in the street.

Knowing how your partner is going to react, and what he probably will do can actually determine one's survival in the war of the good guys versus the bad. It is also important to understand the things that might disturb or annoy a partner. For instance, looking at Tony, one would not fathom that his fear of heights even bothered him in nightmares – Marty knew. Likewise, no one would suspect that Marty, who conducted college seminars and addressed large audiences in his police career, was an inherently shy individual even to the point of abnormality - Tony knew. Being long time partners involuntarily breaks the personal and confidential barriers that we all hold so dear. It is no secret that police spouses envy the relationship that builds between partners, since it is said that partners know each other better and spend more time together than husband and wife.

Chapter Three

The House on Maple Street

"Hey Iniddor, these prints came back from forensic for you."

"Thanks Sarge, I've been waiting on them." Marty and Tony had been working on a burglary for a few weeks. The burglar entered at approximately two or three in the morning, surprised the sleeping man and woman, and ultimately had the wife tie up her husband. The perpetrator then took the wife with him throughout the house and chose those items that were most valuable and easily pawned. He put the items in a pillowcase and left the bulging bag at the front door for a quick escape.

However, before he left, he beat and raped the woman in full sight of her helpless husband. There were five such cases with the same Modus Operandi (MO). These particular types of crimes boiled the blood of most police officers, and Tony and Marty were no exceptions to the rule. The burglar-rapist had all of East Flatbush in a state of fear. The last incident, his fifth attack, involved a newlywed couple who had arrived from Germany just six months ago. During the sex attack, the young woman put up a fierce struggle, and amongst other things, ripped off one of her assailant's gloves. Her screams alerted neighbors, and the burglar had to make an unscheduled quick getaway. In his anxiety to silence the woman, he picked up the nearest object to him and split her head wide open. Hedda Fernback was still in a coma, and her husband, Douglas, called the Squad Office every day. The piece of vanity mirror used by the perpetrator caused a deep laceration of the skull, and Hedda had lost an extreme amount of blood. Excellent and painstaking latent fingerprint work produced two readable prints from the mirror.

Marty beamed with satisfaction: "Tony, we got a definite hit on the prints. The son of a bitch's last known address is on Maple Street between Albany and Troy." Tony smiled like the cat who caught the canary: "Hey Medina, how about you and Jones giving us a backup on this guy." Juan had just returned from court, and Jimmy was finishing some paperwork. "Say when," was their joint response. As the four detectives went to their cars, a plan of action for the collar was formulated. On the way over to the house, Marty was perusing the yellow sheet that accompanied the prints. The perpetrator had been arrested six times: three for Burglary, one for Grand Larceny, and two for Assault - the last of which resulted in the issuance of an active warrant for escape. This scum tooth was no novice to the system, and he apparently was improving the quality of his burglary attempts by spicing them up with sexual assaults. What the hell, if he could get away with it, why not? So, besides the local press clamoring for an end to this spree, the squad personally wanted to deal with the guy. Before leaving the office, Del wished them the best: "Don't come back without him!"

The house on Maple Street showed no outward signs of decay as did many of the other surrounding homes. With this one, the decay was inside! At one time, the area was filled with very affluent people, and the community was a prosperous well-to-do neighborhood. However, the past fifteen years showed a slow but noticeable change as white flight hit.

One-fourteen Maple Street was a one family house situated on the North side of the street between Albany and

Troy Avenues. There was no sign of activity inside the house, as the squad watched for a few minutes before getting out and beginning their plan of attack. His past record indicated that Reggie Bennett was not one to usually carry a gun in the commission of his crimes. Although Marty and Tony were not disregarding a gun as a possible option, they felt more relaxed in executing the arrest. They knew from past experience that the perpetrator would try to escape in any way left open to him: crashing through a window, breaking a cellar door or even bursting right through the entrance.

This guy, in particular, did not want to get nabbed because he would be looking at a return to prison for a long, long time. Juan got impatient: "Well, let's get him now before it gets dark and the odds go in his favor." It was approximately 5:30 p.m. and the winter night was beginning to take hold. Marty took charge and positioned the Detective assault: "Juan, you and Jimmy take the rear door and watch for the possibility of a side window breakthrough. Tony and I will take the front. Keep your portable on frequency one." Juan began to go down the side alley when Jimmy stopped him and whispered: "Did anybody bring their vests?" "Yeah", said Juan, "they're in the car."

Iniddor and Ossur were no strangers to announcing arrests, identifying yourself, asking for an invitation inside, and then announcing the collar. Sometimes it went smoothly, other times - well. Just before knocking Marty checked: "You in position, Juan?" The portable squawked back in a low, almost inaudible whisper: "Let's do it." Standing at the side of the front door, Marty knocked. A female came to the solid wooden door and, without opening it, asked who it was. "We'd like to speak to Reggie, is he in?" She repeated her question: "Who is it please?"

"It's the police, mam, we'd like to speak with Reggie." The door opened and a woman of approximately 45 years inquired as to the nature of the visit. Disregarding her inquiry, Tony pressed: "Where is Reggie?" The response came surprisingly quick: "He's upstairs sleeping." As Marty asked her to get her son, there was a yell on the portable: "He's outside the rear bedroom window, and the bastard is going to jump into the neighbor's yard." Tony ran up the stairs and Marty ran out the door to the neighbor's yard which was bounded by huge evergreen bushes. As he ran, Marty laughingly yelled back to Tony: "Whatever you do, don't jump after him." Tony, to offset the degrading humor, determinedly answered: "I'll get the fuck before he jumps."

There was no way Tony would even attempt a jump. Marty knew that his partner didn't like being near the edge - one flight up. Bennett was twenty-four and recovered well from his leap and landing. He was making good his escape through the neighbor's alley when Iniddor turned into the alley, and they came face to face. Being six foot four and swift of foot, Bennett jumped and landed on Marty's chest before he could even yell "Police." As they wrestled and fell to the floor throwing punches, Tony arrived. With one swift kick to the head, Reggie Bennett slumped over and resisted no more. Tony took no shit from anyone. You wanted to play the game, you got caught, you lost. A philosophy that he carried throughout the job. However, where another cop might have added a few more well positioned shots, Tony just assisted in the handcuffing. He had no use for abuse. Getting himself together, Marty looked at Tony: "Hey, I didn't disturb you, did I? Where the fuck were you?"

"I was tiptoeing down from the second-floor rooftop, Hump. You're lucky I came at all after you set me up like that." Marty retorted: "The only way you beat your fears, pantyass, is to face them." Tony grabbed his crotch and ended the quick ventilation session with: "Face this!"

Juan and Jimmy took Bennett to County Hospital and then to the precinct, while Tony and Marty interviewed Mrs. Andrea Bennett about her son. She didn't want to believe that her son was once again involved in something criminal. After informing her that Reggie had been arrested for burglary and sexual assault, and that she could meet him in night court in about four hours, they asked if they could take a look into Reggie's room. Figuring that cooperation might make things easier for her son, Mrs. Bennett accompanied the two detectives upstairs and into the room.

Circumventing a search warrant, they proceeded to look for items that could be connected to the past burglaries. In a closet, on the bottom shelf behind two pairs of sneakers was a shoe box filled with various bracelets, necklaces, watches and rings, none of which Mrs. Bennett recognized. Inscriptions on some of the articles matched the names of past complainants. The detectives had struck gold and were well on their way to an airtight case against the East Flatbush Burglar.

"Congratulations guys on a job well done." Del was happier than a pig in shit. "I notified the local papers and civic groups, and they all want to speak with you two. In fact, channel two news is already on the way." Marty smiled: "Did the Chief mention anything about a promotion?" Del answered: "No, but he said that he'll let you and Tony stay in the squad." These good-natured jabs were only intended to re-emphasize the fact that Detectives felt they were underpaid, and if anyone, especially the bosses, were listening, maybe some type of promotional increase would come as reward for good work. However, as was the case most of the time, the jabbering fell on deaf ears, and as one captain said: "The reward for good work is more work." The captain worked himself into a disability retirement caused by a nervous breakdown - some reward!

As Tony and Marty were processing some of the arrest paperwork, the phone rang: "Hey Iniddor, it's for you."

"Thanks, Jimmy. Hello, Detective Iniddor speaking." "Yes Detective, this is Dr. Rouch at County Hospital." "Hi, Doc. What can I do for you?"

"I have to inform you that Hedda Fernback died at 6:05 this evening. Your name appears on the police report, and I thought you would want to know."

"Yes, thanks Doc." Marty turned to Del: "Charge Bennett with Felony Murder. Fernback just died at the County."

Ira Jacobs overheard and looked up with almost an eye of envy and said: "Boy, the news people are going to eat this one up. You guys will be able to name your own ticket." Marty shook his head in disgust, and Tony looked directly at Jacobs: "Fuck you and the news people. A twenty-five-year-old woman just died for no reason." Del broke in: "The news people from channel two are here, and they want to talk to both of you. I'll go out to them now and bring them in here in about five minutes. Think about what you want to say and remember that they're doing a job just like we are." "Hey Sarge, I have a better idea. Why don't you let Jacobs take the interview? He knows all about the case and it will make much better print - a Jewish cop explaining the death of a German woman." Tony was pissed.

The reporters couldn't wait to begin: "Detective Iniddor, what led you to the house on Maple Street?"

"Detective Ossur and I were able to lift two prints from a piece of vanity mirror which was the alleged weapon used against Mrs. Hedda Fernback the night she was assaulted and killed. Those prints were then matched to those of the suspect, Reggie Bennett."

"Was a search of the house conducted?" "Yes, there was."

"Was any incriminating evidence found?"

"You know that since the case is still under investigation, I can't disclose something like that." Marty's voice showed the strain of annoyance.

"Detective Ossur, have you spoken with Mr. Fernback regarding the arrest?" As Tony began to answer, the outer door of the office opened and a police officer escorted Douglas Fernback into the rear rooms of the squad office. Their eyes met and Tony nodded as Mr. Fernback walked solemnly into the adjoining room. The rear of the office led to two rooms: one a conference and interviewing room, and the other a holding cell room which at present housed Reggie Bennet.

Luckily, the reporters had their backs to the doors and were too intent on the questioning to realize that the victim's husband was now sitting in the conference room. "What was the exact time of death?" Marty answered: "6:05 p.m. this evening."

"Has the District Attorney been notified to change the charges to Murder?" It was like a rehearsed skit which Marty hated: "Reggie Bennett will be charged with Felony Murder in the death of Hedda Fernback."

"Sergeant Dello, how many man hours and what type of special task force was set up to apprehend the suspect?" As Del began to answer, he heard commotion and a yell from the conference room.

"Hey, Stop!" Douglas Fernback ran from the room with the officer's gun in his hand. He pushed past Possidos who was at the fingerprint cabinet and ran into the holding cell area. The office was in total surprised confusion, and the cameras were rolling. When Tony and Marty ran to the door, Douglass Fernback was holding the gun out in front of him and pointing it directly into the cell at Bennett.

"Doug, put the gun down. This won't make things right and he's going to go away for a long time. Hedda wouldn't want you to do this. Think about what you are doing. You'll be as bad as he is. Give me the gun." Marty was trying desperately to stop another real tragedy from occurring. Bennett didn't say a word and was cowering in the corner of his cell.

"Detective, I thank you and everybody for trying to help me and Hedda, but there is no more reason for me to live without her. My life means nothing, and I cannot let this animal live to possibly kill someone else." Marty tried again:

"He won't be able to do anything again, he'll be in prison for a long, long time."

As Marty talked, heading away from the doorway entrance and trying to keep Fernback's attention, Tony moved slowly in the opposite direction, sliding along the wall, to the rear of the distraught man. The strategy had worked at other times and places, they were hoping it would work now. Fernback continued talking: "In my homeland, he would not escape the punishment he deserves, but here, it is possible that he will be out on the street in a few short years to kill again. For Hedda's sake, I cannot let that happen." He leveled the gun at Bennett, and as Tony leaped, the report of the gun shot rang out throughout the office. Reggie Bennett lay dead with a bullet hole in his chest. Douglas Fernback was under arrest for Murder, and the press had a field day!

Chapter Four

The Caller

"United Flight #417 to New York City's LaGuardia Airport now boarding at Gate # 12." Chicago's O'Hare International Airport is one of the busiest airports in the world. With the Thanksgiving holidays only a few short days away, it was busier than ever. In addition to those travelers who were going to visit relatives for the holidays, the airport bustled with college students who were heading home for the intercession. Besides the two local schools, the University of Chicago and Decatur College, students throughout the country crammed into O'Hare as a stopover for connecting flights.

"Your boarding pass please." Alex Hassid fumbled for his phone and finally produced the boarding pass with the QR code. All the confusion and chaos added to his already strong dislike for air travel. He looked ahead with dismal anxiety at the idea of being enclosed with 170 other people, all as anxious as he to get home and all as annoyed at the overcrowded conditions. However, if he wanted to get home for the holiday, this was the only option available to him. So, he presented his pass and boarded. The take-off was delayed approximately forty-five minutes due to incoming traffic, but this was nothing new to O'Hare. It just made the trip even more unbearable.

"This is Captain Anderson. We are number two for takeoff and should be taking off shortly. It is 43 degrees in New York, and it is an overcast day. We will be flying at 33,000 feet and with the present weather conditions, we are anticipating a pleasant, smooth flight. Have a good day and an enjoyable trip. The attendants will assist with any problems or requests that you may have. Thank you."

"The Captain has turned on the 'Fasten Seatbelt' sign, so please remain in your seat and fasten your seatbelt." The airline attendant was a middle-aged woman who seemed both competent and confident. It made Alex feel just a bit better. The other two attendants were younger but also expressed an air of confidence. However, Alex realized that they were trained to demonstrate this attitude, whether or not they felt it.

The two-and-one-half-hour flight allowed for a lot of thinking time. Alex's mind was turned to thoughts of his father and older brother who were being held in an undisclosed prison somewhere in Israel. Alex, and his sister were living in New York with their uncle for the past six years and contact with his father and brother Chail, was at best minimal. Holidays, therefore, were not a time for rejoicing, but rather a scheduled family conference to determine what actions could be taken to help free the remaining family from Israeli tyranny.

Alex's dark complexion, black hair and brown eyes were indicative of his Arab background. He had, however, assimilated very well into the American lifestyle and was awarded an education grant to Chicago University to study in the field of science. His intelligence and hard work had earned him a possible shot at a fellowship award for graduate work at New York University. He was looking forward to attending school in New York. He would be attending a university whose reputation for scientific research is second to none and whose location puts him about twenty minutes away from his often-missed family.

Brooklyn, New York was a far cry from a small hamlet on the outskirts of Palestine; however, it was now

Alex's home, and he anxiously awaited arrival at LaGuardia. Maybe, in part, because of the many things presently going on in his life, and maybe because of the thoughts he had regarding the strange phone call he had received right before he left, the flight seemed to speed by and once again the "Fasten Seatbelt" sign was lit. Knowing that the landing and take-off are the most dangerous parts of air travel, Alex was apprehensive as the plane approached LaGuardia out of a dense fog, or what pilots might refer to as "pea soup."

Alex caught sight of the Whitestone Bridge as it lit up a small area of the darkening night. He saw the outline of Rikers Island Prison, and it immediately triggered thoughts of his father and brother. As the plane banked, he saw the dim guiding lights of the runway approach. He knew that in a few short moments, he would be landing in what has been termed one of the most dangerous landing airports in the country. Its short approach, deep descent, and brief runway caused many pilots to wonder if they had chosen the right profession. However, Alex's worrying was over, and the landing turned out to be smoother than on some of the other flights where conditions had been more ideal.

As soon as the plane came to a halt, Alex was the first to rise. He was most anxious to deplane and meet his family who he had not seen since the end of August. Seated to the rear of the plane became an apparent obstacle to his quick departure. He had to wait for the slow methodical line of passengers as they reached for baggage, smoothed their wrinkled clothes, and stretched with the intensity of those in attendance at the seventh inning of a baseball game.

"Hey Alex, take it easy; you're going to have to wait anyway. We got in a little early, so relax." Vin Falco had been assigned the seat next to Alex and had shared some brief conversation with him during the flight. Two-and-one-half hours was a long time to have to remain silent. It was Vin who had initiated the conversation and who, in fact, did most of the talking. Since it had allowed for the time to pass more quickly, Alex hadn't seemed to mind.

Alex stepped back: "You know you're right. I do it all the time, and I just wind up standing and waiting for the front to unload." Since Vin was also from Brooklyn, he suggested that the two exchange telephone numbers with the idea of possibly getting together during the break. Alex reluctantly gave his number - not reluctant because of Vin, but rather the fact that he was by nature a loner. Finally, they were up and walking toward the long tunnel that led to the passenger and baggage pick-up area where Alex was to meet his family. It made Alex feel good knowing that, as usual, the whole family would be at the airport for his arrival.

The crowded conditions persisted at LaGuardia as they had at O'Hare. The baggage pick-up area was a zoo! Alex had his attention divided between looking for his luggage and trying to locate his family. He wasn't succeeding well with either. Vinnie saw that Alex was having a bit of a hard time and inquired: "What color is your luggage? I'll get it for you, and you can scout around for your family. I'll meet you at the exit door all the way to the right." Alex was visibly relieved: "Thanks Vin, there are two pieces, both dark green with a tan stripe in the middle, shouldn't be hard to spot."

"Go ahead, Alex. I'll take care of it. My parents won't be here for another forty-five minutes anyway." Alex left in search of his mother and sister, but found no familiar face, no waving hand or smiling "hello." After a while, he even went to the courtesy desk and had them paged. There was no response. Twenty minutes passed, and Alex headed to the exit door where he was to meet Vinnie. Vin was there with four pieces of luggage, two were green with a tan stripe. As Alex approached, disappointment masked his entire face. Vin tried to make light of the situation: "They are probably caught up in traffic. It's a madhouse out there. I wouldn't worry about anything." Alex was still concerned: "They always leave in plenty of time; they're never late. Could you just wait here for a few more minutes? I want to call home to make sure everything is OK."

"Go ahead Alex, but I'm sure all's fine."

The phone rang for the tenth time with no answer. Alex hoped that it only meant that they were on the way. However, he couldn't shake the uneasy feeling in his stomach, and they were already forty-five minutes overdo. He thanked Vin again and informed him that he was going to stick around and wait for a while. Vinnie headed off to a pre-arranged meeting point but assured Alex that he would check back with him before he left the airport.

As Vinnie approached the United Airlines courtesy desk, he saw his mother pacing and his father patiently awaiting his son's delayed arrival. His folks were proud of him. He had won an athletic scholarship to Arizona State and was now carrying a 3.5 index. This was one middle-class family who wouldn't have to be burdened with the financial problems inherent in a college education. His mother was the first to see him.

"Hi Vincent. You look good. How was your flight? Do you have all your luggage? How is your new roommate?" That was Vinnie's mother. She would ask four questions before you could start to answer the first; and in fact, none really got answered because then his dad would start talking. This time was no different. The scenario was true to form. "Let me take a piece of luggage, son, and let's get out of here before the traffic gets any worse." He knew it really couldn't get any worse than it already was, but that was his way of saying to get a move on.

"Just wait one minute dad, I want to see if my friend, Alex, got his ride." To the grumbles of Mr. Falco, Vin ran down to the baggage area where he saw Alex, one of the last few people remaining. Trying to remedy the temporary situation with some humor, Vin said: "Hey, are you sure you get along with your family?" The comedic attempt failed, however. Alex was visibly concerned and worried about them.

"Listen Alex. Why don't I give you a ride home? We both live in Brooklyn, and you're only about fifteen minutes away from my house anyway. We'll leave a message at the courtesy desk just in case they come after we've gone. They'll know you're okay and on your way home." It was obvious that his family was not coming, and Alex was running out of options. Alex agreed to his friend's generous offer.

"Mom, Dad, this is Alex Hassid. We met on the plane. He's a student at the University of Chicago, and his ride is late. I offered to take him home. He lives in Marine Park." They smiled a forced smile and welcomed Alex aboard. There was the usual trite conversation on the way home, as Alex's thoughts were concentrated on the whereabouts of his family. Considering traffic, the fifty-minute ride wasn't that bad. The car pulled up in front of the address on East 31st Street - a neat one family house with a small well-kept lawn, bounded by evergreen bushes. Alex anxiously got out of the car and thanked the Falcos for the ride. At Vinnie's insistence, he promised to keep in touch. Alex walked up the front steps to a totally dark house. It was obvious that no one was home. As he opened the front screen door and placed the key in the lock, he heard a car pull up in front of the house. Alex turned and a man in a dark gray suit got out.

"Excuse me, are you Alex Hassid?" Alex was surprised and caught unaware as his low wavering voice indicated: "Yes, who are you?" The man approached displaying a gold police department badge and said: "I'm Detective Iniddor." Alex looked puzzled and immediately asked Iniddor if there was a problem.

"Your sister, Rachael, was hurt at a high school rally. She was taken to Inter-County General Hospital, and the rest of your family is there with her now." Before Alex could ask, the detective added: "She isn't hurt badly, and I came here to give you a lift." The color drained from Alex's face as he became a picture of worried concern. The ill-feeling of anticipation had turned out to be a reality. His younger sister was hurt, and his mother was probably worried sick. His stomach was turning, and his complexion was white. Because of the particular continuing family crises affecting them, his family and he reacted more sensitively to family emergencies than most. He tried to regain a little composure. He thanked Detective Iniddor for his thoughtfulness and asked him if he could wait: "I just want to put my luggage inside and I'll be ready to go."

Rachael Hassid was a very pretty and intelligent 15-year-old who was totally involved in anything that went on at Thompson High. She was one of the student council officers and was probably going to run for Student Council President next year. The ride to Inter-County was approximately fifteen minutes - a very long fifteen minutes for Alex.

"How was my sister hurt, Detective?" Iniddor lowered the Department radio and responded to Alex's Question: "Apparently, Rachael was seated on the dais during a political rally at the High School football field. There were over a thousand people in attendance, and all the various political factions and candidates were represented. If it wasn't one group protesting, it was the other demonstrating over some issue or standpoint." Sometimes Iniddor was too thorough and exact. "Halfway into the rally, Assemblyman Stalker was giving his views on the redistricting issue when shots rang out in the crowd." Alex interrupted: "Gunshots?" Iniddor continued: "Approximately four gunshots were heard, according to witnesses, but we're still checking on that. When the smoke had cleared and the panic subsided, there were three people injured. Your sister was one of them. She's been shot in the left shoulder, but the bullet seems to have passed right through without doing any real damage. She's in no danger but will probably have to stay in the hospital for a couple of days."

Alex listened carefully and then asked: "Do you know who did the shooting?" Iniddor answered: "No, but we have a pretty good description, and I'm sure we'll come up with something soon." Uncontrollably, Alex blurted out: "You'd better get him, because if you don't, I will." Iniddor understood the gut emotion and didn't respond. Instead, he picked up the radio: "Brooklyn South Detective Auto to Central-K"

"Go ahead detective auto."

"One male to Inter-County General. Will be 10-62 on an investigation thereat." "10-4"

Alex hurriedly opened the car door and ran into the emergency entrance. "Alex, Alex," his mother broke into tears upon seeing him. "They hurt Rachael. They shot her." Alex's macho overtook his emotions, and he was able to hold back his tears. "I know, Mom. How is she and can I see her?" His uncle came over to explain and told him the room number. Alex saw a doctor and asked if he could go to see his sister. The doctor gave the okay and directed him to the room, but warned him not to stay too long since the loss of blood had made Rachael weak. She needed rest more than anything else right now.

If Rachael was asleep, Alex did not want to wake her. He opened the door to Room 202 very quietly and slowly. However, as soon as the door left the jam, Rachael looked up and saw Alex. She appeared very weak and helpless, and the array of tubes going into her arms did not make for a very comforting sight.

"How are you doing, Rae?"

"I guess I'm okay, Alex. I have a little pain but I'm mostly numb, and I think the Doctor gave me some sedatives." Alex's concern was apparent on his face: "Tell me what happened, sis." Alex could not have expected the response. Rachael began to cry.

"It's okay, Rachael, It's okay." Rachael took a sobbing breadth: "No, it's not, Alex. That man meant to shoot me." Alex attributed the statement to the fact that shock, excitement, pain and confusion were all combining to distort the reality of what actually occurred. She raised her voice to impact the seriousness and truthfulness of her story and repeated: "Alex, he stood up in the crowd, took aim directly at me and fired. It was after he fired at me that he fired into the crowd." Alex, in an attempt to calm her down, patronized her with a question: "How can you be sure he aimed directly at you and intended to shoot you?" She unhesitatingly answered: "Because before he fired, he mouthed my name and smiled. I thought he was pointing a camera at me, but instead I felt a sharp pain in my shoulder. From that point on, I really don't remember anything else."

"Rachael, did you tell the police that?"

"No. I'm too frightened, and I don't even want mom to know. But I had to tell somebody. You are the only one that knows. Promise me that you won't tell anyone yet - at least not until we can think about it some more. Alex, promise me." Against his better judgment, Alex promised as Rachael slowly drifted off to sleep.

As he left her room and entered the main hallway, his mind was racing in thought about someone intentionally shooting his sister. He was deep in thought and obviously disturbed by even the possibility that Racheal was right. The bright lights of the corridor brought him back to the needs of the moment. He had to concentrate on comforting his mother now, and tried to, at least temporarily, place his sister's revelation to the back of his mind.

The trip home was a silent and somber one. Alex reviewed all the questions that the Detectives had asked. He had been tempted many times to break his promise, but the strength of Rachael's appeal was so strong that he remained silent about her convictions. The family would again be talking to the police tomorrow at the hospital, and Alex would have another opportunity to discuss the shooting with Iniddor and Ossur. They said they would come by again, and Alex believed they would because, as far as he could tell, they seemed both concerned and sincere in their efforts to console the family and find the shooter.

It was about ten o'clock when they arrived home. Mrs. Hassid was totally emotionally and physically worn by the day's events; so, the usual "catching up" family discussion would be delayed at least until tomorrow. The rest of the family lingered for a short while, but then they too retired for the evening, leaving Alex alone downstairs in the living room to try and unwind. He had so many things to sort out, so many new obligations to meet and so many questions to answer. He closed his eyes and took a brief minute to relax and weigh his options. Not realizing how really tired he was, before long he drifted off to sleep in the all too comfortable sofa-chair. Abruptly awakened an hour later by the resounding ring of the telephone, Alex jumped and ran into the kitchen to stop the God-awful noise that, at this time of the night, sounded like a fire alarm that would surely awaken the rest of the house. He glanced at the kitchen clock. Who would be calling at 11:30 at night? He froze, mentally pushing back the possibility that it could be the hospital calling, and the hospital would only call if there was bad news. He picked up the receiver and hesitatingly said: "Hello." The caller responded: "Hello Alex, I'm sorry to hear about your sister. How is she doing?"

Still in the throes of sleep, Alex answered: "She'll be all right, thanks." As he spoke, Alex tried to recognize the somewhat familiar voice, but could not readily place it. In an effort to demonstrate how late it was and how fatiguing the day had been, Alex groggily asked: "What time is it?" The caller answered promptly and apologetically: "About 11:30. I'm sorry for calling so late, but I just found out about your sister, and I wanted to speak to you as soon as possible. I know that the incident was not an accident, and I must talk to you." Alex, who had been slowly awakening, was shocked into attention by the caller's statement.

He was also now aware of where he had heard the voice before. It was the same person who had called and spoken to him before he left college. It was a low, soft, calm voice, but one that was deadly serious. The caller had told him earlier in the day, when he called him on campus, that he was aware of Alex's father and brother and how unjustly they had been imprisoned. The voice also stated that he and a group of others were anxious to work out plans to free them. The caller not only knew the details of the arrest but was also familiar with the history of the entire family. He had also mentioned that he would soon be in touch with Alex to arrange a meeting. When Alex had inquired as to whom the caller was, he had simply stated: "For now, it suffices to know that I am a friend."

Alex was already irritated at the time of the call but the surrounding mystery really annoyed him. "Who is this?" The voice simply answered: "You will know soon enough." Then again, shrouded in the mystery associated with a spy novel, the caller continued: "For now, consider me as one of a group who is concerned about you and your family." Alex wanted to hang up. He did not like dealing with a person who would hide behind the anonymity of a phone call.

However, Alex couldn't dismiss the fact that the caller knew the details regarding his father's and brother's arrests and even more so, couldn't disregard the fact that someone, be he unknown, was adding credence to his sister's story.

"I will be in touch with you before the vacation ends, and we will meet to discuss items which will be of great concern to you. Good night, Alex." As quickly as he had entered the night, the caller was gone. If Alex had been confused before, his mind was now a shattered mass of thoughts screaming to be heard and his consciousness, a tangled web of questions wanting to be answered.

He knew tomorrow would be another long day, so he decided to try and get some sleep. He would have to be fresh and alert to cope with the new problems that would surely arise with the morning. He wearily climbed the stairs burdened with the effects of an emotionally and physically draining day. Enroute to his room, he peeked in on his mother. He often internalized all the suffering she had gone through in her life, and now, sadly empathized with her feelings regarding the day. As he closed her bedroom door, he silently promised that one day, he would make things right again for her.

Because his mind was working overtime, he laid in bed for what seemed like an eternity before he was able to drift off to sleep. The soft light of the candle that his mother always placed in the room to protect him in the night reflected on a face that revealed the strain and sorrow of the day. The unwiped residue of tears gave testimony to the insecurities of a boy plunging into the harsh realities of a man.

Chapter Five

The Wino

If the majority of a cop's time is not spent with the dregs and downtrodden of society, then they usually spend much of their time as the bearers of bad news or the city agent who is responsible for curtailing some "guaranteed" freedom. In an effort to offset the certain depression that sets in, cops are always looking for a party or a good time. The holidays, therefore, were very special to most police officers. The men assigned to Brooklyn South were no exception. With Thanksgiving quickly upon them, they decided to get together for some holiday cheer, and as the schedule went, it was Ossur's turn to do the hosting.

Within the tightly guarded society of police officers, there are two kinds of celebrations, however. There is the traditional family socialization process which includes husbands and wives and which for the most part is self-explanatory, and then there is the extra-curricular celebration which promotes a setting where the guys would get together with people other than their wives. These depression-relievers would usually take place in a local gin mill or a favorite restaurant, or even sometimes at one of the girls' houses.

The girlfriend-socials seem to occur a lot more often than the family cloches, and as a result, the girlfriends, ironically, seem to enjoy a stronger friendship bond than do the wives. With their common denominator, they remain a special breed of woman. They know that they are the "other woman", yet they will go through most of the heartaches of having a married man as a boyfriend, as long as somewhere down the road, they can see even the smallest glimmer of hope that one day they might become number one. I guess what they fail to realize is that the day they become number one, there already exists another girl vying for that coveted position. I don't know if law enforcement draws the type of personality who must always socially assert him or herself, or if the "job" turns one into that type of person. These two opposing positions have been the research work of many a psychologist, and a definitive answer still remains elusive.

Whatever the reason, police officers rate among the top ten percent in divorces in the nation. So, in an unconscious effort to ward off the demon of divorce, Tony invited the guys and their wives, the weekend before Thanksgiving, for a few drinks at his house. Now for Tony, his house meant Myrna's home in Staten Island. He had been seeing Myrna for about eleven years. They met during the City-wide festivity events on July 4th, and for the past eleven years their relationship has been intermittent - sometimes "on," sometimes "off." Myrna was the one who was there to pick him up out of the throws of, at that time, a recent divorce and bring him back to level-headed thinking. Tony will be the first to admit that he owes her an awful lot, but he will also be the first to admit that he doesn't love her. In his words: "I love her like a sister." But her house and her company is the only semblance of home that he has; so, he remains with her.

Although the squad enjoyed getting together with the wives, many times it was done out of necessity. The social situation demanded it, and although the meetings were usually friendly and congenial, it was at these types of gatherings that an accidental slip of a name or reference could cause a negative ripple effect which would last for weeks. So as the guys relaxed and enjoyed themselves, they were always on the alert for that one person who would alcoholically imbibe beyond his limit and become vocally dangerous. It was just another exercise in the art of policing. They all realized if things got out of hand, that one of these small get-togethers could become the basis for a future divorce suit. So, although necessity demanded these sometimes-enjoyable parties, the Brooklyn South Squad, although off duty, was ever vigilant for the "loose-lipped ship sinker."

"Hi Tony. It's eight o'clock and nobody's here yet?" Marty and his wife, Lisa, were the first to arrive. It was a chance for Tony and Marty to quickly discuss whatever had to be arranged, if anything, and it allowed for Lisa to help Myrna prepare last minute items. Within a short time, the rest of the office began to arrive. By eight-thirty, seven couples had sipped their first drink of the evening.

Jim Jones, Angel Torres and Ira Jacobs were working the duty so they could not attend; and Mary Austin had come down with the Flu, so Frank was stuck on a nursing assignment. Whoever was left was in attendance, and for Tony, that was plenty. Everyone seemed to be having a good time except the host. Tony was obviously preoccupied with other things. And the more Tony drank, the more distant he became. It was obvious to Marty what was happening because he had seen Tony react this way a number of times before. Tony was apparently having troubles with Donna, the woman he denied addictively loving. Tony had found that one woman who he couldn't forget and felt he couldn't do without. I think we all harbor feelings for that one special person, and ironically, it is that one who gives us the most trouble, and the one with whom we rarely settle.

So it was with Tony. He was suffering a very real attack of feelings. Sometimes, upon observation, one can see a little of each woman in all the girls a cop dates. However, Tony covered both ends of the spectrum. Donna was tall and skinny, while Myrna was short and shapely. Donna lacked personality while Myrna appealed to everyone, and Donna always spoke with a double-edged meaning while Myrna's words always detailed sincerity. To top it off, Donna personified the calculating demeanor of the typical German she was, while Myrna's ancestry could be traced to Hebrew speaking grandparents. In an attempt to save Tony from a fate worse than death, Marty asked him for another drink, and the two headed for the kitchen and out of the sight of the curious gathering.

"Tony, what the hell is the matter with you?" Tony stood in silence. Marty continued: "Whatever it is, you're making it obvious to everyone, including Myrna, that you would rather be somewhere else, maybe with someone else. I know it has to do with Donna. What did she twist your balls about this time?" Donna was not one of Marty's favorite people, but he tolerated her for Tony's sake.

In referring to Donna, Tony's reply was typical: "For a long time, that bitch has been living with a beer-bellied asshole with three kids. That means she was going out with him while she was still seeing me. When you think about it, I'm the asshole." Tony was beside himself. He had stopped seeing Donna in August and had recently learned that she moved in with this new guy at the end of October. Although there was no proof positive, it seemed obvious to him and everyone else who he told, that Donna would have had to have contact with beer-belly before August to be able to move in with him into a new apartment in October. Donna had, of course, vehemently denied any outside social contact while seeing Tony.

Since he had learned of the turn of events, Tony had successfully tried to suppress his gut feelings of frustration, revenge, betrayal, love and hate. But now, after a few drinks and the party atmosphere, which served to depress rather that cheer him, and the fact that the holiday season is of itself a depressing time - it boasts the highest rate for suicides - Tony's hodge-podge of mixed emotions began to uncontrollably surface for all to see. Tony gulped his drink which served to fuel and intensify an already raging fire.

"That bitch will pay. As much as I love her, that's how much I hate her." This sentiment was nothing new. Tony had always expressed this apparent contradiction of feelings. Knowing Donna as well as he did, Marty could understand where Tony was coming from. All during the kitchen conference, Tony had been raising his voice. Marty's constant efforts to lower Tony's tone had failed. Now, his vocal outrage was developing into physical movements and symbols. He had raised his fist, symbolically choked his own neck, and clasped his hands together in pagan prayer of seeing her again. It was during this revenge prayer that Myrna walked into the room.

The kitchen was small, but all of a sudden it was like standing in a closet with the air getting chokingly thick. Myrna looked at Tony, then to Marty and back at Tony in a cold condemning stare. Looking directly into Tony's eyes and with uncharacteristic scorn she spoke: "It's her again, isn't it?" Under booze-influenced emotional trauma, Tony mockingly yelled back: "It's her again, and it always will be!" Marty stepped in between the two and tried to diffuse the inevitable explosion. Over Marty's efforts and pointing directly at Tony, Myrna yelled: "I want you and your God-damned friends out of my house. Maybe you can pick it up at Donna's, they probably all know each other anyway." Myrna was livid and began to mutter some indefinable expletives.

In the living room, the rest of the party could not help but overhear the verbal assault, and they began to exit quickly and quietly before they might be ordered to leave by the wounded, rage-filled, exploding female who just a few short moments ago had been their charming host. The whole transposition brought back memories of the bedroom scene in the "Exorcist." It was as if she was possessed. Maybe, she had reason to be. A party that should have been good medicine for all turned into an instrument for the creation of even more tension.

For those wives present who did not know about Tony's other girl, it raised questions as to the loyalties in their own relationships. It was certain that the office would not be happy with Tony come Monday morning. They might understand, but they wouldn't be happy. The incident had created an air of doubt, and it seemed that there was a lot of explaining to do all the way around. There were very few pleasant conversations on the way home for the men of the Brooklyn South Squad. Jim, Angel, Ira and Frank, they were the lucky ones.

Following a few more well-chosen words, Tony left the kitchen into the already barren living room, picked up his jacket and exited with a bang through the front door. Although Marty looked at an angry stone-gazed Myrna, he felt that Tony might be the one in more need of immediate help. He was hoping that Tony would head for the office dormitory where he could sleep it off. This type of scenario was no stranger to Tony's lifestyle, and Marty was assuming that Tony would follow past precedent and head for the squad room.

Marty and Lisa got to the outside steps just as Tony started his mustang and left rubber along the service road of the Staten Island Expressway, Myrna's front street. They hurriedly got into their car and followed Tony from a distance, hopefully monitoring Tony's safe arrival at the office. The mustang negotiated the toll booths with ease and was now beginning to put distance between the two cars. As the mustang sped toward the middle of the Verrazano Bridge in route to Brooklyn, Marty got caught behind a car that didn't have the E-ZPass displayed, and as the driver slowed to a stop struggling to produce it, Marty lost sight of Tony's car.

Passing through the toll booth, Marty kicked down the accelerator, but by the time he reached the hump of the bridge, Tony's vehicle was nowhere in sight. Although Tony had been driving quicker than usual, Marty saw that he had been in full control of the car and, therefore, was not that worried about his partner. Anyway, Marty couldn't totally concentrate on Tony's dilemma, since he was in the midst of answering a barrage of questions about the evening's events from Lisa. It seems he too had become suspect of extracurricular activity which the scene tonight had served to intensify, and which Marty had hoped would lay dormant a while longer.

Although Marty had judged Tony's driving abilities correctly, he didn't realize in how bad of a psychological state Tony was floundering. With the effects of the alcohol, the high emotional conflict, and the holiday season, Tony was working on psychological overdrive. Instead of proceeding directly over the bridge to the 65th exit of the Gowanus Expressway (prior to the bridge being built, this was the old 7th Avenue), Tony had turned off at the Belt Parkway exit and was enroute to the Sheepshead Bay area of Brooklyn, and in particular, the neighborhood of East 36th Street.

As Tony Ossur approached Avenue R and East 36th Street, he turned off his lights and slowed the car down to patrol speed (3 to 5 miles an hour). Tony turned south down East 36th and surveyed the block for parked autos. He was looking for one in particular. There, in the middle of the block, was a very familiar sea blue Nissan. It was her car. The car that Tony had bought for Donna when she was practicing to get her license. She failed the test but drove anyway. He parked!

Donna was a creature of habit, and Tony knew those habits very well. It was Sunday evening, and every Sunday Donna would visit her parents on East 36th Street to have a sit-down dinner, German style. Tony stared and relived the memory of when he had been an integral part of this Sunday ritual. He checked the time. It was eleven-thirty; Donna always left before Midnight. In less than thirty minutes, he would be seeing her and getting that same old gnawing feeling again. His stomach was already beginning to react in anticipation. He knew that seeing her would bother him, but up until now he didn't realize just how much. He didn't need the pain; he should leave. He wanted to go; he couldn't.

The waiting was getting worse. However, fate was on his side. Fifteen minutes having gone by, the front porch light at the residence on East 36th Street went on. Donna, saying good-bye to her parents, exited alone. Apparently, she had visited alone, and had left her beer-belly partner at home with the kids - his kids. Maybe it was lucky for everyone that the other guy wasn't there. Having consumed a good amount of alcohol and feeling the way he did, Tony didn't know how he would have reacted seeing that "lardass" escorting his girl. As she waved goodbye and crossed the street to her car, Tony eyed the long shapely legs exposed by the brevity of the mini skirt she wore. He became lost in the daydream of those legs that at one time had wrapped tightly around him as the passion of love making began. His dreamy thoughts were interrupted as the Nissan engine started, and Donna proceeded to pull away from the curb.

Tony was now in his natural habitat, and he was at his best. He could follow a stranded woman on a deserted island and never leave proof of his existence. Following

Donna was no big problem. The problem would arise when she finally arrived at her destination and continued her co-habitation with beer-belly and the kids.

Although there were previous times when Tony hadn't given into emotional urges and followed her without incident, this time his rage, jealousy and overall frustration was further being fueled by the handy bottle of scotch he carried in his car's portable bar. The usually clear-thinking Brooklyn South Detective was beginning to lose a psychological battle that could bring about irreparable harm.

The ride to her apartment in the Gravesend section of Brooklyn was only about ten minutes. It was the shortest ten minutes that Tony had ever experienced. There were so many things racing through his mind, so many emotions struggling for juxtaposition, and no time to mead anything out. His anger and frustration, like cream in a milk bottle, rose to the top and became paramount as they began to take control.

Since he had done some personal, clandestine work there previously, he knew the exact location of the apartment. He raced to arrive there before Donna. As Donna's car approached, Tony was already parked and hidden in a very dark spot about 50 feet away and across the street from the entrance to the apartment which was a second story walk-up. He noticed that the lights in the apartment were all off, and that the street was all but deserted except for a wino sprawled out on the corner of the block.

Donna had not known that Tony bought a new car, trading in his silver Toyota Supra for a new silver mustang - silver being his favorite auto color. So, Tony was even more secure in his hiding. He took another swig from the scotch bottle and watched as Donna parked about five spaces behind him. She locked the car and walked across the street proceeding down past Tony toward the front door entrance of the building. It enraged him to see her dressed like that and going home to someone else. He and the alcohol decided to do something about it.

As if experiencing a flashback to military tactic maneuvers, he exited his car and silently ran directly behind her. Knowing that his reflexes were not at their best, he was surprised at what an easy target she was. If she were the enemy, he would have accounted for another silent kill. However, killing might have been too good for her. That was not tonight's assignment. Having armed himself with duct tape before leaving the car, he grabbed her from behind in a choke hold and kept her quiet long enough to tape both her mouth and eyes. The Army Ranger training had worked so well that it was almost easy dragging her across the street to his car. So far, the capture technique was textbook. So perfect that the wino, a relatively short distance away, never even budged.

As headlights from the next block began shining down the street, she started to struggle. He had to get her into the car. He could not take the chance of being seen, so he open-handedly slapped her across the face. Her resistance slackened, and he pushed her into the car. He shoved her over to the passenger side and slammed the door shut. He smothered her to keep her out of sight of the quickly approaching motorist. The car passed without incident, and Tony released the immobilizing hold he had on her, just a bit.

With the twine he had taken from the glove compartment, he tied her wrists and extended the line down to her ankles which he quickly fastened. He was quite adept at what he was doing, and Donna was hogtied and gagged in a very short time. It was a new experience for him, and he was reaping the usual excitement a potential rapist would enjoy. As Donna moaned under the tape of Tony's handiwork, he started the car and proceeded to a deserted area of Gerritsen Beach. Her mini dress was now exposing the pubic hairs that sneaked out of the side of the black thong she wore. Tony was harder now than he had been in months. He found a dark secluded spot and proceeded as a doctor preparing to operate. He got great excitement and pleasure in the sightless and voiceless dilemma of his prey, and further joy in the fear, embarrassment and humbleness she had to be feeling.

He was free to work with total anonymity. He was all too familiar with his victim, and for a long time just rubbed around those areas he knew to be her erogenous zones. Because of his acute skills in roping, Donna could hardly move away. And with her eyes being taped shut, she could not anticipate his next touch. Although she flinched upon touch and tried to recoil, her efforts fell far short of success. He began rubbing the tips of his fingers lightly across her nipples which protruded from under the black silk blouse now exposed by her open jacket. The more that she moaned her frustration and helplessness, the more satisfaction he got. Tony Ossur had become the typical criminal sex aggressor who he had always abhorred. However, he was personally and emotionally involved with this victim, and the influence of alcohol combined with the exacerbation of other emotions dictated the actions of his wounded psychological state.

Prior to entering her, Tony had decided that he would fuck her until she hurt. He carefully released the lever for the front passenger seat and laid her back as the seat reclined. Then in one solid swift motion, he cut her ankle bindings and forced his body into the middle of her resisting opened legs. Her hands, however, were still bound, so her efforts at escape were of no real threat. As a matter of fact, her reeling, twisting attempts at avoidance became a turn-on for her aggressor, who at this point was acting out all his anger, frustration, and hate in this one alcohol-influenced frenzy.

Tony ripped at the black thong that covered her sex zone and exposed the blond shaved silken strip. Many times, he had pressed his lips against that intoxicating mat, and many times they both shared in inexplicable joy. But tonight, he would not give her that satisfaction. He would penetrate as deeply and vigorously as he could and continue to pound with all his might. He wanted her to hurt with the same degree of excitement he felt. He expertly spread her apart as he worked his pants down. His joint was throbbing with the anticipation of entry. His legs effectively stopping her lateral movement and the rope restraining her sweaty struggling hands, he had a very little problem thrusting his tool of hate into her. His weight burying her down with each stroke, he ripped the tape from her mouth and languished in the pain and anguish he heard.

Although his plan had called for the ultimate infliction of physical pain, the thrusting excitement was too much, and Tony squirted his sexual venom before any real damage could be done. Physically, he felt that he had failed in completing the level of pain he had hoped to impart; however, he was assured by her continuous rantings that the psychological damage was severe and would be long lasting.

Surprisingly, in a few short moments, Donna ceased to resist and just laid limp. She was sobbing and whimpering as a scolded child would. Instead of enjoying this scene to its fullest sadistic climax, Tony's joy slowly started to fade, and he felt a sudden unexplained urge to take her back as soon as possible - and just go. Sober reality had begun to filter into the nightmare of the evening. He dressed her as quickly as he could, cleaned her up a bit, and then raised the chair. It was difficult for her to help, being bound and sightless. However, with her now limp reactions, untying her would not have been a threat. His anonymity, of course, had to be guarded at all costs. He started the car and drove quickly but carefully from Gerritsen Beach back to her apartment in Gravesend. As he turned the corner of her block, at the far end of the block - approximately in the front of her building, he noticed two police officers and the flashing lights of a police car. The lights also outlined what seemed to be the straggly figure of the wino who had been sleeping at the corner. Tony abruptly stopped the car, cut her wrist bindings and ushered Donna out. Her eyes remained taped.

As soon as she heard the car backing out of the street, Donna began yelling and ripping at her eyes. The uniformed police officers heard the screams and immediately turned toward her. They started running up the block with the wino in the lead. As Tony hurriedly turned his car and accelerated in escape (lights out), he thought he saw the reflection of the street lamp bouncing off a piece of metal hanging from a chain around the wino's neck. The shape of a chain and a shield became clear. The wino - an undercover decoy cop - was rushing to Donna's aid.

Chapter Six

Three's A Crowd

Monday morning brought with it the residue of the ill effects of a party that caused grief and concern for the majority of the Brooklyn South Squad. However, the open hostility that had been anticipated by both Marty and Tony was not apparent. I guess the consensus of opinion was that Tony had enough problems going for him without additional squawks. They were not as congenial, for lack of a better term, as they usually were, but they were not as nasty as they could have been. Tony was ahead of the game - so to speak.

The Monday morning tour in Brooklyn South is a very busy tour. Today was no exception. As Tony and Marty entered the squad room, they saw Del partially hidden by the stack of case progress reports that he had to check for the past weekend's work. He was sitting at his desk apparently in the process of interviewing or interrogating, from their vantage point they weren't sure, a young white male.

Alex Hassid was already waiting for them. He was sitting at Tony's desk patiently awaiting their arrival. Alex was concerned with the progress, or lack of it, regarding the shooting case involving his sister. Tension and concern masked his face. This concern was obvious to Tony as he started talking with Alex. Although the squad had no new leads, information or evidence, Tony thought it better, at this time, not to give Alex the impression that the detectives had come up against the proverbial "stonewall." As Alex battered him with a deluge of questions, Tony skillfully danced around most of them. However, Tony was beginning to read an "I'll do it myself" attitude. The tone of his voice and the characteristic body language emanating from Alex was indicative of someone who is ready to take things into his own hands. Tony now found himself in the unenviable position of trying to convince a very concerned, strong-headed young man that the police department should be the only one investigating and enforcing the law.

Tony housed his warnings of vigilantism and interference in a passionate plea for just a little more time. It became obvious, though, that the pleas were falling upon deaf ears. It was especially difficult for Tony to be as sincere as he would have liked, since the facts indicated "no new information."

"Iniddor, Ossur, come into my office." In addition to Sergeant Del seeming tired, he was apparently disturbed about something. Tony and Marty, having heard that tone of voice on numerous other occasions, reported directly to his office. As a door shut behind them, Del introduced Detective Paul Staffio, formally of the Narcotics Division, and the newly appointed third member of the Iniddor-Ossur detective team. Surprise, annoyance, reluctance, and resentment simultaneously surged through the both of them and not necessarily in that order. However, remembering the tone of Del's voice, they said absolutely nothing – not even an "hello" to their new team member. Marty and Tony continued to stare directly at Sergeant Del, as he spoke more of Detective Staffio and tonally indicated that Staffio had been dumped out of Narcotics into the confines of Brooklyn South. Del was not happy; Iniddor and Ossur were definitely not happy; and for that matter, Staffio had experienced happier days. All in all, an air of "aw shit" permeated the Sergeant's office.

As is the routine procedure when a new guy is transferred into an office, Tony was on the phone, out of earshot of Staffio, with a contact who worked narcotics. As Tony got the "dope" on Staffio, the beginnings of a strong burning sensation started to develop in the pit of his stomach. It was a burning that would ultimately result in an ulcer that he knew would plague him for the rest of his life. Tony returned to the general working area of the squad room and with a nod, indicated to Marty that he had completed his mission.

Detective Paul Staffio was a younger guy, but compared to Ossur and Iniddor, every guy was a younger guy, and his job immaturity didn't allow him to make an easy transition into a squad atmosphere. Having lost the prestige of a specialized detail, he was bitter and somewhat embarrassed. Of all punishments, he was transferred into the Brooklyn South Squad which had possessed a somewhat dubious reputation. He had been a super sleuth in the Narcotics Undercover Division, and now he was just another detective doing routine detective work – work which he knew was far below his capabilities. However, there were going to be obstacles to his immediate rise and ultimate regaining of stature. It was certain that he had not come upon the likes of a detective team as Iniddor and Ossur. They were not going to take any of his sanctimonious shit. In fact, they were now going to have to be a lot more careful

in how they operated, until this new guy could be trusted –
and that time may never come!

Leaving their newly assigned team member to
familiarize himself with the paperwork procedures, Marty
and Tony went out to lunch. Paul was left behind by design
and by the mere fact that they were not yet ready to have
this supposed dethroned hot shot shoved down their throat.
Besides, Marty wanted to know what Tony had learned from
his contact regarding Staffio. Marty waited impatiently to
hear the scoop, but Tony was forever taking his sweet time.
"Okay, do you want me to read your fucking mind or are you
going to tell me what you found out?" blasted Marty. Tony
was caught by surprise and seemed very reluctant and
hesitant to discuss the issue. This was totally out of
character for him. Marty pushed: "He's a turnaround cop
who has homosexual tendencies and snorts coke. Am I
close?"

Tony broke the silence and finally started to reveal
the influencing factors which ultimately placed Staffio into
Brooklyn South, and the burning started to pain again. Tony
was not his usual flowing self. Every word seemed labored
and weighted with an undue amount of concern. It was
obvious to Marty that his partner was disturbed. Someone
else might not have noticed a difference, but working
together for a long time enables you to absorb certain
inflections and emphasis that would be wasted on someone

else. This was one of the few times that Marty, even though he had a number of questions, allowed Tony to continue the story without interruption. Marty had to consider Tony as a complainant or a witness, and resort to training that instructed the investigator to "let the person finish and make mental notes of questions to be asked later."

Tony was explaining how Staffio had screwed up an undercover surveillance assignment. Although the faux-pas was not directly related to the narcotics watch, his inability to stay awake allowed an assault and rape to take place on the same block as the surveillance, and probably less than 30 yards away. Tony continued: "Apparently Staffio had come to work directly from an all-night party. He can put away the booze. He was tired and probably would have blown a 1.5 intox, so he just nodded off." Marty couldn't help himself: "You mean hot shot, fell asleep on the job." Tony confirmed: "His surveillance vantage point was in a prone position, and he slept through a kidnapping, assault and rape." "Talk about fucking up," was Marty's response. All Marty could think about was how this young and shining star was now the third member of their team, and also what kind of supervisory attention he was going to bring along with him.

"I'm surprised they didn't bounce him out of the Detective Division with charges and specs," Marty said. "Charges and specs" is the police jargon associated with disciplinary action taken against a cop which can result in transfer, loss of pay or days, suspension and/or termination, according to the severity of the accusations. Tony answered: "Apparently, he had a hook, or he definitely would have been bounced to patrol."

"It might be good for us to find out who that hook is. Do you have any leads yet?" "No," Tony said, "but I already put out my feelers." Marty asked: "Where was the rape?" The answer came quickly: "Brooklyn South."

"I'm surprised that we didn't hear too much about it."

"Why should we? I'm sure that the Sex Crimes Unit will catch it, especially with the SNAFU attached to it." Marty unknowingly continued to needle Tony: "Do you know how bad the victim is? We might have to do the preliminary." Tony answered: "I think she is more in shock than anything else."

"Any description on the perp?" Tony hesitated: "No, I think the victim was blindfolded the entire time. And before you start asking a thousand and one other questions that I can't answer, let's eat!"

"Okay. Last question and then we eat. Just in case we get anything on it, what's the complainant's name?" Tony quickly retorted: "I knew we weren't going to pick up the case, so I guess I just forgot to even ask."

Now, for sure, Marty knew that something was wrong. Tony was too good of a detective to let an item like identification go unquestioned. Marty's intuitive investigative juices began to mix with comparative observations, and an uneasy feeling grew in the pit of his stomach. It was obvious that Tony was visibly bothered by Staffio's assignment to Brooklyn South, and in addition, Tony had become close-mouthed and possibly even lying about facts relevant to the rape case. Tony was definitely out of character, and Marty was at a loss to understand his strange behavior. After all they had been through together, what could possibly be so secretive that Tony couldn't discuss it with him? Nothing! So, having faith in Tony's judgment, as he always had, Marty felt that when the time was right, his partner would level with him. Sometimes it was better to let things slide.

Their lunch was quick, quiet and queasy - none of the usual conversation and hardly any shop talk. In fact, for the amount of sandwich they consumed, they could have ordered only one and still had some left over. Tony picked up the tab and in another unprecedented move, told Marty that he would meet him up in the office. As Marty was leaving, he heard the usual: "Give me a pack of Marlboros." Ordinarily, this would have been Marty's cue to start breaking Tony's balls about smoking. This time there was no comment.

As Marty opened the office door, Detective Juan Medina was just hanging up the phone: "Hey Marty, where's your partner?"

"He'll be right back; he's picking up some smokes."

"When he comes in, tell him to call Detective Sergeant Debbie Noldir from Sex Crimes. She said it was important." Partners are involved in each other's cases, even though they are individually responsible for their own closeout rate. Marty knew that neither one of them was involved with anything connected to the Sex Crimes Unit, so Marty curiously awaited Tony's return. He looked over at Paul Staffio as the new addition inattentively thumbed through some paperwork. Subconsciously, Marty began to blame Staffio for the uneasiness, the tension, and the difference the two partners now felt. This blame gave way to an anger and attitude that began to obviously permeate the entire office.

From the information they had received, Marty knew that Staffio had gotten flopped out of a specialized detail, because he fucked up. The unfortunate thing, however, is that he landed in Brooklyn South, and Marty was concerned that other people were now going to get fucked because Staffio, through a hook, didn't get bounced out of the detective division, but landed here in Brooklyn South. Fueled by the rift that now existed between him and Tony, Marty's feelings went from anger and disgust, to hate and disdain. As he stared at the new arrival, Marty decided that Paul Staffio would never fuck up again!

Chapter Seven

Rachael's Gift

Alex had left the squad room shortly after Iniddor and Ossur had been called into the boss's office. His disappointment and dissatisfaction were apparent. For the first time since the shooting, he felt that he might have to start taking matters into his own hands. His sister had been the apparent victim of an assassin's bullet, and it seemed that the detectives were no closer to finding out who the gunman was. He knew that after visiting his sister, he would have to start doing things himself. He would have to start asking his own questions and call upon some street people who might be able to help. However, he could not visit Rachael without first picking up a little present. Although she argued with him not to spend his money, he knew that she would be disappointed if he did not arrive with some sort of surprise. He knew his sister well. Since he had to make a quick trip to the mall anyway, he would pick up a gift there.

Three Kings Shopping Mall was crowded again, as usual. Even during the week, people manage to fill the walkways and corridors so that bumping and shoving become part of the normal shopping rhythm. Although this holiday season was already reflecting record-breaking sales, the relentless hue and cry from the never-satisfied merchants would again portray a lean margin of profit and a just-making-it attitude. For them, there was never enough.

After a frustrating and nerve-frizzling search for a parking spot, the privilege for which cost one dollar, Alex found himself almost involuntarily ushered into the entrance doors with the excited hordes of holiday shoppers. They were excited to the point that they didn't mind, or even notice for that matter, that they were being pushed, shoved, squeezed, spat upon, cursed at and cheated. They were getting their holiday shopping done because this was the season to be jolly. Alex now became one of a wandering mass of humanity, anxious holiday shoppers, being pushed from store to store. With a very angry, stout, determined, package-ladened woman running interference for him, he was able to finally weave his way to a familiar small novelty shop. He entered the store and felt relatively safe for the time being. The store was crowded, but compared to the general walkway areas, it was a ghost town. Alex now concentrated on his original mission – a gift for Rachael.

After what seemed to be an eternity of looking, examining, picking up, and price searching, Alex saw the special item. Trying to be practical, and at the same time thinking of his sister's likes and dislikes, he decided on a set of writing paper and matching pen. The set contained pink, purple, and yellow envelopes with fancy squiggly lines on the top that matched the printed design on the color coordinated stationery. The best part, however, was that the whole package only cost five dollars. The stress filled trip might have been worth it, since this very appropriate gift was well within Alex's financial reach. He picked out the stationary and went to the cashier's line behind approximately twelve other shoppers. His quick calculations told him that possibly within ten minutes time, he would be exiting the store and on his way to the parking lot. All in all, not that bad. He was certain that Rachael would like his choice. It was so in line with her personality that Alex knew she would assume that he spent a lot of time picking out such a special gift. It would seem that he had put genuine effort into her surprise.

"That will be five dollars and forty cents, please." Alex had the five dollars ready but had forgotten about the tax. He embarrassingly looked into his pockets for change. He came out with thirty-seven cents, three dimes, a nickel and two pennies. He began to reach for his wallet as the murmurs of disgruntled and impatient shoppers began to grow. He would gladly break another dollar, just as long as he escaped the vocal frustration which was about to begin. The more quickly he tried to get at his wallet, the more-clumsy he became.

However, in line with the true values of the holiday season, a good Samaritan behind him online offered the necessary three cents. Alex said no, but was thankful that the man insisted. Alex repeated his gratitude and found himself in small talk with the man. In fact, without realizing it, Alex had waited for the man to pay for his item. As they exited the store, Alex closed his conversation with a " thanks again," wished him a happy holiday, and braced himself for the unceremonious entry into the main flow of shoppers in the walkway, which seemed to have even grown to greater proportions since his departure. As Alex turned to leave, the man placed his hand on Alex's shoulder and turned to him with: "I told you that I would be in touch with you before the vacation ended, Alex." Confusion gave way to curious suspicion as Alex now connected those words to the voice on the phone – a voice that haunted him since he had left school.

The man continued: "Alex, I'm concerned for you and your family. Can we speak for a few moments?" The stranger had whet Alex's appetite for curiosity. How did this man know so much about Alex and his family? Maybe some nagging questions would be answered. Alex Hassid agreed to stop for a cup of coffee and listen for a few moments.

The coffee shop was reflective of the crowded conditions at the mall. It was chaotically noisy and not really conducive to serious conversation, but it was the only close oasis available. Alex did not have the luxury of time, since his visit to the hospital was his first priority. The man had a mild demeanor and spoke in very soft tones, sometimes so low that his words became inaudible and difficult for Alex to understand. The man's sincerity was obvious to Alex, and it became apparent that trust was the only thing exhibited on the man's face. He was a fellow countryman who wanted to help undo some of the injustices that had beset the Hassid family.

Alex listened with attentive concern as a stranger gave a brief account of the perceived inequalities existing in Israel, which had ultimately led to the unjustified and arbitrary incarceration of Alex's father and brother. Since this was a subject that was undoubtedly of interest to Alex, he forgot about the time and his commitment to Rachael. A young lady walking nearby in her nurse's uniform suddenly jogged Alex's memory, and he abruptly interrupted the storyteller: "Excuse me, but I have very little time left, and when you called you said that you had information about the shooting of my sister, Rachael." His brother and father were an ever-present concern for him, but right now, Alex's sister occupied the sustenance of his brain power. She was the priority, her safety was of paramount importance, she was here!

"My sources tell me that the shooting incident was not that of an indiscriminate madman. Your sister was the target of an assassin's bullet." Over the past days, Alex had entertained this thought many times, but to hear it verbalized chilled his entire body. His face became a mirror of concern, and he could not hide the obvious fact that this stranger had confirmed Rachael's original story. However, Alex would not accept the face value of the man's statements and wanted more convincing evidence of the man's convictions.

"Why would my sister be targeted for murder? She is fifteen-years-old, well-liked by almost everyone who knows her, and has few or no enemies. Also, how reliable are your sources anyway? What makes you think that you know the real story?"

The man looked directly into Alex's eyes and said: "It is the activities of your father that have dictated the actions against your sister." Alex remained mute. He had heard what the stranger said but wasn't sure he understood what was meant. The stranger continued: "Your father and brother have been accused of organizing and leading a rebel group in guerilla warfare. Even while they were in jail, they were accused of directing the raids against the Israeli regulars. They are being held responsible for the Basah attacks on Israeli bases and for the destruction of government property as well as the deaths of Israeli soldiers."

Before Alex could interrupt with questions, the man continued: "However, because Israel is convinced that your father and brother exercise strong influence over the rebel actions, the government wants them kept alive. They hope that by putting pressure on their two captives, your father and brother will ultimately influence the rebels to peacefully surrender. What pressure, however, could be exerted on these prisoners? Both have come to accept that their lives are expendable; but what about the pressure that does not affect them directly, but those they care about? How would your father feel if he knew that the lives of his family in America were being threatened?"

The stranger took a breath then directed his comments as a professor emphasizing a lesson: "Your sister was not meant to be killed. She was to be shot and wounded as a warning to your father and Chail that their family does not have the sanctuary of another country, and that what they do in an Israeli prison could determine the family's safety or lack of it. By this time, your father is well aware of what has occurred here. The incident is right now being used as a wedge for his collaboration."

The stranger began to answer Alex's second question which by now Alex had almost forgotten he asked: "Secondly, there is very little that the group does not know concerning events that affect our people. We want to help you and your family, but we will also need assistance from you. However, that can wait until we meet again. Now, I'm sure you want to get going and visit with your sister."

His sister - he almost forgot about visiting her at the hospital. So much had impacted on Alex that his physical and mental reaction time was laboriously slow. He was trying to mentally digest an unbelievable but believable story. The man got up and began to leave. Alex lunged and grabbed the man like a child who tugs at the end of a parental visit. "Who are you? When will you contact me?" So many questions, but he was able to verbalize only these two. In a caring but business-like tone, the man answered both: "You'll be contacted before you return to school, and I am called Dunait."

Once again, in his mysterious and almost spiritual manner, the man was gone. As his mind tried to put the events of the last few moments into some organized framework, Alex Hassid walked absentmindedly amongst the crowd toward the parking area. When he finally reached the general vicinity of where he thought he parked, his car became one of the hundred non-descript vehicles that weary shoppers searched for as they ended a trying day. As with many of the mall dwellers, whose minds were on everything but the parking lot, he did not even mentally record the color of the section in which he parked.

As the present vividly came to the forefront of his consciousness, panic started to set in. The hour was getting late, and he feared that he might miss visiting hours at the hospital, an action that would be unforgivable as far as Rachael was concerned. He had lost track of time during his meeting, and now he wasn't even sure where to look for his car. After what seemed like an eternity of walking in circles, there right in front of him, was his car. It was almost as if a higher power said: "Okay, I've put you through enough for today, here's your car." However, he was not going to ponder the how's of the situation, he was just glad to be able to get in and head for the hospital. Now more than ever, he wanted to be with his sister as much as possible. He would just feel better if he were there.

Driving up Kings Highway was a challenge for the most attentive drivers, so Alex knew that he must keep his mind on the road. Although he tried to be attentive to his driving, his mind was filled with so many questions, especially about the safety of the remaining members of his family. If they could so easily attack Rachael, why not his mother and even himself? He would have to more closely scrutinize the activities of all family members and offer unalarming guidance. He worried about surroundings, people, places, and situations. No matter how he tried to tell himself that this man, Dunait, wasn't right, a nagging feeling of insecurity permeated his present stream of consciousness. How could he go back to school and leave his family when it seemed that they needed him the most, now? Even they didn't know how much they might have to depend on him. How could he leave his family as unguarded prey, according to Dunait, for the sick, obediently sick, robots working for the ruthless wardens of Israel?

As his imagination brought the possibilities of reality into focus, the validity of Dunait's story seemed solid. From a puzzle of indecision, he came to the point of certain convincement. He made a mental commitment to help his new friend in any way possible. He needed alternatives to free his brother and father, and also ensure the safety of the remaining family. In his determinedness to finally do something tangible to help, Alex did not know how much would be asked of him. He couldn't even dream of the tasks and responsibilities that awaited him. Soon, when he was at the point of no turning back, he wouldn't believe the demands that this self-appointed savior would make of him. Dunait had appealed to the dormant macho feelings that lay in wait to bring the family safely together. The seeds of injustice, tyranny and inequality had been placed in the fertile mind of Alex. They would germinate, however, into a viny, jungle-like growth that ultimately developed into terrorism.

Chapter Eight

The Tete - e -Tete

Jalecya Prison was located on the southeastern edge of Israel in the town of Netivot. It was shaped in the form of a semicircle with the administrative operations building in the center of the horseshoe shaped opening. The three-story institution housed most of the political prisoners that Israel had considered a formidable threat to the efficient workings of the Israeli Government. It was here that Amir and his oldest son, Chail, had spent the last two years of their life. Both father and son had been arrested for their alleged participation in attacks on government installations and the deaths of numerous Israeli soldiers. Ordinarily, once found guilty of such crimes, the criminals would be put to death under Israeli law. However, it became known to the Israeli government and the Commanding Officer at Jalecya, Major Berman Yithak, that Amir and his son were not only active participants in the rebel cause but influential leaders within the group.

Major Yithak convinced his superiors that the two political prisoners would be more valuable if kept alive. He was certain that he could persuade them to cooperate in either convincing the rebels to retreat and discontinue their attacks, or even maybe supply information that would lead to the military dissolution of the rebel organization. However, the Major also knew that personal threats against the two would not result in the desired outcome. There had to be potential jeopardy for those who were dear to both father and son. It was with this plan in mind that Rachael Hassid had been shot and wounded at the rally.

The news of the shooting quickly reached the prison, and Amir knew that it was meant to be a message that he should cooperate or face the prospect of more family members being hurt or even killed. After speaking with his son and carefully evaluating the situation, Amir made the decision that he would at least listen to what Major Yithak had to say.

Chail was not of the same mind as his father, but he did not openly oppose the decision. Chail knew that an attempt to persuade the rebels to retreat would fall on deaf ears, and he also knew that no matter what, his father would not offer information that would lead to a calculated and devastating attack on the rebel stronghold. Amir would not let that happen, and Chail would make sure that his father would not sway from his determination.

Letting a few days pass and having allowed the seriousness of the situation to sink in, Major Yithak ordered the guards to bring Amir Hassid to his office. By this time, the concern and worry for his family was readily visible on Amir's face. The Major started by asking if Amir had heard the troubling news that his daughter Rachael had been injured and was the victim of a gunshot wound. Amir knew that the Major was aware of the fact that the news of the shooting had reached the prison that following day.

Berman Yithak showed his "sincere" dismay over what had occurred at Thomson High School and following a positive response by his prisoner, Amir, the Major asked: "Do you know of anyone who would do something like that?" Amir answered that it had been a crazed individual, and Rachel had unfortunately been the victim of an errant gunshot. With a very discerning eye and the sneer of a cobra ready to strike, Yithak said: "That is not what I heard." He went on to say that there were strong indications that the gunman had singled out Rachael as the intended target. Not wanting to give the Major anything to support his allegation, Amir vehemently denied the circumstances that the Major had described. The cat and mouse game continued for a time until Major Yithak ran out of patience. In a focused, determined and loud voice he said: "Do you want to make certain that another 'accident' doesn't happen to her or anyone else in your family? Your son and wife could also suffer the consequences of such an accident. If we work together, we can possibly protect your family from further harm. As you know it is a dangerous world out there."

Amir Hassid just stared at the Major and waited to hear what he had to offer. However, Yithak offered nothing but silence, waiting for Amir to squirm and bite at the prospect of protection for his family. The psychological tete-e-tete was in full swing, and the Major played his cards well. With no comment coming from his prisoner, he ordered the guards to take Amir back to his cell. Yithak wanted Amir to really consider whether he would want to risk the safety of his family versus the extermination and inevitable short-lived existence of a mis-directed rebel group.

Amir and Chail's cells were next to each other, so communication was not difficult. Chail was anxious when his father returned. His immediate question to his father was: "What did the Czar want?" Amir hesitantly answered: "I think he was implying that he could ensure the safety of our family if we cooperated with him." Chail was concerned: "What does that mean? What does he want from us?" The next response weighed heavily on Chail. "The Major wants us to convince our group to give up peacefully; and if that doesn't work, and most likely it won't, I'm sure he will want us to help in eliminating the group."

Because of Amir's tone, Chail felt that his father's determination was wavering in the face of possible harm to the family. Although Amir was a leader and highly regarded by the group, he did not have the same reckless and savage instincts as Chail. Chail was very worried that at the next meeting with his father, the Major would break Amir and get the information that was needed to stop any further action by the Alliance. Chail felt that his father was very close to betraying the cell in an effort to save the family from further harm. Chail could not let that happen.

During their one-hour exercise time in the courtyard, the Hassids were walking together and discussing some options that might be available. They both knew that the Major would be calling Amir into his office that afternoon to get the results that he wanted. As the two were walking, they were stopped by two other inmates asking if there was any additional news from the outside. As Amir and Chail faced one of the inmates, the other went to the back of the two. It was then that Amir grimaced in pain and let out a cry as a sharp object penetrated his back. The assailant nodded to

Chail in a positive manner and melded into the crowd of inmates that gathered around Amir. Chail held his father as he lay on the ground. Amir's last words to his son were: "You have signed a death warrant for our family. May Allah forgive you."

Chapter Nine

The Cell

The Alliance Cell had already met a number of times, but following his brief sit-down with Alex, Dunait called for another meeting to discuss Alex's potential participation in the future actions of the cell. The meeting took place in the backroom of a Halal Butcher Shop located in the Hicksville area of Long Island. Including Dunait, there were eleven other members of the cell in attendance. Everyone was talking until Dunait asked for their attention. Now, you could hear a pin drop. He explained where he was with Alex, and that he was almost certain that Alex would join them in their efforts. Although Alex did not know to what extent his participation would be, the accident that his sister suffered was a convincing element in his full cooperation.

Among the other eleven members was a man named Ismul Rahej who worked as a security officer at Three Kings Shopping Mall. He would be very important in the execution of the terrorist plan scheduled for Christmas Eve.

There was much talk regarding the recent shooting of Amir Hassid's daughter, Rachael. The group was incensed that the Israeli government would stoop as low as they did by placing Rachael in danger of serious injury or even death. However, they were also very worried that the pressure being brought to bear on Amir might break his determination in not offering information that might cripple the cell's upcoming plan. Dunait assured the group that he was confident that Amir and Chail would be strong, and no matter the circumstances, the Christmas Eve plan would not be jeopardized.

A number of the members had already done surveillance at the Shopping Center, and they were depending on Security Guard Rahej for certain specific information that would facilitate their planned terrorist action. Additionally, two of the members had applied for custodial positions and were scheduled to begin work the week before Christmas - two weeks from now.

Ismul had obtained maps of the internal diagram of the mall in addition to the surrounding outside areas. The group continued to view the maps as each member of the cell reviewed his specific positioning and responsibilities. To take on such an outrageous attack, specifics and particulars had to be committed to memory so there would be no doubt as to each individual's actions. Dunait went from member to member asking what the responsibility was and an alternate plan if an unexpected event was to occur. Nothing could be left to chance if they were to succeed in bringing Israel to its knees regarding the freedom of twenty political prisoners housed at Jalecya – two of which were important leaders in the Alliance Network. Amir and Chail had to be freed as they were an intricate part of the Alliance Hierarchy and had developed plans for future actions.

With the aspect of having inside information and assistance, the take-down of the Three Kings Shopping Mall would be greatly facilitated. Ismul had gotten close to Bob Baxter and was a personal favorite of Reginald Winsten, the General Manager of Three Kings Shopping Center. Guard Rahej had been able to create an attitude of trust, and because of this, became privy to many things that the other workers never knew. In fact, a number of times both Reginald and Bob Baxter had brought Ismul in to discuss specific problems and concerns regarding the overall operation of the mall. Rahej acted as the informal site supervisor for the security activities involving the safety of the shoppers as well as the security of the facility. This level of trust would facilitate the successful execution of the Christmas Eve attack.

Although it was not the intention of Dunait or the other cell members to kill anyone, they had accessed a number of weapons that they would carry with them – anywhere from a Glock automatic pistol to a semi-automatic assault rifle. They also had a number of explosive devices. If they were ultimately confronted by armed law enforcement officers and were in danger of not completing their plan, they would have no recourse but to attempt to eliminate the threat by opening fire on any and all who stood in the way of success. The cell was determined to execute their plan no matter what the cost.

Dunait knew that very shortly he would have to meet with Alex again to explain his part in the terrorist plan. There would have to be a serious discussion with him emphasizing that this plan could be the only way that Alex would be able to see his father and brother again. Although this was part of the intended result, the overall focus was to free approximately twenty of their countrymen who could, once again, join the ranks of those who fight the perceived tyranny of the Israeli government.

Having been satisfied with the attention the members had given to their individual responsibilities,

Dunait closed the meeting with a guarantee that there would be additional meetings scheduled before the attack day, and these meetings would now include the attendance of one, Alex Hassid. What Alex would be unaware of was the fact that his new friend, Vin, would also be attending the meetings as a willing participant in the Christmas Eve terrorist attack on the Three King Shopping Center.

Chapter Ten

The Revelation

Alex went back to college for the two weeks before his Christmas vacation was to begin. He was very worried about his family, but they insisted that he return for the two weeks and finish with his final exams which would lead to the end of the semester. It was now the Friday before the vacation began, and he was very anxious to once again fly home and be with his family. During the Thanksgiving break, Vin Falco had called him a number of times, but because of all the worries that were consuming his every waking thought, Alex just ignored the calls. He had no time for socializing and meeting with friends. He also had not heard from the mysterious Mr. Dunait who said that he would be in contact with Alex shortly. He wondered why someone who knew so much about Alex and his family and who had a possible plan to help eliminate some of the problems that the family faced and seemed so seriously enthusiastic about his help, would stay so elusive for so long. Why hadn't he called? Why hadn't he met again with Alex before he went back to school? Why was everything so mysterious and cloaked in secrecy? Also, how was Alex to help in freeing his father and brother? What would he have to do?

As all these things bombarded his stream of consciousness, his cell phone rudely interrupted his train of thought. The screen lit up with Vin Falco's name as the caller. Since he hadn't answered the calls from Vin when they were on vacation, he felt an obligation to answer it now. After all, Vin did him a solid at the airport, and the least he could do now was to answer the call. "Hello Vin, how are you doing? Sorry, I couldn't get back to you on break, but I was dealing with a number of family problems. In addition to my sister suffering a serious accident, I am worried about my father and brother back in the homeland. Things are just piling up, and I have no real time for myself." Vin listened carefully and astonished Alex with his response: "I know about your problems, Alex, and I'm here to help with whatever I can. In fact, the next time you speak with Dunait and ultimately meet with him, I am going to be there."

Alex couldn't believe what he was hearing. How could Vin know what was going on, and how was it possible that he knew Dunait? It sounded like Vin knew more about what was taking place than Alex did. Alex was both confused and alarmed as he questioned Vin: "I don't understand Vin. How do you know so much and what's your connection to Dunait?" Vin answered: "Dunait and my father have been friends for a very long time. In fact, they grew up together. They share the same ideals and commitments to the people who are suffering under Israeli tyranny. My father has been working with Dunait for a long time, and I, as well as my dad, have been recruited to assist in the present "freedom" operation - the one where you will be needed to bring the plan to a successful conclusion."

These new revelations were a lot for Alex to mentally comprehend. In fact, it was hard for Alex to really believe what Vin was saying. Alex continued: "So our meeting was not just a chance meeting, and your contacting me is not out of mere friendship. It seems like you are on a mission to help Dunait get my cooperation. I do not like being duped and played for a fool. I want to know right now what is going on, and who you really are." Vin felt that he might be losing Alex, so he offered some insights into the planned mall activities: "My father and I are part of a group known as the Alliance

Cell, and we are organized to fight against the unjust treatment our people receive from the tyrannical Israeli government. Your father, my father, and Dunait have been working together to plan an action that would push the United States into pressuring their ally, Israel, to abide by the demands we will make of them. These demands include the immediate release of your father and brother as well as twenty other political prisoners being held in Israeli prisons."

Vin stopped abruptly realizing that he might have gone too far. It was for Dunait to offer the explanation to Alex, and for him to address any concerns Alex may have. He might have jumped the gun, but he was afraid that Alex was not fully on board. Still, it was for Dunait to address the situation, not him.

To steer the conversation in another direction, Vin told Alex how his father had Americanized the family name to facilitate the family's absorption into the American culture as well as "grease the rails" for possible employment. It had been successful, and his father's previous experience as an engineer allowed Mr. Falco (formerly Falcohaetj) to land the Director of Facilities position at the Three Kings Shopping Center. The information slowly sinking in, Alex became increasingly apprehensive, but even more so, somewhat fearful about what this seemingly organized rebel group would be asking of him. Now the anticipated meeting with Dunait was even more troubling.

Alex asked Vin when Dunait would be contacting him since it had been a while since the last communication. Vin did not know and was reluctant to discuss anything further regarding the operation. However, Vin did say that he would be contacting Mr. Dunait to let him know that they had spoken. Alex pushed forward and asked if Vin would give him Dunait's number so that he could initiate contact. Vin answered: "Absolutely not. I have divulged too much already. Mr. Dunait is not going to be happy with me, and if I gave you his contact number, I don't know what he would do."

Alex almost felt betrayed by Vin. He was more than the person who he portrayed to be. He won Alex's trust only to influence Alex to become a part of a group that would be pitting the United States against Israel. Alex had to get his thoughts together, and so, he very abruptly told Vin that he was hanging up. In the middle of him speaking, Vin heard the disconnect, and now he had to speak with Dunait as quickly as possible to smooth the way with Alex. Vin knew that there would be hell to pay. He couldn't be more right!

Chapter Eleven

The Travel Agency

Seven days until Christmas and, as usual, the burglaries, robberies and assaults were mounting up. Friday night, Tony Ossur and Paul Staffio were part of the working Detective team for the night tour. Marty had taken off both Friday and Saturday with Sunday and Monday being his scheduled days off. So, he had a four-day swing. Ordinarily, it would be no big deal for Tony, but Marty being off now meant Tony would be coupling with only Paul for both Friday and Saturday.

They were on their way to interview a victim of an assault and robbery which had occurred in the Marine Park area of the 65th precinct. The female victim sustained injuries to her neck, back and arms as she tried to fight off her assailants. The detectives were met by her husband who answered the ringing doorbell. He was very much concerned regarding his wife's well-being and was somewhat reluctant to have the Detectives speak to her so soon after coming home from the emergency room. Tony explained to the husband that they wanted to speak to his wife while descriptions and circumstances were still fresh in her mind.

Actually, they should have already interviewed her at the hospital, but because of the increased caseload, they couldn't get to her until now. Mr. Jacobs understood and opened the door for the detectives and escorted them into the living room where they found Mrs. Jacobs reclining on the sofa. Tony apologized for interrupting but explained to her that it was necessary to get all of the information as soon as possible so that an investigation could begin.

Leslie Jacobs explained that when she left the Three Kings Mall, she was carrying a number of items including a hand bag with her wallet containing approximately $250.00 and a number of credit cards. She was walking home because her residence was within walking distance from the shopping center. Apparently, she had been followed by two males who attacked her while she was walking. One grabbed at her bag while the other pulled on her arm and wrapped his hand around her neck to immobilize her and reduce any resistance. When they ultimately got her bag, they released her by throwing her to the ground where she landed on her back.

At this point, Mrs. Jacob was in tears and shaking from the nerve-racking experience. Nothing that Tony had not seen and dealt with before. He allowed her time to compose herself and then questioned her some more. "Can you give me a description of the two males?" She answered: "There was one white male and one black male."

"How tall would you say they were and what were they wearing?" In an effort to facilitate the description, Detective Staffio stood up and said that he was approximately 6 feet tall. He said: "Were they taller or shorter than me?" This helped Mrs. Jacobs to come up with a height and weight approximation. However, what Staffio did was to interrupt Tony's flow of questioning, and Tony was not happy with that. He would definitely have to set down some ground rules when the interview was over. Ground rules that any other Detective who was assigned to case work would already know.

Mrs. Jacobs answered: "They were both about 6 feet tall and maybe 200 pounds. The white male was wearing a brown sweater with jeans. He was also wearing a white baseball hat with a big 'C' in front. The black male had on a red sweatshirt with a hoodie, and he also wore jeans. I couldn't tell if he was wearing a hat because of the hoodie." Tony followed up: "Did they have any facial hair or markings that would distinguish them from others?" She could not remember if the black male had facial hair, but the white male had a goatee. Once again, Paul chimed in: "Did you see which way they left, and did they escape on foot?" Leslie Jacobs could not remember in which direction they went, but she did not see or hear a car so she assumed that they were on foot. Tony thanked Mr. and Mrs. Jacobs for their time and told them that if the Detectives found out anything, that they would be in touch. Mr. Jacobs escorted them out.

As soon as the car door closed, Tony began his chastising. Surprisingly, Paul just listened and tried to explain that he was only trying to help. Tony emphatically yelled that he didn't need his help. Tony might have been somewhat over-reacting just because he knew of Paul's involvement in the recent rape case concerning Donna Uhrich.

As they pulled away from Mr. and Mrs. Jacob's residence, and after he had been bombarded with Tony's criticism, Paul asked Tony if they could stop at the mall for a few minutes. Since they were just blocks away, he didn't think that it would be a problem. Tony was hesitant and wanted to know why the stop was necessary since they had a number of cases to investigate. Paul explained that it involved a complainant from a previous case, and he just wanted to follow up on it. Tony reluctantly agreed. They pulled into one of the reserved spots on the street adjacent to the west side of the mall. These were spots reserved for emergency responder vehicles, and there was a guard assigned to secure the area. Paul exited the vehicle with Tony close behind. They went up to the second floor and to the other end of the shopping mall. Tony lagged behind as he was going into an area in which he was all too familiar. Paul stopped at the entrance to the Compass World Travel Agency. He went directly to the desk assigned to Donna Uhrich, who worked for Compass.

Tony was beside himself, but had to react in a way that did not give any indication that he was either involved professionally or personally. Unbeknownst to Tony, the phone call that Paul had received from Detective Sergeant Noldir from the Sex Crimes Unit, was a directive to assist with the investigation and follow-up with an interview. As Tony entered, he came into eye contact with Donna. He nodded and she returned with an obvious "hello." Paul was speaking with Donna, and Tony did not want to interrupt.

When there was a lull in the conversation, Tony showed his concern and asked what had happened. She explained in detail what had occurred and began to tear up.

Tony displayed his false concern and shock, but was beginning to feel those same pangs of guilt that he had started to feel that night. Paul did not stay long and told Donna that he would be in touch with her again. Tony was within earshot and did not like the idea that Detective Staffio would again, at a later date, be in touch with Donna.

They left, and Tony could not wait until they were back in the car so that he could pump Paul about his involvement in the case. Paul explained that since he had been in the area the night of the attack, and since the Sex Crimes Unit was understaffed, his former commanding officer committed Paul to assisting in the assault and rape investigation. Tony carefully inquired as to where they were with the case and explained that he had a former relationship with Donna. Paul answered that he knew that, and they were exploring the description of the escaping vehicle. After canvassing the immediate area, it was learned that the vehicle was a late model sports car, either silver or gray. Tony was concerned that Paul already knew about the former relationship and also the particulars about the vehicle.

Although Tony had turned off his lights that night, the reflection from the street light apparently was enough for a witness to mention a late model silver or gray sports car - Tony's new, silver, Mustang. Tony, in some way, had to mis-direct the investigation, and get to the complainant,

Donna, or find a patsy to take the hit. He needed help, and hopefully that help would come from his long-time partner, Marty.

Chapter Twelve

A Son's Betrayal

Alex arrived home early and surprised everyone. He was anxious to see his sister, and how she was recovering from her injury. Rachael seemed to be physically fine, but Alex could tell that she was still worried about her safety. Following the usual elongated greetings, Alex was able to get Rachael alone and have a serious conversation with her, letting her know what had been occurring in his life. Although she was young, she was mature above her years and would understand what was actually taking place. He explained his secretive conversations with Dunait and what the focus of his organization was. He also let her know that he was awaiting another contact where he would be informed of his potential role in the plan to free their father and brother, as well as other political prisoners.

Rachael was shocked to hear that such a plan was being proposed, and even more shocked that Alex would be a part of it. For fear of Alex getting hurt and possibly killed, Rachael warned against his participation, but Alex was determined to help in getting Amir and Chail to freedom and safety. Rachael teared up a bit. She did not want to lose another brother, another family member. However, after seeing how determined Alex was, and knowing that she could not persuade him to not get involved, she asked if there was anything that she could do. Of course, Alex told her that there was nothing for her to do, not wanting to get her involved in a potentially dangerous situation.

Just when they were finishing with the conversation, they were interrupted by the doorbell. Alex went to the door, and to his astonishment, opened it to Mr. Dunait. Recovering from the shock, Alex asked what Dunait was doing there. Without hesitation, Dunait answered: "It is time that you meet with me and the rest of the group. Please come with me now so that you can truly understand what we are about to do, and your participation." Without hesitation, Alex let the family know that he had some errands to run, and that he would be back shortly.

He left with Dunait. He attended that meeting and a number of other meetings with the group and was perplexed that he had not seen Vin or heard from Vin Falco. At one of these meetings just five days before Christmas Eve, Alex asked why Vin was not there. He was very directly told that Vin had become a risk to the operation, and that he was given other non-related duties. Alex did not know what that meant but thought better of asking for any clarification. However, it was clear as to what specific duty and responsibility Alex would have. His target and concern was none other than the General Manager of the Three Kings Shopping Mall, Mr. Reginald Winsten.

At the same time that these meetings were taking place, tension was building in Jalecya Prison. Major Yithak was being pressured by his superiors to come up with results. It was going to be now or never if he was to get information from Amir. As the Major was about to send for Amir, one of the guards burst into the office to let Major Yithak know that Amir Hassid had been stabbed and killed in the exercise yard, and that they had no idea who committed the act. Yithak was beside himself. He had guaranteed to his superiors that he would be getting information that would lead to the dismantling of the rebel group. His only hope now was getting cooperation from Amir's son, Chail. That was going to be difficult, but the

Major's future depended on it. His future and his possible life.

He told the guard to bring Chail to him immediately, and prepare Amir for a proper burial. Chail appeared before the Major in a matter of minutes. In an attempt to disarm Chail, Yithak told Chail that he would find out who had killed his father and would have him executed. Chail remained quiet and waited for the Major to continue: "We were about to settle on an agreement that would guarantee the future safety of your family. With Amir unfortunately gone, I am depending on you to enter into the agreement. Amir understood what was at stake, and he realized that the efforts of his organization would not bring victory to the rebel cause. He valued the safety and security of his family over the useless cause of the rebels. I am certain that I can depend on you to keep your part of the bargain."

He paused and waited for Chail's response which was a long time in coming: "I will not bargain with you, and I will not betray my comrades. My father died for the cause, and I will not let his dying be in vain. All will know that the monster of Jalecya killed Amir because he would not cooperate with Israel and betray his countrymen and the cause. My father's death will strengthen the determination to take down unjust Israeli rule." He concluded his statement by spitting at the feet of Major Yithak.

The Major became incensed and lunged at Chail in an effort to choke the life out of him. The guards outside the door heard the commotion. They entered and separated the two as Chail was fighting for his life. Major Yithak ordered Chail to solitary confinement with a reduction in food and water. Things now had gotten worse for the Major, especially if word got out that the prison Commandant was responsible for the death of one of the cell leaders. This news would only serve to bolster the participation in the cause. The Major realized that he only had a short time to make things right with his superiors and an even shorter time to break Chail. Or had he run out of time?

Chapter Thirteen

The Delay

Many cops moonlight (work second jobs) to supplement their police salaries. Marty and Tony were no exceptions. Especially during the holiday time, private security demands are very high. So, although Marty had a few days off from police work, he met with Tony at the Jewelry Store that they were protecting during the holiday season. "Best Jewelry" was located on the first floor of the Three Kings Shopping Center and was the nearest store to the front entrance of the mall. Although the spot was great for sales, the location was also ideal for a "grab-and-run," hence the hiring of security to deter losses.

Although both Tony and Marty were vigilant in their watching for potential thefts, it also gave them time to discuss a number of things. Marty had done a little investigating and discovered information regarding the recent assault and rape case. Detective Sergeant Noldir was a close friend, and Marty was able to speak directly to her regarding the case. He learned that the incident took place the same day as the party at Myrna's house and during the time period that Tony had stormed out. He learned that the victim was Donna, and he also found out that an eye-witness had given a partial description of the vehicle believed to be involved in the crime – a silver or gray late model sports car. The witness had also stated that the right rear light was not working.

Marty was almost one hundred percent sure that Tony wouldn't do anything that would hurt Donna, but he was well aware of how Tony had this love-hate relationship with her. That night when Tony stormed out of the house, no one, including Marty, knew what Tony was going to do. However, from past experience, Marty just assumed that his partner would head back to the precinct to sleep it off in the dorm.

Marty had checked with the desk officer who was on duty that night to see if he remembered seeing Tony come into the precinct. The desk officer wasn't certain for sure but was almost positive that Tony didn't come into the precinct. Where did Tony go? What did he do? Could he have possibly gone to Donna's neighborhood? Did he confront her? All these questions were unanswered and nagging at Marty. Now, out of the confines of the squad room and in the Jewelry Store, he was able to toss these questions directly to Tony, fully assuming that Tony would have an explanation for his actions.

He started: "Tony, I found out about the kidnapping and assault incident, and I understand why you are so reluctant to talk about it. I'm curious though. Where did you go when you left Myrna's house? I checked with the precinct, and they said that you did not go back there. Did you head toward Donna's?" Tony couldn't hide his anger and concern from his partner: "I went to Donna's mother's house and waited for her to leave to go back home. I waited for about twenty minutes to a half-an-hour before I saw her leave. I was pissed, and the wait just added to my anger and anxiety. When she drove away, I followed her to her apartment." Although Tony was revealing information that would ultimately confirm his guilt, he felt somewhat relieved to get things off his chest, and who better to confess to than his partner, his friend. Marty picked up the questioning: "When you got to Donna's, what then?"

"I got there first and waited for her to arrive." Marty interrupted: "So you were there right before the assault? Did you see anything before you left?" Tony answered: "I saw the whole thing." Marty was confused: "So you just allowed it to take place? I don't understand. You could have stopped the whole thing and you just let it go down?" Tony looked directly at his partner: "That bitch deserved everything she got and more, and I gave her as much as I could." Marty felt like he just got sucker-punched to the gut: "What are you saying, Tony, that you raped her? You're the guy they're looking for? You're the one who is guilty of kidnapping, assault and rape? Tony, what the hell were you thinking?" He answered: "I wasn't thinking. I was just reacting to the anger I felt, and it was being fueled, I guess, by the alcohol."

"Tony, you have to turn yourself in. You can't let this go on. Throw yourself at the mercy of the court and hope that Donna has more sympathy for you than you have for her." Tony knew that Marty was right but asked Marty a favor: "I will turn myself in right after the Christmas holiday, and I need you to understand that. Don't mention anything until after Christmas. Please." Marty did not want any part of the delay but reluctantly agreed to wait for Tony to surrender after Christmas. He also realized that he could be considered as "obstructing a criminal investigation." He knew that, but he owed Tony a lot and would wait the three days. They would both be working the security at the

Jewelry Store up to and including Christmas Eve. Marty would make sure that Tony would not renege on his commitment.

It was difficult for Marty to feel the same toward Tony. He no longer felt the camaraderie, and loyalty he once had, but was inundated with feelings of pity, disgust, guilt and shame. How could Tony put himself, and now his partner, in such a compromised position? Marty couldn't wait for the three days to pass. He was now working with a criminal sex aggressor, the type of person that they both abhorred.

Tony was ultimately going to be found guilty of the crimes against Donna and be sentenced to time in prison. However, having had many a conversation with his partner, Marty knew that Tony would not accept the fact that he would have to be remanded to prison for years. It's just that Marty didn't know how Tony thought that he was going to avoid it. The whole situation put Marty on edge, and it was not where he wanted to be.

Following the disconcerting conversation that had just taken place, both men were surprised to hear a familiar voice: "So, this is where you guys hang out. A couple of guys in the squad said that I could find you here." Paul Staffio was front and center: "Just wanted to let you know that the humps who attacked Mrs. Jacobs were collared as they attempted another robbery. They ran, but uniforms picked them up a block away from the scene. They were positively identified by the new complainant and Mrs. Jacobs."

Marty and Tony, still reeling from the previous conversation, only picked up certain things that Detective Staffio was saying. However, when Detective Staffio started giving them a progress report on the Sexual Assault case, they were all ears. He mentioned that they were close to identifying the escape vehicle and had received additional information from a witness. They were also looking at the red light and traffic cameras in the area at the time of the incident to possibly get more on the vehicle. Just what Tony wanted to hear!

They played off the information and asked Paul if there was anything else that he had to say. They also asked if that was the only reason he came to the mall. Paul said: "Actually, I'm here for personal reasons too. I need to get a present for my girlfriend, and I thought that I could get a break on some jewelry, if I come to see you guys."

Marty introduced Paul to the store manager and asked that he show some items to Paul that he might be interested in. The manager directed Paul to the showcase displaying rings and bracelets. Paul said thanks to the guys and followed the manager. If looks could kill, Tony would have murdered the guy, but he had to play it cool, at least for the next three days and maybe after.

Chapter Fourteen

The Preparation

As is the usual routine, an order came down to the Brooklyn South Squad to only keep a minimum of detectives working cases and assign the rest to high trafficked shopping areas. This, plus the constant pressure from the Merchants' Association for better protection, forced Sergeant Dello to divide his squad into two sections: case investigation and crime prevention patrol. The majority of the office went on patrol until after the Christmas Holiday. The remaining detectives were burdened with all of the cases that would come into the office during this time.

Detectives Ossur, Iniddor and Staffio remained in the office, probably because of seniority, while Jim Jones, Juan Medina, Nick Possidos and Gary Glasser were assigned to the Three Kings Shopping Mall area. Frank Austin, Angel Torres, Ralph Clemengas and Ira Jacobs were sent to the downtown market area to supplement the uniformed patrols in that area. There would always be at least two detectives working patrol at any given time, and in the case of the Shopping Mall, when Tony and Marty were working at the Jewelry Store, there would be 4 detectives actually at the Mall.

Public notices were sent out to notify shoppers and potential thieves that security had been "beefed up," and that shopping areas were under constant scrutiny by the NYPD. Although this additional security did not prevent all crimes, it did deter the incidence of criminal behavior in and around the mall. The detectives worked two tours during this time: 8:00 am to 4:00 pm and 4:00 pm to midnight. In the event of an arrest, the detectives would turn over the collar to the uniform patrol so coverage would not be reduced in the mall. The way the assignments had been doled out was unfortunate for Tony. It meant that Paul Staffio would not be bogged down with patrol assignments and could still devote time to investigations, especially one particular investigation.

As a result of the gut-wrenching conversation that took place in the jewelry store between Tony and Marty, there was tension and an uneasy feeling floating in the air between the two of them. Since there were only three detectives working cases, Sergeant Del took an experienced uniformed officer to assist Detective Staffio on the night shift as Marty and Tony took the day shift. Following their shift, Detectives Ossur and Iniddor would then go to the Jewelry Store for their moonlighting job. It worked out well.

Since the squad knew that Marty and Tony were at "Best" during the night tour, the detectives assigned to the mall mostly concentrated on the other wings of the shopping area, knowing that Tony and Marty would respond to anything that came up in their location. The guys assigned to the mall were somewhat happy with their assignment because just like the majority of shoppers, they also waited for the last minute to decide on what presents to buy. That was why Christmas Eve was one of the busiest shopping days of the holiday season. Everyone waited for the last minute because people thought that prices would be reduced as it was the last day, and merchants wanted to sell as much as possible to reduce their inventory and realize a decent profit.

Mixed in with the normal shoppers were members of the Alliance Cell who were familiarizing themselves with the mall, and the position that they would take during the attack. They knew that the Shopping Mall was divided into three separate wings, however, the cell members were only concerned with the west wing since they were going to be able to isolate that wing from the rest. The west wing included the main entrance to the Three Kings Shopping Center and, for the most part. was the busiest section.

The electricity, doors, lights and ventilation systems in the mall were electronically controlled from the administrative offices where the Director of Facilities, Erman Falco, shared office space with Security Director, Bob Baxter and the General Manager, Reginald Winsten. This building also housed the security camera room and would become most important in the success of the planned attack. It was also the location where Alex Hassid would actively participate in the "take-over." However, getting into these offices presented a problem because the entrance doors to the administrative offices were electronically locked, and unless a person had an authorized pass card to enter, the doors would remain locked. The only other way to enter was to be buzzed in by someone inside. The entrance was also under camera surveillance.

Alex and the rest of the cell members were even more determined now since they had heard that the prison commander at Jalecya had ordered Amir's death because he wouldn't cooperate. He died for the cause, and it was imperative for every member that they succeed in making certain that Amir did not die in vain. Chail had worked his magic, and the entire Alliance network knew of how Amir died at the hands of Major Yithak, the Commandant of Jalecya Prison. This bold and outrageous move by Chail had the desired effect on the cell members. Those who were originally on the fringe of participation were now emboldened to wage whatever war they could to bring down the unjust tyrannical regime. As the news spread, many of his countrymen were now interested in the clandestine activities of the cell and wanted to become a part of the organization. Even though he was still in prison, things were going Chail's way, and he would soon become the designated leader of the rebel group and would ultimately bring Israel to its knees.

Strongly aware of the potential success of the planned attack, Chail would soon be free to plan future missions and gain, what he believed, were the fruits of victory. Israel would have to bend to the demands of America, their strongest ally. If they didn't, they would be jeopardizing future support and be directly responsible for the possible death of hundreds of American citizens. The rebels were in a win-win situation, and they knew it. Soon America and Israel would also know it!

Chapter Fifteen

The Barbarian

Having only spent approximately forty-eight hours in solitary confinement, Chail, surprisingly, was now being escorted back to Major Yithak's office. He assumed that the Major was going to offer some other bargain or decided that solitary confinement and reduced rations was not a good enough persuader. As he was thrown through the door of the Major's office, he was surprised that Major Yithak was not there to meet him, but General Abel Gollman, also known to many as the Barbarian, was sitting behind Yithak's desk.

Although Yithak was a formidable adversary, there was no comparison to what General Gollman could and would do. Chail knew that he was in for a real rough time, and that the General would live up to his reputation. The General greeted Chail with: "Do you want to continue to live or would you rather suffer a tortuous death?" Chail did not answer. Gollman nodded to one of the guards who had what looked like a cattle prod in his hand. The guard proceeded to jab the weakened Chail in the back. Electric current flowed through his body and he went to the ground screaming out in anguish and pain. The General shaking his head said: "Consider that just foreplay. Do we understand one another?" As he lay on the floor, Chail could only nod "yes'" to General Gollman's question. The General ordered the guards to prop the prisoner up in one of the chairs in front of the desk. Chail swayed like a rag doll and needed the guards to stabilize him.

The General continued: "I need information regarding your organization, the headquarters, their leaders, and what they are planning. I know that the group is planning an action to possibly free some of their countrymen who are imprisoned here and at other prisons. Just to let you know now, no matter what is planned, it will not happen. So, the information that you give us, although useful, will not be our only resource to stop the rebels. We are collecting information as we speak."

Chail responded to the General: "If that is the case, why do you need anything from me?" Gollman answered: "Only because there are some gaps that we have to fill, and we do not want to waste our time and efforts. It is my understanding that your father was ready to cooperate with us before his untimely demise. It is also my understanding that you have filled the network with propaganda that we are responsible for Amir's death. Although you might have thought it was really smart to spread that rumor, it will come back to bite you when we find out who did it - and we will. But for now, I need information! To start with: where are the rebels working out of?" Chail slowly responded: "There is no specific headquarters. We meet at different locations all the time so that someone like you cannot come in with guns firing and kill innocent people." Gollman interrupted: "I don't believe you, but I will accept it for now as long as I get more information. Other than you and your father, are there any other leaders here at Jalecya?"

The electric shock treatment to his body began to wear off, he started feeling a little stronger and somewhat obstinate. He answered: "There are no real leaders, we all contribute and decide as a group." The General shouted "bullshit," and nodded once again to the guard. This time the electric contact was longer and more focused. Chail again went to the ground swearing and uncontrollably shaking. Gollman stood over the tortured prisoner and let him know that the electric charge was only at half power, and that he was very capable of increasing the current. He ended his comments with the warning that a full charge can ultimately stop the heart, but it was the journey up to that charge that was an unforgettable and tortuous trip.

General Gollman then sent Chail back to his cell with the guards almost carrying him. The General would see him later in the day so that the weakened Chail could regain a little strength and focus on how bad things could really get. Chail really didn't care what happened to him, but he started to have the same guilt feelings about his family in America, as did his father. He was sure that sooner or later when Gollman saw that punishing him didn't produce the desired results, actions would be directed at his family. It was not beyond the Barbarian to maim, torture, or kill to get what he wanted.

His father gone, it was up to Chail now to protect the rest of the family, especially his young sister, Rachael. He was torn between furthering the "cause" and securing the welfare of his family. It was a difficult decision, and one that Chail was not willing to make. As he sat in his cell, he thought about all of the suffering that his people have gone through, and how he could not allow it to continue. He also thought about his father, who had to be sacrificed to protect the cell. And he was now also plagued with the idea that his family would become unwilling allies after the application of the Barbarian's persuasive methods. He wished his father was here now, but Chail knew what decision his father would have told him to make. Chail also realized that there were others who could also step up and lead, maybe not as experienced, cutthroat, or determined as he or his father, but men who would forge ahead to bring about freedom.

Chail knew that in a very short time, General Gollman would once again be sending for him. It would be time for another question-and-answer period, where the wrong answer or no answer at all would result in excruciating pain. He was not up for that, and didn't know if he could withstand another session where electricity rushed through every part of his body and turned him into a pile of squirming flesh. He wouldn't sell out his countrymen, and he would not allow the Barbarian to put the Hassid family in harm's way.

Approximately one hour later when General Gollman felt that he had given Chail enough time to recover and also think about the ramifications of a "no cooperation" attitude, he once again ordered the guards to bring the prisoner to his office. This would be the final interrogation. Chail would either give him what he wanted or suffer consequences for himself and ultimately for his family. The guards left to escort Chail to the General's office. As the outside corridor doors of the cell block opened, other prisoners who knew what was going on, started to warn Chail that the guards were on their way.

It was an extended walk to the end of the block before the guards would come to Chail's cell. All during that time, the prisoners whispered warnings to Chail. However, there was an eerie silence that absorbed all of the cautions that were sent to him. The guards arrived at Chail's cell to see what appeared to be a red sheet covering his body. They entered and realized that the red coloring was a result of the blood that had flooded from Chail's wrists. The guards tried to revive Chail, but their attempts were in vain. They would now have to tell General Gollman that other efforts would have to be employed to collect the much-needed information. The Barbarian would not be happy. He did not see this one coming. Chail Hassid had escaped the no-win decision making – but at a great cost!

Chapter Sixteen

The Shopping Spree

The day before Christmas Eve, and the mall was hopping. Marty, Tony and Paul had finished a very busy day tour in the office with many cases still pending; but now Tony and Marty were back at "Best" looking for potential "grab-and-goers." Things still weren't right between the two, and the possibility existed that they never would be. It was a lot for Marty to carry, knowing that he was now intimately involved in obstructing an investigation. Over the past few days, he had questioned his earlier decision many times; however, it was done, and there was no turning back. Tony felt the coldness and regretted pulling Marty into the mess, but he had no choice. Somehow, he would ultimately make things right.

They had just left Detective Staffio in the squad room, but here he was again showing up at the jewelry store. He acknowledged his partners, and then went to see the manager who had originally helped him. Apparently, he wanted something engraved and needed it for the holiday. Marty was mildly annoyed that Paul was using their contact, but there was nothing he could do about it now. On the other hand, Tony was really uptight about Paul being there, not only because he was abusing their contact, but mostly because Paul was heavily involved in the sexual assault investigation. A slip of the tongue by anyone could result in a disastrous outcome for Tony. As Paul was waiting to see the manager, he kept looking around as if he was waiting for someone. It didn't take long before that someone arrived.

Having mentioned to Laura Noldir that his partners moonlighted at a jewelry store for the holidays, Laura said that she was looking for a piece of jewelry for her wife. Paul invited the Detective Sergeant to meet him at "Best" after his tour. Tony had never met Laura, but Marty knew her well. They warmly greeted each other, and Marty proceeded to introduce her to Tony. When Tony realized that this is the boss who is responsible for commanding the Sex Crimes Unit, the blood began to drain from his face. Hiding his concern as much as possible, he extended his hand to the Sergeant. Laura went on to say that she had mentioned to Detective Staffio that she was looking for a piece of jewelry for her wife, and Paul had invited her to meet him at the jewelry store. There was no love lost between Tony and Paul as it was, but now Tony wanted to kill him. Marty acted as a buffer so that Tony would not explode. Marty mentioned to Laura that he was sure she would find something nice. He directed her to the back of the store where Paul was still waiting for the manager.

Two stores down from "Best Jewelry" and right next to the mall florist was the gold mine known as Starbucks. But for Tony, the florist was a constant draw. His favorite flower, the Narcissus, the Daffodil, was always on his desk. To Tony it was a symbol of beauty and strength rolled into one. It usually bloomed in late winter and was the color of his detective shield - gold. When other flowers died, the strong daffodils flourished. To him, it reflected who he was, and so a day did not go by without Tony getting just one daffodil for his desk. When they weren't in bloom, he had a fake one displayed.

Since he was a frequent customer at the florist shop, his floral taste was well known to the owner, Miriam Howard. In fact, over the years, Tony had become good friends with Miriam, who just happened to be a cousin of the sitting President of the United States. So, in befriending Miriam

Howard, Tony satisfied his floral appetite as well as securing a valuable resource he could possibly call upon, if needed, in the future. That was Tony.

Although there are other coffee shops in the Mall, it seemed that wherever you worked in the shopping center, you came to Starbucks for your coffee break. It was always crowded either with workers or shoppers, but no matter — it was always busy. Donna was no exception to the coffee rule and working extra hours for the holidays, she needed an energy boost. She was now in line at Starbucks.

Standing right outside of the jewelry store, but keeping a vigilant eye on what was going on inside, Tony and Marty were in conversation about the unexpected visitors to the store. Donna, who had seen them talking, walked over with her coffee in hand to say "hello." This was turning out to be just a real banner day for Tony. He now had one of the investigating detectives, the Detective Sergeant and the complainant of the sexual assault case all together with him and Marty. You couldn't ask for more if it was a Hollywood movie plot.

Once again, Tony inquired Donna she was doing and fostered his false air of concern. Marty, who had no strong liking for Donna, also forced a concerned demeanor. However, he now looked at Donna, not as someone who was in a relationship with his partner, but someone who was attacked and still visibly shaken by the events of a harrowing night.

Donna asked them both if they knew anything further regarding her case. They both stated that it was not their case so that they knew very little about any results. As they were talking, Detective Staffio noticed Donna and proceeded to greet his complainant: "Hello Donna, how are you doing?" She answered: "I guess the best that I can. I have trouble sleeping, and I am in constant fear that the person might return." Paul tried to comfort her and emphasized that the Modus Operandi of these types of attackers showed that they very rarely returned. He also mentioned that they had new evidence regarding the description of the escape vehicle, and he was sure that they would soon come up with an identification.

Donna looked somewhat relieved but became curiously alert when Detective Staffio described the vehicle. In fact, she took a quick look at Tony as Paul continued to speak. Although it surfaced in her mind, the idea that Tony would do something like that quickly evaporated, and she thanked Paul for all of his efforts. She said good-bye to all of them and went back to work. Paul also had to leave and told his partners that he would see them in the office.

Tony sweated that one out and was wondering what was going through Marty's mind. He wondered, but he did not want to discuss it. This had been a really bad day so far, and Laura Noldir was still in the store. When she leaves, they would both be able to take a deep breath of relief.

During this time, they had been watching two individuals who were acting in a suspicious manner, looking all around and not focusing on any one area of the store. They had refused help twice and were still just walking around. As they began to exit the store, after what seemed to be an extended stay, they were met by another male who looked familiar to both Detectives. Alex Hassid now joined the two other males.

Having now identified a third person, the detectives approached Alex: "Hello Alex. How is your sister doing?" Marty assumed that Alex would remember him, and his assumption was correct. However, Alex looked quite nervous, and it seemed that he did not want to get involved with the detectives. He answered: "She is doing okay." Very curt and to the point, he seemed to be looking to his two friends for support. Marty continued: "Are you shopping for last minute holiday gifts as we all do?" He answered "no," and with a nudge from one of his friends, said that he had to go. He did not inquire how the investigation involving his sister was going, and that was quite odd. He hurriedly said "good-bye," and all three quickly left the Mall. Tony looked at Marty, and they both had that questioned look on their face. Why was Alex so nervous, and what was his involvement with the other two males who were at least ten years older than he?

Tony said: "What was that all about? For someone who was so concerned about his sister and for the safety of his family, he couldn't get out of here quick enough." Marty agreed, and then Tony sarcastically asked: "By the way, are we also going to run into the Pope today? Maybe, he has to do some last-minute shopping too."

Chapter Seventeen

The Final Prep

Dunait called for the last meeting of the cell on the night before Christmas Eve. To his satisfaction, everyone once again went over their positions and responsibilities. It was at this meeting, however, that Dunait was going to decide where the explosives would be placed, and what weapons each individual cell member would carry. Once again, Dunait emphasized that their main intention was not to injure people, but to have the threat of injury and/or death serve as the element that would persuade the powers-to-be to abide by their demands.

However, if necessary, injury and death could very possibly be the end result of their mission. Injury and death not only for the mall hostages but also for the cell members. They all knew that this was a possibility, but it did not weaken their resolve to carry on. In fact, following the news of both Amir's and Chail's deaths, the anticipation and enthusiasm for a victory was paramount in their minds, especially since they "knew" that the two deaths were a result of Israeli torture and mistreatment. Chail's original idea of Amir's death being carried out at the hands of his Israeli captors, and now, the same account of his own death, spurred on the rebel cause.

At one time or other during the past weeks, all members of the Alliance Cell who were involved with the Christmas Eve attack surveilled the mall to become familiar with the idiosyncrasies that were germane to its operation. They timed the rounds of the guards, and they noted the entrances and exits – both employee and public. They observed the goings-on of the stores in the immediate vicinity of what would be their assigned post, and they calculated what they thought would be the best locations for the cell's explosive devices. These devices, if triggered simultaneously, would surely take down an entire wing of the shopping center. Of course, this would be a last resort, but the possibility had to be realized.

Gathering all of the information that he received from the members' visits, Dunait now planned out the specifics of the attack. Although all of the members would be armed, only half of the team would have the automatic assault rifles, while the other six would be armed with the Glocks. These six would also have the triggering devices for the planted explosives that could be detonated by each cell member so equipped, or could be triggered by a member at a central location. That member of course would be Dunait, himself.

Erman Falco, the Director of Facilities, would arrange for the placement of trash disposal cans at specific locations in the mall. Explosives detonated at these locations would cause the most damage, and since they were placed in metal containers, the impact would act in a manner as if a dirty bomb exploded. Although not wanting it, they were prepared for war. The informal security site supervisor, Ismul Rahej, would arrange the patrol rounds and postings so that there would be a minimum of guards in the west wing when the attack actually went down.

Dunait directed his attention to Alex. Alex would be one of those armed individuals who also had access to an explosive device which would be located in the Administrative Building. In fact, the bomb would be planted in Reginald Winsten's Office – Alex's post and responsibility. That specific device was on a timing fuse so that when it was triggered, the explosion would be delayed for thirty seconds, indicating to Alex that there would be time for him to exit and be clear of the impact.

This was a new wrinkle for Alex to digest. He knew that he would be in the Administrative Building, but didn't realize that he would also have the responsibility of maintaining, protecting, and possibly detonating an explosive device. He was concerned but was not going to visibly display that concern to the rest of the group, and especially not to Dunait. All of the cell members would be connected by a state-of-the-art radio communicator, and it was through these ear phone equipped portables that members would get the order to possibly trigger an explosion. No one would do so, however, unless they were so ordered directly by Dunait. Dunait would be located in a van that would be parked on the street outside of the mall.

Director Falco would arrange wireless camera coverage of the entire shopping center to the van where Dunait would be able to control and see the actions of his members. However, the full capability to trigger individual explosions or detonate a simultaneous blast rested with Falco. This capability rested in Falco's office in the Administrative Building, but Erman would do nothing unless directed by Dunait. The leader, under the protection of the van, would be responsible for the successful execution of the attack while being removed from any immediate danger.

The two cell members who were employed as custodians in the mall would be responsible for the operation of the air intakes which were located in the middle of the west wing. Each wing had its own individual ventilation system. If worse came to worse, the gas in the vents would have to be used to put down hundreds of people shopping on Christmas Eve. Dunait did not plan on utilizing this tactic, but he had it at his disposal. This too would be a last resort because its employment would also mean the possible extermination of his fellow cell members. The only other person who knew about this option was Erman Falco, who had previously planted the lethal gas explosives at the entrances to the ventilation shafts.

Apparently, nothing was going to be left to chance, and Alex was impressed with the strategy and organizational planning that went into such an undertaking. It became even more apparent to him how much effort went into the planned attack when it was pointed out to him that Reginald Winsten, the General Manager of the Shopping Center, was a Jew and ardent supporter of the Israeli government. In fact, he had traveled to Israel on a number of occasions and donated over a million dollars to Israeli efforts. He was also responsible for creating an organization that had an annual fund-raising event for support of the Israeli military. So, what could be better than taking the Three Kings Shopping Center from an Israeli supporter who would have to give an assist in completing the demands made by the anti-Israeli rebel squad known as the Alliance Cell. The attack had been well planned, but as a wise man once stated: "Even the plans of mice and men sometimes go astray."

Chapter Eighteen

A Call to the Squad

Maybe it was a woman's intuition, maybe it was residual feelings from the break-up, or maybe it was the lingering effects of that awful night, but things just didn't feel right to Donna Uhrich after the brief meeting with Tony and Marty at the mall. She knew that Tony was really uptight about how their relationship collapsing, and she assumed that Tony thought that she had been seeing someone while Tony and she were still involved (he was right to assume it), but it seemed more than that as the three conversed in the mall. Also, she couldn't get Detective Staffio's comments regarding the description of the car out of her mind. She fought against the idea that Tony could be involved in any way, but he had recently told her about his new car, the car that clearly matched the description that Paul had given. Would Tony be that upset to actually want to hurt her? She couldn't believe that would be the case. However, because it stayed nagging in the resources of her conscious thought, she decided just to run it past Detective Staffio. She hesitated; maybe, she should approach Tony one more time and see if that same nagging feeling persisted. If it did, then she would speak with Detective Staffio or Detective Sergeant Noldir about it.

Donna made it her business to "run into" Tony and Marty again as she purchased another energy shot from Starbucks. She went into the jewelry store, and, in what she thought was a sly and non-alarming manner, began to talk to Tony again about the kidnapping and sex attack that she had endured. She housed her questions and comments in the framework that if he was there, maybe it would never have happened. However, being very much aware of his own involvement in the incident and having a great deal of interviewing experience–she was not speaking to a rookie cop - he very readily saw that she was fishing for information that may or may not incriminate him. He had seen her initial reaction to Paul Staffio's comments and description about the escape vehicle, and actually was surprised it had taken her this long to possibly connect the described vehicle to his.

In her best Scotland Yard attempt, she roundaboutly got to the point where her next question was going to be: "Where were you when this happened?" However, Tony stopped the questioning when he preemptively mentioned that he had been at a party with other members of the Squad, and he had been there all evening on the night of the attack. Donna realized that Tony had seen right through her weakly veiled interrogation and felt somewhat embarrassed that she had even entertained the thought that Tony could be involved. She sort of apologized, and then turned to Marty who had been within earshot and nodded in an "I should have never entertained the thought of Tony's possible involvement" way. Marty just stared at her, not acknowledging her compromised position.

However, it was difficult for Marty to stand by and listen to the lies coming from Tony. Even though there was no love lost between Donna and Marty, he felt that no one should be subjected to the physical and emotional trauma that Donna had endured. It was getting harder and harder for Marty to just say nothing. Hopefully, he would only have to do it for another day or two, and the Christmas holiday would be over. Tony would then turn himself in and suffer whatever the consequences. If Donna really wanted justice, and it seemed that she did, Tony would be sentenced to substantial jail time. The courts did not look kindly on sexual assault cases, and this one involved the additional charge of kidnapping. Many times, the District Attorney wants to make an example of a bad cop, and the court sentencing usually reflects that attitude. As it is, the New York Judicial System does not look highly on police to begin with; so, Tony should expect something other than a sympathetic decision.

As mentioned earlier, Tony and Marty, on numerous occasions, had discussed hypothetical "jail time" and the "what if" of their actions, as did most cops. However, in Tony's case, he always and emphatically mentioned that jail time would never be an option for him if he were to be found guilty of an infraction or crime, either connected with the job or in his personal world. So, Marty was somewhat leery about Tony's commitment to turn himself in after the holiday. Tony had to know that his previous actions involving Donna would surely result in imprisonment, and at this point, Marty didn't think that Tony was going to be able to convince Donna to drop the charges. In fact, it seemed to Marty that because of the original aggressions, and then the further deceit, that whatever she wanted from the courts, she would get.

Donna was somewhat relieved that she got it off her chest, but still wasn't totally convinced of Tony's innocence. She had been in a relationship with him for a long time and he was not one to easily forgive and forget. However, unless there was more evidence, and the investigation then showed his involvement, she would have to let it go. She had wanted to approach him first before she did anything else. She did that, and although he seemed somewhat sincere, she knew that he could convince a smoker that smoking was a healthy exercise for the lungs. So, she wondered if she fell prey to his ability to persuade. She had seen him in action before, and he was good. So, giving herself the benefit of the doubt and thinking "what harm could it do," she decided to contact Detective Staffio. She would inform him, if he already didn't know, that Detective Ossur's car closely fit the description of the escape vehicle that the eyewitness described in her statement.

"Hello may I please speak with Detective Staffio." Donna was contacting the 65th Detective Squad.

"Who's calling Please?"

"It is very important, and I don't want anyone else in the office to know who I am. Please may I speak with Detective Staffio. It is important."

"Hold on, please. Hey Paul, it's some woman who wants to talk to you, but she won't give her name." Detective Frank Austin was completing some paperwork, and he took the call. Detective Staffio picked up the phone: "Hello, this is Detective Staffio."

"Hello Paul, It's Donna Uhrich, and I just didn't know if Marty or Tony was in the office. I didn't want them to know that I was calling."

"Okay, what can I do for you.?" She answered: "Well I had some thoughts about my case and was wondering if you identified the escape car yet?" He answered: "not yet, why?" She continued: "Well I don't know if you know that the description of the car may closely resemble what Tony's car looks like. I am not saying that it is his car or it is him, but I just wanted to cover all bases." Detective Staffio answered: "Yes, thanks. We are well aware of that and have already included that information into the investigation. We will not leave any stone unturned. If you think of anything else, please don't hesitate to call or contact me."

"Thank you." And she hung up.

Both Tony and Marty happened to be in the office at the time and were curious as to the mysterious phone call.

"What was that all about?" Paul said: "It was a woman from a previous drug case, and she is just very leery of everyone. I was the lead detective, and she trusted me and only wanted to speak with me regarding the case. Every once-in-a-while she remembers something she feels might be important, and she calls me. We closed her case a long time ago."

The office seemed to accept the explanation and everyone continued with what they were doing. However, the investigative juices began flowing in Tony's mind, and maybe they were influenced by the burden of guilt he was carrying. He left the office, under the pretense of hitting the "John," and went to a private office in the precinct and contacted a personal friend who worked for the contracted phone carrier. He asked her to give him the last number that called the squad office. She hesitated, knowing that she could lose her job, but Tony had done many favors for her. In fact, Tony had gotten her that job. She told him to hold on and returned in about a minute. Tony asked her to repeat the number, and there was no mistake that it was a number with which Tony was very familiar. The number belonged to Donna Uhrich, and now he knew for sure that he could not trust Staffio.

Chapter Nineteen

The Visitors

Jalecya prison was buzzing with the news of the two deaths. General Gollman knew that he had to do something and do it quickly. He had to resort to desperate measures because all else seemed to fail. His thinking centered around the Hassid family, of course; however, what was left of the family was in the United States. Did he dare to put together a clandestine operation in another country, especially one which was a strong ally? The answer had to be "yes." Of course, he would need the unofficial approval of his superiors which he was sure he would get. That approval came with the caveat that if the mission failed, and it came to light that a clandestine operation was in effect in the United States without the latter's approval, Israel would have plausible deniability. The brunt of the blame and responsibility, then, would fall on one rogue General Gollman. He communicated with his contact in the Israeli Mossad and explained his need. The wheels of secrecy and operation had begun. Agents from Israel would travel to the United States and persuade the Hassid family to cooperate. It wasn't certain, however, that the rest of the family had any useful information, but if they did, the prime focus would be on Alex.

Dunait, having been the key figure in a number of planned attacks, knew very well that Israel might stoop to some unorthodox and risky plan to secure whatever they wanted. To thwart such an operation, he had assigned a cell member to surveil the Hassid residence. Also knowing that if an attempt on the residence would occur, it most likely would take place in the evening under the cover of darkness. Therefore, the cell member assigned would take up position mostly at night. Any law enforcement officer could tell you that this type of surveillance was not only tedious but boring. It taxed one's mental acuity. That is why law enforcement always assigned two officers to a surveillance operation. This allowed for a break from the constant attention.

However, the Alliance Cell did not have the luxury of inflated manpower, so only one person was assigned to a non-descript van. In an effort not to alarm anyone in the Hassid family, especially Alex, the surveillance was known to only two cell members - Dunait and the cell member assigned to the task. If anything suspicious was detected, the member would call a number and help would arrive within minutes. Although the van was equipped with excellent camera surveillance equipment, having just one person constantly focusing on the house becomes mentally exhausting and could lead to "dozing off." The cell member knew this, and since he had screwed up once before, he was not going to let that happen.

Alex was returning from a late meeting and noticed that the house was totally dark. This was not the usual routine. No matter what family member was out, and no matter what time that person returned, he or she would always be met by the welcoming warmth of a house light. The odd rarity concerned Alex, and he felt uneasy as he approached the front door. He opened the door and called out to both his mom and sister, but got nothing in return. He switched on the living room light, and everything seemed to be okay. He called out again as he entered through the kitchen door. Turning on the light, he was surprised to see both his mother and sister just sitting stoically at the kitchen table. As he passed through the door, he was thrown to the ground by an Israeli agent who was hiding behind the door. Another agent appeared from behind a cabinet. Israel had come to the Hassid house.

As far as the cell member assigned to the house surveillance was concerned, everything seemed to be okay except for the fact that now there were lights on in a number of rooms. He guessed that the family just had a hard time getting to sleep and was biding time until sleep finally came. He looked at his watch and realized that thirty minutes had passed since he last looked. Could it have been that he dozed off for a full half hour. Although he was confident that nothing was really going to happen, he was concerned that the family was still up.

Vin Falco decided to take a peek inside the house just to make sure that everything was okay, and that he had not managed to botch another assignment. He carefully climbed the front porch steps and peeked inside. He saw the living room well-lit with nothing really to raise his concern. He did not see any of the family members and couldn't get a better view without going to the rear of the house. Not wanting to alarm anyone nor give away the fact that there was surveillance at the house, he tiptoed to the back yard where he came face-to-face with an armed man dressed in black. The man directed Vin into the house via the back door. As the man pushed Vin into the house, he fell at the feet of Alex who was also in a prone position on the floor. There was a look of shock and surprise on Alex's face, but one of concern and distress on Vin's. He had once again screwed up, and this time it was a bad one.

Things were working out really well for the agents, they now had another possible source of information. By the end of the night, they would report back to General Gollman with all of the information he needed. They would get it one way or the other. On the advice of General Gollman, they were going to start their interrogation with Alex; however, with the introduction of someone new, apparently an active cell member, the strategy had changed. Since Vin was apparently assigned to the house, the Israelis now had a person who was intimately involved in whatever was being planned.

The lead Israeli agent, Fahad Usteth, started speaking in a soft but direct tone: "We are here to find out what the Alliance Cell is planning, and how they are expecting to free their countrymen. We do not want to hurt anyone, but if we are pushed to do so, we will not hesitate. Do you understand?" He directed most of his comments to Vin Falco. Alex's mother was thoroughly confused and was somewhat in shock as the event unfolded. Although Rachael was aware of certain things, Ficera, her mother, was totally in the dark. She kept asking what was going on, but her inquiries were ignored as Fahad now concentrated on Vin. He asked again, but in a stronger tone: "Do you Understand?" Vin just stared at him and nodded his head.

"Let me start with the correct name of your group. Is it Alliance or Allegiance Cell?" Vin just looked and did not give an answer. "Do not let me repeat myself. What is the group's name?"

Following a pregnant pause by Vin, Fahad pistol whipped him to the side of his head and knocked him off of the chair. "Maybe you didn't understand my initial comments. If you push me to the extreme, you will regret it. The name of the group?" Vin uttered in a whisper: "Alliance." Somewhat pleased, Fahad continued: "Okay, now we are getting somewhere. Where is the rebel stronghold, their headquarters?" Vin answered: "There is no specific headquarters, we meet at different locations all the time." Fahad had been briefed by the General, and he knew this to be the case. He was testing Vin to make certain that he was telling the truth. "Who is the leader of the group? What is his name?" Vin couldn't bring himself to say Dunait's name, so once again he became the recipient of another blow to the head. He was now bleeding from both sides of his face. Alex yelled to Fahad to stop and earned a punch to the kidney by the agent standing next to him. He groaned as it became difficult to breathe. Fahad repeated his question: "What is the name of the leader of the Alliance?" Vin weakly said: "Dunait."

"How many cell members are involved with Dunait?" Vin answered: "Approximately a dozen." In a threatening tone Fahad addressed Vin directly again: "If I find out that you are untruthful in any of your answers, I will make certain you suffer a painful death and track down your family and kill them. "Understand?" Vin nodded.

Fahad continued: "Where and when is Dunait going to execute whatever he has planned?" Vin spoke: "I am just on the outside. I don't know any specifics. Dunait doesn't trust me with that information." Fahad smiled and said: "I could understand why. Why were you outside the house tonight? What was your assignment?"

As Vin tried to stall for time and before he could answer, Fahad's questioning was interrupted with the sound of three smothered thuds. The agent who was standing by Ficera and Rachael collapsed to the floor; the one guarding Alex fired his weapon in the direction of the back door, and Fahad fired at the rear window. The return fire, however, felled Alex's guard and mortally wounded Fahad. Guns drawn, Dunait and other members of the cell charged into the kitchen and secured the area. All three of the Israelis were dead, Alex's mother collapsed, and Vin Falco lay on the kitchen floor, the victim of an errant gunshot. Alex leaned over his friend and comrade and listened to Vin's final words: "He would have killed me anyway."

Dunait had told Vin to call in every half hour and give a status update. Apparently, as a result of his snooze fest, Vin neglected to make his half hour ring. This triggered an emergency response from Dunait and the group. It was a good strategy, and it definitely paid off but at the cost of Vin Falco's life. Now comes the difficult part. How was Dunait going to tell Erman Falco that his son was dead. Dunait needed Erman. He was a trusted member of the group and also a friend. However, Dunait did not know how his friend was going to react to the news; but it couldn't wait. Erman would have to be told as soon as possible, but should it wait until after Christmas Eve so that his attention remained solely on the operation? For Dunait, that was the better way to go.

Chapter Twenty

The Failure

The Hassid family was in shock. Alex's mother finally regained consciousness and couldn't believe what she saw. Both Alex and his sister Rachael were also stunned as to what had just occurred. There were so many questions, and Dunait did not have the time to go into detail about the situation, nor did he want to. He explained to the family, however, that the men who had invaded their home were agents from the Israeli government. They had come here to gain information about a rebel group to which he, and Alex's father and brother had belonged. Looking down at Vin

Falco's body, he nodded that Vin had also been a part of the group. Dunait then broke the difficult news that both Amir and Chail had been killed while they were imprisoned at Jalecya. This was the first time Ficera heard it, and she cried out in disbelief. Alex and Rachael took the news as if they had always expected the worst. However, this was not the time for Dunait to go into a long-drawn explanation of what was occurring and the family's participation. He explained that he would take care of disposing of the unidentified invader bodies and would see to it that Vin received a proper burial.

It was the practice for an agent involved in a clandestine operation to not carry any identification so that their home country could not be formally involved in an "unauthorized" activity, if things went south. So, disposing of the bodies would be relatively simple. For the family, this was the first time that they had witnessed such violence and death face-to-face. It was traumatic and it would take a lot of time to recover, but for Alex there could be no luxury of time for recovery. He had to be at his best in twenty-four hours as part of an operation that could change the lives of others who were suffering in Israel. Alex looked at the body of Vin Falco and shook his head in disbelief. He also realized that in a very short time, it could possibly be him lying on the floor in the mall. Thoughts of death and violence flooded Alex's thinking. He was afraid to die and didn't want to end up like Vin. However, both his father and brother had died for the cause, and no matter how difficult and in their memory, he would not shrink from his responsibility.

Since it was late in the evening and all of the combatants used silencers on their weapons, no one in the vicinity was alerted. The New York City Police would not be notified, and everything would be handled by the cell. The last thing that Dunait wanted was for the NYPD to be involved. Their involvement would destroy everything that the Alliance Cell had been working for and could ultimately result in incarceration, as the investigation unfolded.

Alex understood this and with a little persuasion, Rachael also followed Dunait's lead; but Ficera was insistent on calling the police. She wanted no part of what was taking place and did not agree with the violence and killing. She mourned for her husband and son, but did not want their deaths to become a catalyst for more carnage and possibly innocent people being killed. She could not be persuaded otherwise even with both Alex and Rachael pleading with her. Ficera turned a deaf ear to their efforts and attempted to rise from her chair and head toward the phone in the living room. Dunait reacted quickly and harshly. Ficera was pushed back in her chair and warned again that she could not call the police. Alex did not like the way Dunait stopped his mother. In addition to being disrespectful, it was rough and jarring. It was sinking in now to Alex that he was dealing with hardcore terrorists who would do almost anything to ensure the success of their efforts.

As Ficera kept insisting, Dunait took both Rachael and Alex to the side and explained to them that he was going to arrange for their mother to be brought to a "safe" house. This afforded two things: it would make certain that she was safe from any future potential attack, and it would guarantee that the police would not be notified. Dunait strongly suggested that Rachael accompany her mother to the new location. For Alex's sake, she nodded in agreement and understood why they had to move, but was very worried for the safety of her only remaining brother.

Alex allayed some of her fears and asked that she take extra care of their mother who still hadn't recovered from the killing field that had been her kitchen. While Alex remained behind, one of the other cell members gently removed Ficera from the kitchen and escorted her to an awaiting vehicle.

Rachael and her mother got into the car, and as it pulled away, Rachael waved a forlorn goodbye as Alex pondered the thought that it might be the last time that he saw them. Recent events weighed heavy on his mind and Alex, once again, had doubts as to whether he could contribute to the success of Dunait's plan. The loss of his brother and father, the death of Vin Falco, the killing and violence at the house, the potential of facing serious jail time, and the strong possibility of injury or death did not encourage positive thinking. He was worried that he might be the weak link in the whole operation, and if that was determined by Dunait, Alex was almost certain that Dunait would find a way to eliminate that weak link. So, focusing on self-preservation, he made a strong and determined effort not to outwardly reveal his innermost feelings.

When General Gollman did not receive a progress report from the Israeli commandos, he panicked and was out of alternatives. He had asked for and received the unofficial okay for a very dangerous and desperate mission – a mission now that was deemed a failure. For sure, the ax would be coming down on him.

All this time, the Israeli suspicion centered around the possibility of an attack in America that would force America to require specific cooperation from its Mid-East ally, Israel. However, no one had officially notified the American Embassy in Israel regarding the potential for attack. The idea was to find out about the attack, prevent it from occurring and present that whole secure package to the United States with the identities and whereabouts of the suspected terrorists. However, this apparently was not to be.

Abel Gollman was now a desperate man, living in desperate times which prompted him to take desperate measures. He decided that he was going to go to the

American Embassy and personally notify them of the potential for a terrorist attack. He had learned from other prisoners, trustees, that the attack was going to take place at a shopping mall somewhere in Brooklyn, New York. He did not know when, how or exactly where, but he would share whatever information he had with the State Department Representative in the U.S. Embassy. General Gollman also realized that by this action, he would be embarrassing the Israeli hierarchy and would have to disappear to escape the severe punishment or even death that would be meted out by his superiors.

Unfortunately, he was not giving the Americans much time to investigate, and if something did go down, the United States would want to know why they were not notified immediately regarding any potential for violence. This might jeopardize an already politically shaky relationship between the two countries. Gollman's plan for protection and escape was only a delaying tactic for the inevitable consequences he would, at some time, have to face. He used to be the minister of pain, the Barbarian, now soon enough, knowing that there would be nowhere to hide, he would become one of its victims.

Chapter Twenty-One

The Favor

Unnerved by Paul Staffio's response to the mysterious woman's phone call, Tony needed to vent and discuss the situation with his partner. The way it seemed; the Sex Crimes Unit would want to speak with Tony Ossur any moment now. He believed that they did not have enough evidence to actually charge him with a crime, but he did not want to come under the constant scrutiny of that unit and possibly Internal Affairs.

He approached Marty asking what he thought the next move should be. Marty in a serious and concerned tone advised Tony to come clean and not to make it worse by delaying the inevitable. Tony responded: "Marty, remember that you agreed not to say or do anything until after the holiday. I told you that I will turn myself in right after Christmas, and I will. I'm asking for your advice on what to do now about Staffio." Marty, knowing that it was an impossibility but not having a suitable answer, just advised Tony to stay as far as possible away from Detective Staffio.

Tony just snickered and responded: "Like that's possible. He is going to stick to me like bees to honey. I need you to run interference. You have to be the buffer. I have no one else." Marty inquired: "Just how would you like me to do that? We work in the same office and are assigned to the same holiday tours. We feed off of each other's cases, and we are in constant touch with each other. I really don't know what I could possibly do other than tying him up and putting him in a closet somewhere." Tony nodded his head in approval and said: "Exactly!" Unfortunately, Marty believed that Tony would actually want something like that done. However, Marty would only go so far to cover for his partner. Something like kidnapping was a stretch too far. They had to come up with a plan to divert Staffio's attention away from the sexual assault case.

Tony decided that the only way he could help himself was if Detective Staffio, for some reason, couldn't come into work. He could get sick, or he could be suffering from an injury that would prevent him from actively continuing his investigative function. Nothing really serious but an injury that might put Staffio out of commission for a short time. After all, Tony only needed a couple of days.

A plan came to Tony in a flash and just before he was about to confer with Marty regarding it, he decided that his partner would definitely vote against it, so he said nothing. It would be a plan between him and whoever he got to help out. He knew just the type of injury and just the right person for the job. In fact, he knew a number of people who would help out as long as confidentiality was guaranteed. A wave of relief flowed over Tony as he was sure that he was going to buy himself more time.

Having been on the job for quite a while and having dealt with many savory characters, some street people owed Tony. He was now going to collect from one of them. He reached out to a past acquaintance known as Sug. Sug was definitely surprised and also worried to hear from Detective Ossur who he had encountered on a number of unpleasant occasions. However, this time, the tables were somewhat turned, and it was the Detective who needed help from the street.

When Sug first saw Tony approaching the auto mechanic shop where he worked, his initial instinct was to run. Tony knew that this would be the case, so he disarmed Sug by immediately stating that everything was alright, and that Tony just wanted to talk to him. Although leery, Sug remained in his position and asked the Detective what he wanted to talk about. Tony ushered Sug out of the shop and out of ear-shot from any other workers inside. He then carefully explained to Sug what he needed, and that there was very little time left for his street friend to complete the task. In fact, it had to be done almost immediately.

After hearing the proposition, Sug was both nervous and amused that Tony would be asking such a favor. However, he was not going to ask "why," he just wanted to make sure that it would not come back to bite him. He was out on parole and couldn't afford to be put in a situation that would violate his parole and send him back to prison. Tony assured him that only the two of them would know and, if discovered, Tony would be in just as much of a jam as Sug. Tony would make sure that no one else would know. With this assurance, Sug reluctantly agreed and said that he would do the favor before the day was out. Tony knew that Sug would not disappoint, because if he did, Tony would never let him forget it.

Tony, having returned to the Squad Room, was working with Marty and Paul completing some paper work on past cases when the door to the Squad Room opened, and Detective Sergeant Noldir, Commanding Officer of the Sex Crimes Unit, walked in. Of course, Paul gave a warm "hello" to the Sergeant and welcomed her into the office.

Both Marty and Tony were apprehensive and on edge by the unannounced visit. Marty also welcomed Laura while Tony just nodded. Knowing that it was close to the end of their tour and having been in the neighborhood, Laura invited the Detectives for a few drinks at the local "cop" bar. Of course, Marty and Tony could not accept the invitation since they had to go to the jewelry store for their moonlighting job; however, Paul Staffio eagerly accepted - almost too eagerly.

It was now time to go, and they went their separate ways. Paul and Laura went to Paul's car, and Tony and Marty went to their own vehicles to meet up at "Best." It was close to 5:00 pm, and dusk was beginning to welcome the night time sky. It is said that dusk is the most dangerous time to drive. Statistics show that it is the time of the day when most accidents occur.

Tony and Marty had about a two-mile drive to the mall, while Paul and Laura would arrive at the watering hole after only a ten-block jaunt. Paul was driving his black Honda Accord that he bought just a couple months ago. It was detailed to the hilt and couldn't have looked any better. Laura was impressed with the car and could understand why he wanted to drive and show her his new toy. They were almost there and were waiting for the light to change. It turned green, and they were only a block away when everything went black. A dark gray truck blew the light and t-boned the Accord sending it careening into a telephone pole. The occupants were unconscious and bleeding. According to witnesses, the truck had no plates and never attempted to stop. In fact, it sped up after the accident. Tony now owed Sug!

Chapter Twenty-Two

The Caper

She was born into a very religious family. She had been going to Holy Mass with her mother and father every Sunday since she was five years old. It was obvious that she was going to catholic school from the first grade right through high school and then even college. She really had no choice. The influence of her catholic school teachers and the everyday guidance of her parents naturally led Mary Balacieri to think about a religious vocation.

Although the convent was an honorable and respected vocation, it was not for everyone. And even though her parents would have lauded her decision, they did not know if the convent was the right place for Mary. They also knew, selfishly, that they would lose her to the demands of the church. So, they gently tried to persuade her to look elsewhere for her future endeavors. They were torn between praising her religious zeal and losing her to something much bigger than themselves. Mary Balacieri went into the convent at seventeen years of age, right after high school. She lasted one year and came out with a totally different view of who she was and where she was going.

Mary went to college for Business Administration, and became quite the party girl. You couldn't tell if this was a knee-jerk reaction against the strict and disciplined life that she was forced to live in the convent, or if this was just part of a typical college life routine. No matter which, she enjoyed going out, partying and meeting people, especially guys. She was always first to suggest something outrageous or adventurous, and that is what most people liked about her.

One of her suggestions was to arrange a party with other than the guys from a traditional college, but rather with those who were the regular blue-collar workers: painters, mechanics, plumbers, etc. She wanted to interact with the mainstream males. So, she arranged for a "mixer" with the trainees in the blue-collar trades. This decision changed her life forever.

Frank Suggaro had decided that college was not for him; so, with the insistence of his parents, he went to a trade school. Ever since he could remember, he loved anything to do with cars, and he was good with his hands. He was now learning the intricate parts of vehicle repair and maintenance. He was becoming a good mechanic. Sug, that was his street name, grew up in a neighborhood where no one was identified by their real name. His friends were: Steps, Hotfoot, Smiles, Treetrunk, Rails and various other nicknames. They used these street tags so often that, at times, they forgot their friends' real names.

Sug met Mary at the mixer, and they were inseparable from that time on. It was love at first sight and lust every night. He would go to the trade school during the day, work on cars until evening, and then visit with Mary at night. Mary was working for a large corporation, and Sug was hired as a mechanic at a local repair shop. It was a repair shop that did a lot more than fix cars. Not saying that these types of businesses can be somewhat shady, but this shop was. Sug saw that he could make a lot more money working on jobs that were "off-the-grid." He became involved in many illegal activities including doctoring the vehicle identification numbers of stolen vehicles. This paid a lot more than just routine mechanic work, but it also came with a great risk.

Sug and Mary made plans to get married and making extra money really came in handy. They were saving for the wedding and also for the house that they would ultimately buy together. At one point, Mary became suspicious of the additional money that Sug bragged about making, and she nagged him until he finally told her where the extra funds were coming from. Mary wanted no part of the arrangement and insisted that Sug stop the illegal work activity. She didn't care about how much money he was making because she knew that sooner or later his luck would run out, and he would be arrested and sent to jail. She would have a hard time dealing with that.

After much resistance, Sug agreed with Mary and told her that he wouldn't do anything that was illegal. However, once you're involved in that sort of business, it is difficult to just get out. Although he intended to quit, his fellow partners pressured him, and the draw of the additional money was still there. He lied to Mary and continued to doctor vehicles while keeping the money a secret from her. In fact, he was spending most of his time now working on the stolen vehicles.

One Friday afternoon, Sug saw a man come into his boss's office for what amounted to a closed-door half hour meeting. It was later learned that this man was an associate of the head of one of the crime families in the area. Apparently, an agreement had been reached at the meeting, and the repair shop workers were told to prepare for a huge job that was coming in. Everyone would be making great money, and this was only the beginning of what could turn out to be very lucrative for everyone.

Sal, the crime family front man, told Sug's boss, Lenny, that he needed thirty high-end cars doctored within the next two weeks. That was a tall order, but Lenny agreed to do it. That also meant that Sug would be working many additional hours. He would just tell Mary that he was working overtime for the boss. With this new influx of work, Sug would be able to pay for a wedding as well as having funds available for a down payment on a house. This work couldn't have come at a better time.

Sal ultimately introduced Lenny to the guy who would be handling the hands-on operation for the family. Philly became a steady fixture at the shop. He handled the scheduling, the delivery, the transporting and the problem-solving. Things were going along fine, and Sug's boss knew that Sal and Philly were happy with the arrangement, which meant that there would be more business and more money rolling in. Philly was there every day from morning till night, making sure that things were going according to plan. He was also a trusted associate in the family.

The day before the shop got the last of the vehicles was the only day that Philly didn't show up. However, whether he was there or not, the shop worked with the same vigor as they had been. The quicker the shop finished with the job, the quicker they would get the money, and the quicker they would get additional jobs. Things were really looking up.

Surprisingly, just before quitting time, Philly walked through the door. He checked on everything, looking particularly closely at the vehicles on hand and eyeing all of us as we finished up. He apparently approved and nodded affirmatively heading for Lenny's office. Philly spent a few minutes in the office, and then exited through the front door. As soon as he left, all hell broke out. There were cops coming through every door, smashing their way in if there wasn't a door, yelling specific orders to get down on the ground. They had their guns drawn, and their cuffs ready. There were uniformed cops and plain-clothes cops, and there had to be at least twenty-five of them.

One of the plain-clothes cops approached Sug and handcuffed him before he realized that he was under arrest. The cop identified himself as Detective Tony Ossur. That was the first time Sug met Detective Ossur, but it was definitely not going to be the last. Apparently, the New York City Police Department's Auto Crime Unit was working with the Federal Bureau of Investigation for quite a while to disband the stolen car ring. Philly, the trusted associate in the crime family, was an F.B.I. agent working undercover. He had been working with the family for the past two years and got enough information to really destroy the family, putting a lot of people behind bars. The stolen car caper was the icing on the cake.

Tony Ossur, in his inevitable way, worked on Sug. He met with Sug many times, and got a lot of information on places and names that would be used in future cases. Because of Sug's cooperation, and Tony working the system, Detective Ossur was able to get Sug a reduced sentence of three years with five years-probation. Mary would wait for Sug because she loved him, and she had no other choice. It could have been a lot worse for Sug, but Tony had kept his part of the bargain.

So, when Tony, Sug's arresting officer, came to the new shop where Sug was working, he only anticipated the worst. He never expected Detective Ossur to be asking him for a favor, but Tony did. It was a very big favor, and Sug enjoyed the predicament that Detective Ossur was in. Sug would do it, but he would never let Tony forget it. It was something he could hold over Tony's head forever. He loved it!

Chapter Twenty-Three

The Vindictive Mother

At age eleven, Laura had already been introduced to three different men who her mother had taken into the residence. To Laura, her mother seemed to be more concerned about these different men, than she was about her own daughter. Although it bothered Laura, slowly but surely, she was getting used to the idea and becoming immune to the lack of attention. She found herself depending on her own instincts to survive. Laura turned to the street for comfort and friendship. She attended school on a regular basis, but never came right home after school. She looked for her street friends to hang out with.

Laura's friends ranged in age from twelve to twenty, and only a few finished school or completed their education. Although her mother got money from her male acquaintances, it was never really enough for Laura to benefit from the funds. So, Laura joined her friends in getting money anyway that they could. This meant that she would get involved in stealing and robbing, in addition to duping others into "donating" monies to help in supporting her survival. She and her friends would share in the spoils of the day. Some days were better than others, but in the long run, at least Laura had money.

One night about six o'clock, Laura was home in her room and counting the profits of the day. Her mother surprised her and opened the bedroom door to find Laura holding cash in her hands. Her mother wanted to know where she got the money from and how much was there. She needed the money to help support her drug habit that started when her husband just woke up one day and left to never come back. Since the bond between mother and daughter was anything but strong, Laura fought to maintain possession of her ill-gotten gains. However, her mother was able to wrestle the money from Laura.

Laura had reached her twelfth birthday and decided to get back at her mother while making money in the process. Her mother had held onto her most recent male companion for a good six months, which might have been some kind of record. Laura also thought that this relationship might have been somewhat different for her mother. Her mother showed signs of really caring for big Matt, and it might have been reciprocal. Laura strongly held on to the grudge she had for her mother and saw an opportunity to get back at her.

Although Laura was only approaching her thirteenth birthday, she was well developed for a young girl. She had already refused the advances of many of her friends and other male acquaintances. So, she knew that with a little coaxing, she could seduce Matt into a sexual interaction that would hurt her mother. She also intended to bilk a good amount of money out of Matt for the experience of having a pretty, young girl offer some sexual favors. Laura had dabbled in sex before and was not necessarily thrilled by it, but this time, there would be results that would make it all worthwhile. She just had to wait for the right time.

One evening when her mother left the apartment to go shopping, the opportunity for Laura to carry out her plan arose. Matt was in the living room watching television. Laura decided to leave her bedroom, where she mostly stayed, and pass by Matt to go to the kitchen. She wore very sheer pajama tops and lace panties. She knew that Matt would notice because she caught him many times just looking her over. As she took her glass of water, she approached Matt and asked if he wanted anything. Matt looked at her with surprise and repeated "anything." She nodded her head and smiled seductively at him. He rose from his chair and began to hug her.

She had him! She pushed herself away and told him that for a price, he could enjoy her sexual company. He was so excited at that point that he would have paid anything to be with her. So, for a hundred dollars, Laura brought him into her bedroom and began her sexual performance. She left her bedroom door ajar so that her mother would have no problem in finding Matt. She took her time in sexually pleasing Matt so that she would be sure that her mother would arrive in time to witness the scene. Her plan was executed without a hitch. Her mother not only witnessed the sexual interaction, but she also heard the moans emanating from her male companion. She reacted violently with a glass vase, sending Matt to the hospital with a large gash to his head. Their relationship was over, and Laura was a hundred dollars richer. Laura was rather proud of herself, but she couldn't know how vindictive her mother would become.

Laura's mother, who was also above average in looks and appeal, brought other men into the apartment. However, she brought them in with the caveat that for a reasonable fee, they could have sex with a young, pretty girl. Laura's mother had been systematically spiking Laura's food with a drug that lowered any resistance that Laura would muster to fend off potential aggressors. Her mother, not forgetting what her daughter had done, was now pimping her out and making a good profit for her efforts. So, Laura may have won that one night, but her mother was now the overall winner. This arrangement lasted for a while, and Laura had become a sex slave. Her mother was experiencing a good financial upswing, but Laura's health was diminishing as a result of the constant ingestion of drugs.

One day, after her mother left the apartment, Laura was able to struggle to the front door entrance. She opened the door, took two steps forward and collapsed on the hallway floor. A neighbor heard the noise and immediately called 911. Laura was brought to the hospital in critical condition and was placed in the Intensive Care Unit. When Laura's mother arrived back home, there were two detectives waiting for her. She was taken into custody and was arrested for numerous charges including "endangering the welfare of a minor." She was found guilty, and the last time Laura saw her mother was in the courtroom where the judge sentenced her mother to ten years in jail.

Laura's life was in turmoil for a while, but in one of the foster homes where she stayed, she was introduced to a young girl who was approximately the same age as her. They became good friends and kept in touch with each other as they grew. It was that friend who encouraged Laura to take the New York City Police Department exam. It was also that friend who grew to be more than a friend. Laura and her one-time friend were now married. After all that Laura had been through - a father who split, a mother who never loved her, and men who sexually abused her - is it any wonder that she would seek attention, understanding, love and affection from the companionship of a female partner rather than a male?

With all of her street experience and personal tragedies, Laura Noldir was a perfect fit for the Police Department and an even better fit for the Sex Crimes Unit, where she excelled and ultimately became the Commanding Officer. She was a hard but fair supervisor and well respected throughout the Department. Although she held no malice toward the opposite sex, she was going to make it her goal that no one would get away with sexual abuse or any of the related sex crimes. She was determinedly successful and often saw positive results in attaining her goal. Her latest pursuit, the rapist who attacked Donna Uhrich.

Chapter Twenty-Four

The Accident

Just after Tony and Marty arrived at the jewelry store, Marty's phone started ringing. The call was coming from Sergeant Del. It was unusual to get a call from the Commanding Officer so shortly after leaving the Squad Office, so Marty was concerned. Marty let Tony know that the call was coming in, and they both listened as Marty answered the call. The Sergeant was speaking in a both solemn and serious tone which alarmed Marty.

Sergeant Del explained that there had been a car accident involving Detective Paul Staffio and his passenger,

Detective Sergeant Laura Noldir. Del said that they were both brought to Inter-County General Hospital and were in bad shape. They were the victim of a hit and run driver who, according to witnesses, was going approximately fifty miles an hour when the impact occurred. Paul's car was rocketed into a telephone pole and was totaled. Both Paul and Laura were unconscious at the scene and bleeding from various parts of their bodies, including the head. Upon hearing the unbelievable news, Marty told Sergeant Del that he would meet him at the County. Marty turned to Tony who had heard the entire conversation, and told him that he was going to the hospital and would return as soon as possible. They both couldn't leave, so Tony stayed behind.

Tony hadn't counted on Sergeant Noldir being in Paul's car, but the more he thought about it, the better it seemed. He would get no pressure from either one of them now. It was unfortunate that the injuries seemed to be so severe, but he wanted Paul and now Laura out of the way for a while. Because of Sug, he got more than he wanted.

Marty wasted no time in getting to the hospital. He went straight to the emergency room and approached the cop assigned to duty there. He inquired as to Paul and Laura and was told to see the Sergeant in the adjoining room. Sergeant Del had a very concerned look on his face and was waiting for Marty to arrive.

"How are they? What's the news?" Del told him that they were both rushed to operating rooms, and that the injuries could be life threatening. Laura seemed to be in worse shape than Paul, but they were both in critical condition. Marty couldn't believe it, since they had spoken to both of them less than a half hour ago. However, it only takes five minutes to be involved in an accident, and this definitely was the case.

As more police personnel heard about the accident, officers, as is the case, showed up to be of any help and also be available if blood was needed. The sea of blue got so large that the group had to wait in the outside lobby for news. Two hours had elapsed, and there was nothing new from the doctors. Marty contacted Tony and explained that he was going to stay for a while longer, and then he would get back to the mall. He couldn't renege on his responsibility to "Best," and lay it all on Tony's shoulders.

Another hour had passed and Sgt. Del told Marty that he would let both Marty and Tony know of any developments. Marty reluctantly left and went to join his partner in their moonlighting gig. When Marty arrived, he saw uniformed officers with Tony in the store. Tony had collared a "grab and goer" as he ran out of the store with a handful of gold necklaces. His accomplice, however, got away with some of the jewelry. The uniformed officers, as per a former agreement, took the arrest; however, the owner of the store was livid that one of the thieves got away. He kept shouting at Marty that if he was there, as he should have been, both thieves would have been caught, and there would have been no losses suffered. It was the wrong time for the owner to come down on Marty.

In a very soft but focused tone, Marty addressed the boss: "I just came from the hospital where two of my fellow officers are fighting for their lives. My going to the hospital far outweighs my concern for your goods which are insured; and if you ever raise your voice to me like that again, you will be in the same hospital as the two officers." The jewelry store owner knew Marty for a long time and had never seen him this way. Using his better judgment, the boss just nodded and went back to his office and shut the door.

The uniforms took the perpetrator out of the store and into a waiting marked police car. Marty took the opportunity to explain what he saw at the hospital, but Tony, in a very unorthodox move, interrupted him and told Marty that he didn't want to dwell on what had been going on at the hospital. Marty assumed that Tony was feeling as bad as he, but was dealing with it in a different way. No, Tony was feeling the guilt of the carnage that he had planned and directed.

Approximately, one hour later Marty's phone, once again, started ringing. It was Sergeant Del. Marty looked at it and hesitated answering. He didn't know what kind of news he would be getting, and he had a bad feeling that the news would not be good. He forced himself to press the "accept" icon and said "Hello." "Hi Marty." Del never sounded so solemn: "I just spoke with the doctor. They could not save Laura. She suffered massive brain trauma and never regained consciousness. She passed away on the operating table. Paul is still in the operating room, but the doctor said there is a good chance he will pull through; however, he will have some permanent disabilities."

The blood drained from Marty's face, and he just turned to Tony and shook his head. He told Tony the sad news about Detective Sergeant Noldir and mentioned that Paul was still not out of the woods, but the chances for his survival were better. He did mention to Tony that even if Paul made it, he would have some permanent disabilities. Marty was beside himself, and Tony couldn't believe what he was hearing. He couldn't believe it for a number of reasons, one of which was that he was an accomplice to vehicular homicide, conspiracy, and felonious assault. Things were getting worse and worse. Once again, he couldn't confide in his partner. Things were not only getting worse, but confusing and convoluted.

Tony was so far into the dark that he could see no light at the end of the tunnel. He had no idea how he was going to get away with all that he had done, but he knew that he would not, at any cost, go to prison. That was not in the cards, and he would do whatever had to be done to avoid it. He was becoming that person who was despised by law enforcement and who needed to be stopped. However, Tony had the advantage, because at one time, he was the pursuer and knew how the enforcers worked. He was once one of the good guys.

How was he going to deal with his partner, whom he trusted like a brother, and who never let him down? He was always an asset, a crutch, a resource of strength, but now he might very well become an obstacle to freedom. Tony was having a lot of difficulty trying to resolve the partnership problem. He still needed Marty, and he really didn't want anything to happen to him. If he could avoid it, he definitely would. If he couldn't, in Tony's warped mind, freedom outweighed the bonds of friendship. Tony had resorted to panicked thinking and threw all he cared about to the wind. Could he have sunk so low as to disregard a relationship that had at one time saved his life? Desperate people do desperate things, and Tony was now a desperate person.

Chapter Twenty-Five

The Embassy

General Abel Gollman left his office and hurriedly went to his waiting military vehicle. Without saluting the standing guards, he got in his car and sped through the exit gate almost before they were fully opened. He was driving as if his life depended on it, and for all intents and purposes, it may have. He arrived at the United States Embassy in Jerusalem in approximately one hour's time. The usual fifty-five miles from Netivot to Jerusalem should take about an hour-and-a-half, but Gollman knew that every minute counted, so he put the pedal to the metal and violated every speed limit to cut the time down to sixty minutes. In fact, as he approached the Embassy entry gates, his skidding to a stop alarmed the marine corporal on duty to the point that the soldier had his weapon in a "high alert" position aimed at the vehicle.

The General quickly exited his vehicle and told the corporal that he must see the Ambassador at once. The corporal explained to General Gollman that this was not the protocol for visits to the Embassy. He further explained that anyone wishing to see the Ambassador must call the Embassy and make an appointment. Gollman was so infuriated by the soldier that he began to yell and approach the corporal in a threatening manner. One does not threaten an Embassy marine, so the marine went into a defensive stance, pointed his rifle and ordered the General to retreat. This brought Gollman to his senses, and he more clearly explained to the corporal that his seeing the Ambassador was a matter of national security for the United States and a matter of life and death - most likely his own.

The corporal returned to the guard booth and dialed the assistant to the ambassador. He explained what the General had told him and asked whether the Ambassador would want to see Gollman. The assistant told the corporal to stay on the line while she checked with Ambassador Richardson. Knowing that the Ambassador was presently in a meeting, she approached the door to the conference room and gently knocked. Opening the door, she apologized for the interruption and asked to speak privately with the Ambassador. Richardson knew that his assistant would not interrupt a meeting unless something important had arisen. In the corridor outside of the conference room, she explained that an Israeli General, in full uniform, wanted to see him on a matter of urgent National Security for the United States. Ambassador Richardson asked if the General had given his name to the marine guard, and the Assistant said it sounded like "Ghouman."

Donald Richadson knew immediately who it was and told the assistant to allow the General to enter and bring him into the Ambassador's office. Richardson knew that General Gollman, the Barbarian, would only come to the United States Embassy if the matter was of grave importance. The Ambassador was actually shocked that the General would even step foot into the Embassy since Abel Gollman had no liking for diplomacy.

Ambassador Richardson returned to the conference room where he made apologies for having to curtail the meeting. The conference attendees understood and departed with the caveat that they would arrange for another appointment to complete the meeting. Ambassador Richardson left the room and headed for his office. He passed his assistant who nodded that the General was waiting in his office. He entered and addressed the General:

"Hello, General Gollman, what can I do for you?" The General was surprised: "You know who I am?" Richardson answered: "The corporal relayed your name, and your reputation precedes you. I understand you mentioned National Security to the marine. What do you have to tell me?" Abel Gollman parsed his words to deviate somewhat from the fact that the Ambassador was not notified earlier. He explained that it had been difficult to obtain the facts regarding the possible terrorist attack, but that he did not want to prolong the notification any longer. Gollman also explained that since he had not conferred with his superiors regarding this notification, that his safety was in peril.

Richardson kept inquiring as to the specifics of a potential attack, but General Gollman could only respond that he was not able to obtain anything other than what he had already related. Before the Ambassador would initiate an "alert" procedure, he wanted to know the sources from which the General had obtained the information. Gollman explained that at the threat of injury to family members, prisoner trustees had divulged whatever information they had. Richardson knew that there were more than just family threats, after all, he was speaking to the Barbarian, the scourge of the Israeli Penal System. If Gollman could not get any more information, then nobody could. Richardson also assumed that the General's main sources of information had either died after being tortured or, to defeat the Barbarian, had taken their own lives. His assumption was grounded in fact.

Getting his notes together and going over whatever specifics he had obtained from the General, Ambassador Richardson asked Gollman to wait in an adjoining room. He then told his assistant to get the Secretary of State on the line and to emphasize the urgency of the request. Having relayed the information to the Secretary, the Ambassador told Gollman that he could temporarily reside in the Embassy until further accommodations could be made. Donald Richardson had started the ball rolling both diplomatically and tactically. He was sure that the Prime Minister of Israel would be hearing from the State Department, and he was certain that the CIA and FBI were being notified. They in turn would be notifying the New York City Police Commissioner and that Department's Intelligence Division.

It was assumed by all of the agencies that the prime time for an attack to inflict the most damage and the highest body count would be during the Christmas holiday.

Nothing having occurred so far and the focus of the holiday almost gone, the attack could very well come at any time in the next day or so. This would be a major concern for the Police Department who had already deployed their resources to cover the holiday demands. It was going to be one of those times when orders would come down canceling all days off and mandating extended tours.

Officers who were already working past their normal tours were tired and exhausted from the holiday push. However, they would have to bear down and remain even more vigilant as the holiday continued. Additionally, the significance of preventing a terrorist attack far outweighed the bonding of families during Christmas. This hit hard on the senior officers who had already missed plenty of holidays and were looking forward to the time off they had earned. However, when the order comes down, there are no exceptions and the mantra that permeates all ranks is: "You knew what you were signing up for." Explain that to the wife who is preparing the family dinner with the relatives or even more so to the five- or seven-year-old waiting for Santa (who is probably a dad in costume) with only his mom. They might not have known that they were also "signing up."

Chapter Twenty-Six

The Push

Detectives Possidos and Glasser both got the message from Sergeant Del, and they were on their way to make sure that Tony and Marty were on the same page with the information. Nick Possidos spoke first when he saw Ossur and Iniddor: "Did you guys get the alert from the Sarge regarding a possible terrorist hit? It's supposed to be from a reliable source." They both nodded their heads in agreement and said that if the mall was attacked, there would be mayhem just because of the amount of people shopping. Marty said: "We all know that the shopping center is jammed on Christmas Eve with last minute holdouts, so that would be a perfect time for organized chaos." They all agreed, and since it would be the four of them on duty at the mall, a plan was devised to be in contact every half hour.

The alert had also mandated an increase in uniform coverage including specialized units like Emergency Service and the Task Force. So, with so many uniforms in the area acting as a major deterrent, the detectives felt like the Three Kings Shopping Mall would not be the primary target. There were many shopping areas in Brooklyn, but with the increased coverage at the mall, the detectives' instincts told them that the terrorists, if they existed, would be foolish to make Three Kings their focus. In fact, Sergeant Del had authorized extended tours for his squad which meant that the mall had a total of six Detectives at the shopping center for the Christmas Eve holiday. Marty and Tony, however, had to pay special attention to the jewelry store since that is where they were contracted, but they would also be surveilling the common areas of the mall.

Right from the "get-go," the mall was crowded with last minute shoppers. It seemed even more congested than in past years, but maybe that was a result of the detectives paying even more attention this year because of the alert. In an emergency, uniformed cops and detectives would have a difficult time getting to the scene. Tony and Marty took turns being inside and outside of the store. They had a responsibility to Best Jewelry for the store security, but they had an even bigger responsibility for the safety and security of the mall facility, its employees and its shoppers.

It was Marty's turn on the outside, and in the walkway but not far from the store or the main entrance, he scoped Alex Hassid who was, once again, walking in the company of the same two individuals he had seen Alex with before. Marty let Tony know that he saw Alex, and that he was going to approach him. Tony eyeballed Marty, as best as he could, and Marty yelled to Alex to stop. Instead of stopping, Alex and his two companions picked up their pace and totally ignored Marty's call. Detective Iniddor did not want to stray too far from the jewelry store, but he was determined to speak with Alex. The last time they spoke, Alex seemed nervous and almost under the control of his two friends. This was the consensus of opinion by both Tony and Marty.

Things just didn't seem right. Alex showed very little concern regarding what progress may have been made on Rachael's case, and it seemed that his nerves dictated a very curtailed conversation. Both detectives shared the uneasy feeling that things weren't right. Marty rushed through the crowd and finally caught up with Alex, grabbed him by the arm and stopped him. Alex looked annoyed, very nervous and on edge to speak with Iniddor. The detective asked: "Hey Alex, just wanted to check to see how things are. How have you been and how is your sister, Rachael, doing? Is she fully recovered?" Alex, head down and no eye contact, answered with one word: "Fine." It seemed that his two associates wanted no part of this meeting and conversation: "Come on, Alex, we have to go." They pulled him away before Marty could ask or say anything else.

This time their meeting was even more suspect. Marty couldn't believe that Alex showed no real interest in his sister's case, and it seemed that he wanted nothing to do with the investigating detectives - Tony or Marty. Marty remembered how Alex showed frustration and disappointment when the detectives had nothing new to tell him; and Marty also remembered how Alex's look implied that "if you don't do something, I will" attitude. Now, he never even asked about the case. The "why" was troubling Marty. He couldn't let it go and decided to catch up again with the threesome. He wanted to finally find out what was going on, and what seemed to be troubling Alex Hassid. Marty was also suspicious of how much influence his companions seemed to have over Alex.

Iniddor started hustling after Alex and the two males. He called out Alex's name again. Marty started jogging after the group. As he got closer, he saw one of the males look back to see if Marty was following them. Marty was not only following the three but was in a stone's throw of catching up. What Marty saw next; he just couldn't believe. One of the males, the one who noticed Marty in close pursuit, pushed his way through the crowd and, what seemed like an intentional act, pushed an older woman into a man who was wheelchair bound. The woman fell to the ground and yelled out in pain while the man in the wheelchair also fell with the chair on top of him. A large group of people surrounded the injured shoppers, and Marty was forced to stop his pursuit and give aid to the elderly man and woman. He called for police and emergency medical assistance and waited at the scene for uniformed officers to arrive.

Just before Marty stopped to offer help, he took a last look at the racing three. Alex was being pushed up front with the other two males following closely behind. The trailing male, now with his shirt raised above his waist because of the "collision," displayed what Detective Iniddor believed was a portable radio. He couldn't be one hundred percent sure, but it certainly looked like a radio communicator. Why would the male need a portable radio to be shopping in the mall? Why would Alex be involved with these two, who apparently wanted to escape a further encounter with the detective- a detective who just wanted to help Alex? Everything pointed to suspicious behavior.

Alex did not want to talk, did not want to find out about his sister's case and was being rushed off by his two companions, at least one of which was carrying a portable radio. Alex also chose the company of someone who would intentionally injure two vulnerable people, committing a felonious assault. Additionally, he wasn't even able to make eye contact with Detective Iniddor, the lead detective in Rachael's case.

These thoughts and suspicions needed attention and answers, but right now Marty was involved in helping the injured and getting information for the police reports. In speaking with the elderly female, who was initially pushed and whose off-balanced fall caused the man and the wheel chair to tip over, she related the facts of the incident. She stated that when the unknown male first pushed her to the ground and focused on the results of his actions, she was positive that she heard him speaking in a foreign language to the others who were with him; however, the only English words that she could make out were: "Allah is great."

Chapter Twenty-Seven

The Message

Having escaped from the clutches of Detective Iniddor, Alex and his two companions headed toward the shopping center administrative offices. As agreed upon with Dunait, this would be the location where Alex would take up his position during the attack. The General Manager, Reginald Winsten, had made it his focus to hire college students during the summer months to help with the routine tasks that needed attention in the mall. Alex Hassid had been one of those college students, so there was a familiarity between the two. Alex was depending upon that familiarity to facilitate his entrance into the administrative offices at the designated attack time. As was discussed earlier, the building also housed Erman Falco, the Director of Facilities and Bob Baxter, the Director of Security.

Leaving his two comrades behind, Alex approached the controlled entrance, looked up at the camera and pressed the access buzzer. Baxter looked at the camera, recognized Alex and pressed the entrance release button. After entering, Alex nodded an "hello" to Baxter, and mentioned that he was here to see Director Falco. Bob ushered him in as he called out to Falco that he had a visitor. Alex knocked on Director Falco's opened door and waited for the Director to wave him in.

"Hello Mr. Falco. I am very sorry to hear about Vin. He was a good guy and helped me out a lot. If there is anything that I can do, please let me know." Erman Falco, with tears in his eyes, answered: "Thank you, Alex. I miss him every day, but his death will not have been in vain. We will avenge him and everyone else who has suffered from Israeli wrath. How are you holding up?" Alex was glad that Mr. Falco seemed concerned about him.

"I'm okay, I guess." He looked behind him to make sure that no one was within ear shot and said: "To tell you the truth, I am a bit nervous. What's left of my family depends on me, and if something were to happen to me, they would be on their own. I wouldn't want that." Falco responded: "There is always a risk in an undertaking such as this, but Dunait has been involved in a number of these actions, and he is well rehearsed and an excellent planner. So, the risk is reduced because of his organizational leadership. Also, I will be looking out for your safety as well. Just try to relax, and do as you were instructed, and you will be fine. Do it for Amir, Chail and Vin. They deserve the success!"

Alex listened attentively and felt somewhat relieved that Mr. Falco was so confident in the plan and in Dunait himself. He would perform as best as he could and would strictly follow the planned steps. He wasn't going to allow his fear and trepidation to rule his actions. He said "good-bye" to Director Falco and, as planned, headed for Reginald Winsten's office.

"Hello Mr. Winsten, I just wanted to stop by and wish you the best for the holiday season." Hanukkah and Christmas fell at the same time. "How are things going?" Winsten responded: "Things are going well, Thanks. But more importantly, how are things going with you? I heard about the incident with your sister. How is she and the family doing?" As the conversation continued, Alex could not help but focus on the fact that General Manager, Reginald Winsten was his assigned target. Alex, not wanting to raise any alarm or curiosity, continued: "Rachael is doing good, and things are okay at home. I noticed that the mall seems to be even busier than last year at this time, so I guess you'll be working late again on Christmas Eve." Winsten answered: "I will be working late, Director Falco will be working late, and Mr. Baxter will also be working long hours. It comes with the territory." Alex answered: "Well, I will be around for Christmas Eve, and if you need any help from me, don't hesitate to ask. Although, I don't really know what I could do." Winsten was impressed with Alex's offer but told him that they would most likely be able to handle everything that came up; however, he thanked him for the offer anyway.

Alex said "good-bye" and proceeded to the exit when he was abruptly stopped by Bob Baxter: "Hold up, Alex, you could do me a big favor, if you don't mind?" Initially, Alex shuttered with thoughts that Baxter knew something. Alex did not want to get involved with the Director of Security, but he answered quickly and positively: "Sure, Mr. Baxter. What can I do for you?" Baxter said: "Thanks, Alex. Could you just stop by Best Jewelry and tell either Detective Ossur or Iniddor, who are apparently not answering their phones, that I would like one of them to stop by my office as soon as possible? Could you do that for me?" Although hating the idea of having to approach either one of the detectives, Alex said: "Sure." It briefly passed through Alex's stream of consciousness that Baxter was going to tell the detectives about the potential attack; but that probably was just his nerves getting the best of him.

As Alex left, the two cell members approached him and asked how the surveillance went. Alex responded with the information that he had gleaned from the General Manager. Everyone would be working. Then Alex told them what the Director of Security wanted him to do. That information was met with strong consternation. They told Alex that going to the detectives could jeopardize the entire operation. They were concerned that Alex might break down and, in a weakened moment, inadvertently reveal the plan.

Even more so, they knew that Alex was very nervous about the operation, and if his nerves got the better of him, he might just get it off his chest and confess the plan to the detectives. So, in a strong and threatening tone, the two cell members said "absolutely not." Alex was somewhat surprised by their attitude and demanding demeanor. For a second time in twenty-four hours, he doubted his participation in the attack plan. However, for the sake of wanting things to look normal, Alex felt that he should relay the message. He argued with the two that his not conveying the message would bring doubt and suspicion, and that Baxter would be looking for him to complete the favor.

Because the three could not reach a compromise, they decided to contact Dunait and let him decide. Dunait had emphasized the mandate that if any problems arose or anything out of the ordinary was to occur, he should be immediately contacted. So, one of the cell members went out of earshot from Alex and called: "Hello, Dunait. Sorry to bother you but we have a problem here with Alex. He visited the Administrative Building as you ordered, and he made contact with the Security Director, the Facilities Director and the General Manager. He found out that they will all be working late on the Eve; however, on his way out, the Security Director asked Alex to do him a favor."

Dunait, becoming impatient with the delay, said: "Okay, get to the point. What did Baxter want?" "He wants Alex to deliver a message to the Detectives in the jewelry store. We both think it would be a mistake to put Alex in such a possibly compromising and dangerous position. We all know that Alex is not the strongest link in the chain and worry that, either inadvertently or intentionally, he might offer up something to jeopardize the operation. We do not want him to go near the detectives or the jewelry store. What do you think?" Dunait replied: "We have to trust that Alex will be strong enough to handle the matter." So, he agreed to let Alex deliver the message for Baxter. Dunait continued: "If he doesn't do it, Baxter will want to know why. He might even become suspicious. We don't want that. Did Alex let you know the content of the message?" The caller responded: "Yes. Baxter said that he wants either one of the detectives to call him as soon as possible. I don't like it, Dunait."

Dunait answered with a strong and almost chastising response: "I don't care what you like or don't like. Advise him to be quick and careful but deliver the message. The two of you will keep him in sight, and if he takes longer than you think he should, interrupt his conversation and get him out of there. Do I make myself clear?" The cell member answered in the affirmative and disconnected. He then turned to Alex and said that Dunait had agreed with him to deliver the message to the detectives. He also mentioned to him that it should be quick and to the point, and that he should not delay leaving the jewelry store. Additionally, if in their opinion, he stayed too long with the detectives, they would come and interrupt his visit and usher him out of the store.

The cell member emphasized that this was also Dunait's decision. The three of them proceeded to Best Jewelry.

Chapter Twenty-Eight

The Safe House

As Alex and the other two cell members came closer to the jewelry store, they separated so that as Alex got closer to Best, the detectives would only see him. However, they positioned themselves so that they didn't lose sight of the very nervous boy.

Detective Iniddor was looking out at the crowd in the walkway when he noticed Alex coming his way. Marty let Tony know that Alex seemed to be on his way to meet with them. Both detectives were apprehensive about Alex's return. He previously seemed to want to avoid any contact with them, and in fact, had been somewhat involved in the felonious assault perpetrated by one of his companions. Alex had to know that he was taking a risk coming to them. Alex stopped at the entrance, and the detectives approached him.

"Hello, Alex. We're surprised to see you since it looks like you're trying to avoid us at all costs, and the fact that your friend is responsible for assaulting two people in the mall puts you at risk." Marty was the first to speak, and as he addressed Alex, he scanned the area to see if Alex's two companions were anywhere in sight. The cell members, however, were well hidden so they escaped Marty's gaze. After a brief pause and Alex hesitating to say anything, Marty continued: "What's going on, Alex?" Alex looked up and answered the detective: "Nothing is going on. I just have a lot of things on my mind. The reason that I stopped by is to relay a message to you from Mr. Bob Baxter. I visited him and Mr. Falco in the Administrative Building, and before I left, Mr. Baxter asked me to tell you to come to his office as soon as possible. He said that neither you nor Detective Ossur are answering your phones." Marty thanked him for the message, but he was not yet through with getting some answers from Alex.

"The two guys that you are hanging out with - are they from around here? The woman who was pushed over by your friend said that she heard a foreign accent. Also, what do they do if at least one of them needs a portable radio to carry around with him?" Although he tried very hard to hide his angst, Alex was visibly shaken by the questioning. However, thinking as quickly as he could, he answered: "They are both from my home country, and they work for a security company. They are friends of my older brother, Chail. They are also helping out with some of the concerns that my family has right now." Hoping that his explanation would satisfy the detective, he said "good-bye" and turned to leave when Marty grabbed his arm and said that he needed more information.

Now Alex really started to feel the effects of anxiety and stress. He had to leave. Marty, however, was not buying it: "Alex I need to know the names of your two friends, their addresses and phone numbers, and their whereabouts right now. We have an open case on a possible felonious assault with injuries to two people. I need your cooperation, and if you don't cooperate you could be found guilty of conspiring with them. Where are they now, and if everything is legit, why did they and you run from me in the mall?"

"Stop, Police!" Marty heard Tony's voice as he started running after two apparent thieves as they left the store. They both had gold chains hanging from their hands. Marty had to assist in the chase and told Alex not to move from the store. Alex said nothing. The detectives chased the perpetrators out of the main entrance and right into the arms of uniformed cops who were assigned to the outside area. After a brief struggle, the thieves were in custody and charged with larceny; and again, as is the routine, the collar was turned over to the uniformed cops. Marty hurriedly returned to the store, where he hoped that he would find Alex waiting. That was not to be the case.

As soon as Marty left in pursuit, the two cell members gathered up Alex and rushed him away from the store and out of sight. They were about to signal Alex to leave, but the pursuit fit the bill. They started questioning Alex about his conversation with Detective Iniddor: "What took so long? We saw that you were about to leave, and the detective stopped you. What did he want?"

Alex relayed the conversation: "The detective wanted to know why I was acting so strange, and what was wrong. I said that I had some family concerns that were taking up much of my time. He also said that he had an investigation on a felonious assault, that's what he called your push into the old woman. He wanted me to tell him where you were, where you lived and your phone numbers. When he pressed for more information, I just told him that you were friends of my brother, Chail, and that you were helping out with the family. Oh, and he also wanted to know what you did, and why you were carrying a portable radio that he apparently saw. And lastly, he said that the old woman stated that she heard a foreign accent."

The conversation with the detectives alarmed the two cell members, and they told Alex that he was not to enter the mall again until it was time for the operation to begin. Alex understood and left the mall with them.

When Detective Iniddor returned and found that Alex had gone, he conferred with Tony and voiced his suspicions: "Tony, I think that Alex might be involved in something that might move him to do something stupid. I didn't like his answers, and definitely don't like the company that he is keeping. Could it be possible his friends are part of a rebel group? Could he be involved in the planning of something nefarious? We've got to find him to make sure he isn't shanghaied by experienced extremists. He is an innocent kid who just wants the best for his family."

Tony wasn't of the same mind as his partner. He was very suspicious of the way Alex had been acting and now, even after Marty had told Alex to wait, he split. The two males that Alex had been seen with also presented a problem for Tony. They ran from Marty and, by doing so, brought Alex into the fray with them. To Tony, Alex wasn't just an "innocent kid."

Alex and his two companions headed to the safe house where Alex's mother and sister were now residing. After driving for approximately thirty minutes, they turned onto the street where the safe house was located. Their car came to an abrupt stop, however, as they saw police cars and FBI vehicles parked in front of the house. Staying a distance from the police presence, they saw both Ficera and Rachael being led into awaiting vehicles. There was no sign of the two cell members who were assigned to watch and protect Alex's mother and sister. Plans had to change immediately, and Dunait had to be notified. Additionally, another safe house had to be identified so that Alex would stay out of harm's way and be secured before the planned attack.

From their vantage point, and maintaining a safe distance, they called Dunait once again. He was upset with the elimination of the safe house and the apparent capture of Ficera and Rachael, but was not deterred from keeping to the schedule. He directed the three to another location and told them to stay there until the designated time of the operation. While Dunait was still on the phone and as the three were pulling away from the area, they noticed an official-looking white van pull up to the house and into the driveway. It was a van with which they were all too familiar. In big bold letters, they saw the words: "New York City Medical Examiner" painted on the side of the van. They waited a little while longer and witnessed their fellow cell members being carried out of the house with white sheets covering their bodies from head to toe.

The Alliance had just lost another two members, and the attack had not even begun. Worse than that, the FBI and the police had two people in custody now who knew what was about to take place. With a little coercion and the threat of arrest, there was a strong possibility that law enforcement would become privy to the plan for attack. In Ficera's case, officers wouldn't even have to apply that much force, she wanted no part of what was about to take place; however, she really did not know that much regarding the specifics. In Rachael's case, she knew a lot more, and if she gave up the information, the attack would be compromised, and her brother would be arrested. After careful thought, Dunait was sure that Rachael would reveal what she knew because in her mind, Alex being arrested was a much better choice than her brother possibly being killed.

It became apparent now, that the operation could turn out to be a lot more-bloody than anticipated. Dunait would keep that thought to himself and encourage the members to be strong for the cause. While the Alliance members were in more jeopardy now than before, Dunait would remain in the relative safety of his van as he orchestrated movements and directions to his operatives. It was the relative safety of a van that was parked in the area restricted to law enforcement and first responder vehicles.

Although he had the van painted to reflect an official police vehicle, Dunait missed one important item. Police vehicles have designated and distinct license plates. His van displayed a New York State license plate that would be assigned to any ordinary registered vehicle. He had realized this snafu too late to change it, but relied upon police indifference and the official police markings to deter any special attention being given to the van. He was certain that police officers would only see a "police" van parked in the restricted "first responder" parking area. He was unaware of the emergency message that all police officers had received to put them on a "high alert surveillance" status.

Chapter Twenty-Nine

The Raid

When Alex saw his mother and sister being taken into custody, the blood drained from his face. He realized that he failed to protect his family and now more than ever, thought that it might be best if he just went to the police and confessed. He would save Ficera and Rachael from further harassment and anguish at the hands of the police investigators. The two cell members sitting with him in the vehicle became acutely aware of the look on Alex's face. They knew that Alex Hassid was having second thoughts about his role in the mall operation. They also knew that he was never really "gung-ho" about being a part of the plan. He originally had to be convinced that his participation was necessary to ensure the safety of his family members both at home and in Israel. However, his father and brother in Israel were dead, and now his mother and younger sister were in police custody with the F.B.I. and the N.Y.P.D. What purpose did it serve for Alex to continue to be involved?

The two cell members were right about Alex. These thoughts and questions were flooding into Alex's mind, and as he thought more and more about it, he was sure he had to bail out. He turned to the cell member who was sitting next to him in the back seat, and as he started to tell him his concerns and decision, he was met with a hand in his face and the word "Stop."

The member looked at him and facially conveyed the "I know what you're thinking" idea. He spoke to Alex in a very serious and definitely threatening tone: "I was very sorry to hear about you friend, Vin Falco. However, one must learn that with failure comes consequences. He has failed us a number of times, and he reaped what he sowed." Alex interrupted in an effort to correct the member: "Vin was shot and killed by an errant bullet. It was an accident. There were no consequences for a failure. An accident is an accident." His companion shook his head and with a sneer said: "That was not an accident. Vin Falco, because of his failures and the risk that he represented, had to be eliminated. That night in your home, Vin Falco was executed by the Alliance. It was not an accident; it was an execution."

Alex just stared in disbelief and realized that he had just received a veiled threat that no one is immune from punishment for failure or betrayal. If he wasn't afraid before, he definitely was now from both the potential police response and his fellow cell members. Alex just sat there as he pondered his immediate future, and it wasn't looking good. He knew that he would be under the constant scrutiny now of everyone involved in the planned attack. In their eyes, he couldn't be totally trusted, and that might mean he could easily become expendable. They traveled in silence for the rest of the way to the new location which was in the Bay Ridge section of Brooklyn. He knew that he would be a prisoner there until the group had to leave for the Shopping Center.

Ficera and Rachael had been brought to the F.B.I. field office in Manhattan where they were both questioned by F.B.I. agents and detectives from the New York City Police Department's Intelligence Division. On the way to Manhattan, Rachael had emphasized again and again to her mother not to say anything to the police. Rachael wanted to control the conversation between the police and the two of them. She knew that the investigators would question them separately in an effort to weed out the lies and the contradictions in order to get some solid information.

She also knew that time was running out if law enforcement was to thwart a potential terrorist attack.

Rachael was really confused with the two options that she had available to her. There was a possibility that Alex would live through the planned attack and be able to escape any kind of incarceration or injury, and that the operation would yield the desired results of freeing political prisoners in Israel. If she revealed the specifics of the plan now to the investigators, there was a possibility that the terrorist attack would be thwarted, and Alex would be arrested for Conspiracy and sentenced to a long term in prison. The final thought that permeated her consciousness was one that pictured her brother, Alex, lying in a pool of blood on a floor somewhere in the shopping center. This would devastate her and probably kill her mother. There was so much to think about and so little time to make a decision.

In just a few short hours, mayhem would break out in the Three Kings Shopping Center. An entire wing of that mall would be taken hostage with the threat of injury and death to the many shoppers there. Even if she were to tell everything to the police right now, there might not be enough time to stop the possible onslaught. She made her decision. She wanted to see her brother alive, whether in jail or not.

All detectives and police officers were on "high alert" status, but now the concentration of law enforcement efforts would focus mainly on the Three Kings Shopping Center.

Because of the tragic accident involving Paul Staffio and Laura Noldir, the immediate threat of arrest was removed, so Tony could truly concentrate on his job. Marty saw the difference in Tony and was glad he had his partner back, at least for now. Detectives Jim Jones, Juan Medina, Nick Possidos, Gary Glasser and Marty and Tony had been notified about the new information. Special agents from the F.B.I. and the uniformed officers were notified as well.

Everyone was searching for that suspicious person, a group just waiting around and not shopping, and that vehicle that shouldn't be parked where it is. Although Marty and Tony were following the same surveillance parameters as all of the officers, they were looking for an even more specific target. They were searching for Alex Hassid and his two companions. If the detectives' suspicions rang true, the three of them would be somehow involved in whatever activity was planned.

Marty and Tony strained as they stared through the crowded walkways trying to locate any one of the three. They took turns looking out at throngs of people and at the shoppers inside of the jewelry store. They were still responsible for securing the store.

In the interim, Tony had visited the Administrative Building in response to the message that Alex had delivered. Tony pushed the buzzer and was immediately granted access. Bob Baxter came rushing out of his office with both Erman Falco and Reginald Winsten in tow. In an overpowering loud blast Bob shouted: "What the hell is going on? I just got a blurb from one of my contacts in Intelligence that Three Kings might be the main target for a terrorist attack. What the hell is going on? Why do I have to get the information indirectly from Intel when you and the other guys in your squad are here and apparently know the potential problems?" In the normal Bob Baxter flamboyant display and in an effort to demonstrate his sincere concern for the mall and his employer, he huffed and puffed. Tony knew that Baxter was only concerned with his own personal future. If things went bad, it would negatively reflect on his abilities and his further possible employment. So, he took the opportunity to give it his best shot.

When Baxter finally finished, Tony asked Bob, Falco and Winsten to go into the conference room where he would bring them all up to date. He explained that there had been a city-wide alert sent out to notify all the precincts that there was a possibility of a terrorist attack in a shopping center. Although he was sure that they knew about the other shopping centers, Tony emphasized that there were many areas that had to be covered. The NYPD had ordered everyone on extended tours, and the coverage at the Three Kings Shopping Mall had been expanded with the increase of uniformed officers and additional detectives. Tony further explained that they had just received information that the mall was the potential target for the attack.

Tony told them that he had been on his way to the administrative offices when he got Baxter's message. Regional Winsten spoke up: "What do you recommend we do? We can't close the mall on Christmas Eve, but we can't knowingly put our shoppers in danger." Tony knew that there was no way that Winsten would close the mall; there was too much profit to lose. However, Reginald covered himself by just verbalizing his concern. Tony could not guarantee that nothing would occur or the fact that an attack would not take place. However, he emphasized the increased police presence and tried to assure the three of them that the F.B.I. and the NYPD had the situation in hand.

After listening attentively to every word, the Director of Facilities and ally of the Alliance, Erman Falco, hit Detective Ossur with a barrage of questions, most of which the detective couldn't answer or did not want to answer. After summoning up and allaying some of their fears, Tony nonchalantly asked if anyone had seen Alex Hassid. This question coming on the heels of a conversation about terrorism, sparked a concern in everyone's mind, especially with Erman Falco. However, Tony, knowing that it would do just that, diffused their concerns by stating that the detectives needed some additional information from Alex regarding the case involving his sister.

They answered together that the last time they saw him was when Bob Baxter gave him a message to relay to the detectives. Tony nodded an "okay" and asked that they call him if Alex showed up. With only hours left before show time, Falco was very concerned now about Alex and his participation. He would have to keep a close eye on Alex as well as controlling the possible bomb and gas attacks. If doubts arose, and Falco felt that Alex had become a risk, the Director would eliminate that risk. If his only son, Vincent, could be eliminated, then, if necessary, why not Alex Hassid?

Chapter Thirty

The Revelation

The detectives assigned to the mall were keeping in constant communication with each other as they watched for anything suspicious or anyone who appeared to be out of place. That left a whole gamut of possibilities, so they had to rely on their police instincts to sort out things or people who stood out. The paradox being those who were involved in such an operation wanted to blend in and not stand out. It was a definite challenge for law enforcement. They had reliable information that an attack would take place sometime during the holiday, but they did not know what the plot would be, what kind of weaponry might be used, and how many adversaries they would have to face. The major assumption, however, was that the attack would take place in the evening hours since darkness was always an asset.

The Alliance Cell members, employed as custodians at the Mall, were already in their specific areas evaluating the changing conditions. They were in the Three Kings Shopping Center uniforms so they brought no suspicions with their movement. They truly blended in with the busy scene. Other cell members, who would browse along with the rest of the weary shoppers and fit into the crowded holiday scenario, were not yet in place. They would arrive shortly before the designated attack time, a time that would be communicated to all by Dunait.

Of course, Starbucks was just mobbed with one mass of humanity trying to boost their energy to continue on their gift-getting mission. One of these energy seekers was Donna Uhrich. Apparently, the travel agency ran specials on specific vacation trips during the holiday season, since people weren't ordinarily anxious to vacation during that time. It was a way to try and bolster business. As a result, Compass Travel was busy with potential vacationers seeking discounted rates on future planned excursions. Her turn came on the Starbucks line, and she purchased her shot of coffee energy, asking for two additional ones.

Carefully negotiating the crowds, she brought the additional coffees to the jewelry store and offered them to both Marty and Tony. They couldn't be happier with the unexpected offering and thanked Donna for her generosity. She started speaking with them, but realized that their attention was elsewhere as they constantly gazed either into the crowded walkway or the inside of the jewelry store. So, before she left, she went into her purse and came out with what looked like a postcard and approached Tony, handing it to him. She explained that it had been an advertising promotion for one of the Caribbean Islands and when she saw it, Tony immediately came to her mind. Tony turned it over in his hand and saw a picture of a huge field of daffodils surrounding two local islanders. She told him that she knew he had been working long hours and wanted to bring a little relief and cheer to him. She knew about his strong affinity to daffodils, and that he always had one on his desk.

Donna had been in a relationship with Tony for a long time and knew many of his idiosyncrasies. Seeing that they were apparently very busy, she cut the conversation short and said that maybe she would see them later. Marty nodded an "okay" and Tony, once again feeling pangs of guilt, said nothing. It appeared that Donna too was feeling some misgivings at having thought that Tony could be involved in her assault. With her daffodil picture, she tried to ease her conscience and mend fences with Tony. She smiled and left, disappearing into the crowd.

Donna had heard about the catastrophic accident involving Detective Sergeant Noldir and Detective Staffio, and she wondered who was in charge of her case now. She hadn't heard from anyone in the Sex Crimes Unit and feared that her case might be put on the back burner. If she maintained her relationship with Tony and Marty, however, maybe they could push the investigation forward. She had nowhere else to turn.

Marty looked at Tony, the elephant in the room looming larger than ever, and asked the obvious question as to who he thought would be taking over the sexual assault case. Tony just stared at Marty and said: "I really don't care who takes it over. I have time now to put things in order." Marty responded: "Put things in order, you mean before you turn yourself in?" Tony just answered a disconcerting: "Yeah." It was a response that did not convince Marty that his partner would be true to his word about surrendering. With Laura out of the picture and Staffio incapacitated, it would be easy for Tony to change strategies mid-stream. Marty hoped that it would not be the case, because he couldn't let that happen. No matter what, Marty was going to make sure that Tony took responsibility for what he did.

Detectives Medina and Jones stopped by the jewelry store just to see how things were going in that neck of the woods. Juan mentioned that it seemed a lot more crowded where Marty and Tony were than in other parts of the mall. Marty was glad that Juan and Jim came by. It gave him an opportunity to tell them about the suspicions they had involving Alex Hassid.

"Do you remember the complainant we had on the shooting at Thompson High?" Both Detectives answered that they remembered.

"Well, both Tony and I believe that Alex Hassid, the complainant's brother, might be involved in something that prompted the potential attack." Juan questioned: "What makes you think that?"

"Alex's overall attitude and the way he speaks with the two of us. The usual no-eye contact, hesitation in answering questions, and wanting to split very quickly might be indicators of his involvement. He is also hanging out with characters that are at least ten years older than him and one of which is wanted for the felonious assault on the elderly woman and man that we reported." Detective Jones responded: "It's funny that you bring Alex and his sister up. My buddy in Intel told me that the recent information that we got about the pending attack came from his family, mostly from his sister, Rachael. They were picked up at a raid on an apparent safe house used by a terrorist cell."

Although Tony and Marty had received the information, they hadn't known the source. Marty inquired further: "So, Racheal definitely said that her brother was involved." He turned to Tony and said: "We were right!" Jones continued: "My guy also told me that they didn't have to push too hard to get the information. It seemed that both Alex's sister and mother were more concerned for Alex's safety than for anything else. They just didn't want to lose another family member. However, we all know that even if we are able to stop this thing, Alex is going to face charges for conspiracy and spend some time in prison. His family asked about this and apparently the Intel guys were straight with them; they emphasized, on a positive note to the mother and sister, that there would be a time when Alex would ultimately be released from jail and back with the family. It was a much better alternative than never seeing him alive again."

With the advent of this new information, Tony and Marty were even more determined to see if they could identify Alex in the crowded walkways. Marty knew that if he could get to Alex, he would be able to persuade him to retreat from participating and cooperate with the police to stop the potential attack. Where was Alex? He was the stop gap measure, the only one who could help.

The detectives couldn't possibly know that Alex Hassid was under house arrest, tantamount to being a prisoner until Dunait gave the word. They also couldn't know that Alex didn't have a choice anymore; his life depended on his loyalty to the cause and his unquestioning adherence to Dunait's directions, and to the will of the cell.

Alex wondered now how much Erman Falco knew about the raid, the new information that had been revealed to the police and how Alex's loyalties were circumspect. He wondered if Mr. Falco knew the real circumstances of his son's death; that Vin was not the victim of an errant bullet, but the victim of a planned execution. If the Facilities Director knew the truth, would he then be so disillusioned that he might think twice about blindly following Dunait's orders? Could Alex then consider Erman Falco as an ally and help put a stop to the whole operation? At this point Alex did not care about any cause, he just wanted a way out. He'd take a possible arrest in favor of dying and never seeing his family again. Alex was well aware of the risk in confiding to Falco, but he was willing to take that risk. It was his only choice.

Chapter Thirty-One

The Stash

The manager of the clothing store directly opposite Best Jewelry came running out of his store and into the crowded walkway yelling: "Stop that guy, he just stole clothes and hit one of my salespeople. Stop him! The guy with the black baseball cap." The manager's excited shouts landed on the ears of most of the shoppers, but, as usual, no one wanted to get involved. However, the shouts were also heard by Marty and Tony, and also by the other two detectives that were visiting the jewelry store. Both Jones and Medina heard the shouts, saw the perpetrator and started on a foot pursuit. Detectives Iniddor and Ossur followed but were at a distance behind Juan and Jim Jones.

In an attempt to lose his pursuers, the subject initiated a zig zag route through the crowd. People and objects were flying out of the way, but Juan was doggedly closing in on the subject. A shopper, not getting out of the way in time, became a delaying obstacle and slowed down the man wearing the black baseball hat. Juan got close to the perp and estimated his distance before he executed a flying tackle and floored the subject. Both Juan and the perp hit the floor hard, crashing into one of the metal trash cans that was strategically placed in the walkways. The trash can rolled over and spilled some of its contents on the walkway floor. Juan and the guy began struggling, but with the quick assistance of Jim Jones, the black hat flew into the air, and the perp was rendered harmless and smothered by both Juan and Jim.

Marty arrived a few moments after the actual take-down and a few moments before Tony. The contents of the flipped trash can were strewn all over the floor, and as the detectives struggled with the subject, the garbage was kicked in all directions. As Tony looked on, the last one to arrive on the scene, he observed one of the Three Kings custodians pick something up off of the floor and tuck it into his work uniform shirt. Tony thought this odd and went to inquire what the custodian stashed away. The custodian saw Tony coming his way, and not wanting to be confronted by the detective, backed up a few steps and then took flight.

Detective Ossur thought this quite odd and decided to pursue the custodian; however, the Three Kings employee was swift of foot and left Tony in the dust. Tony continued in the general direction to which the custodian had run, but failed to see any evidence of him or his possible route. The first thought that came into Tony was: "Twenty years ago, I would have had him, and it's time to cut out the smoking."

Tony slowly recovered and made his way back to the scene of the arrest and ultimately the jewelry store. As he arrived, Marty asked: "Where the hell did you disappear to? We could have used some additional help." Sarcastically Tony responded: "I saw the ice cream man pass, and I had such an urge for a chocolate fudge cone that I ran after him." Marty just stared and Tony continued: "Oddly enough, as you and the other guys were playing policeman, I saw one of the mall custodians pick something up out of the garbage that you guys spread all over the place, and he stashed it inside his shirt. He saw me looking and decided to back away and ultimately started to run. I followed him and was just about to tackle his ass when an old man with a cane got in my way, and in effort to avoid crashing into the old man, I dove to the floor and lost sight of the custodian." Marty responded: "So, you ran after the guy, he was younger and probably never smoked and he left you in the dust."

"Yeah, that's about the size of it; but it's kind of odd, isn't it, that he would take a piece of garbage from the trash and run like hell to get away from me. I was just curious as to what he thought was so valuable or interesting that he needed to flee. Could it have been an uncut diamond, a gold nugget or maybe even a winning lottery ticket.?" There was a pause. They looked at each other in a confirming acknowledgement of having the same thought. "Could it have been a drop off point for a drug transaction?"

They both assumed the custodian grabbed what had been the results of a paid drug transfer. Tony was the first to speak: "Remind me to let Baxter know that he has drug sales going on right under his nose." Marty responded: "I wonder how many other of his well-scrutinized employees are involved in drug sales. I am sure that Reggie Winsten would love to know how on top of things his Director of Security is. "Boy Tony, if you were a little slimmer, a little younger and a little quicker on your feet, you might have recovered evidence that you could have used to really screw former Sergeant Baxter. Oh, what could have been such sweet revenge!" Tony just nodded in affirming disgust: "Should we let Baxter know that he is down one custodian for the rest of the holiday?" Marty agreed, and Tony called the administrative offices from his cell phone.

"Hello, this Erman Falco speaking." Tony wanted to speak directly with Baxter so he could hold the news over his head, but according to the Director of Facilities, Baxter was not in the office. So, Tony relayed the entire arrest situation and ultimate foot pursuit to Erman Falco. Mr. Falco was noticeably taken aback by the news and asked what the drug was. Tony had to tell him that unfortunately the detectives were not able to retrieve any drugs. In a condescending and questioning manner Falco asked: "So, you really don't know for sure that it was drugs or that my employee was involved in a drug transaction." Tony answered: "That's true, but from my many years in police work, he was carrying a stash of drugs. Also, if everything was legit, why did he run?"

Falco said that he understood, and that he would discuss the entire incident with Baxter when he returned. He also said that he would let Reginald Winsten know since they would be absent one custodian for the rest of the holiday.

When the Facilities Director finished his comments, Tony suggested that a meeting be set up with the Narcotic Division Detectives in an effort to find out who is dealing. Tony offered to set up the meeting, but Mr. Falco suggested that nothing be done until the General Manager was notified. The final decision to meet with the narcotics cops would be up to Reginald Winsten. Tony understood and thanked the Facilities Director.

When Erman Falco hung up with Detective Ossur, he immediately contacted Dunait to let him know what had occurred. He was worried that the detective might decide to have all of the trash cans searched to see if any drugs were found. If that happened, the cell's threat of bombing the west wing of the mall would become moot. Dunait listened carefully as Erman Falco relayed the information that Detective Ossur had given to him. In his calm and decisive manner, he told Falco to try to get in touch with the custodian who fled and make certain that he not come back to the shopping center. Additionally, Dunait wanted Falco to get the explosives from the custodian so that they could be used elsewhere.

The leader was sure that the custodian cell member would race to the safe house closest to the mall. Falco was to contact the house and have one of the other Alliance members bring the device back to Falco. He would then place the explosive in another area of the wing. Dunait saw it as an advantage that the detectives thought that the custodian was involved with drugs. It brought the attention away from terrorism and onto drugs. That was a good thing.

Erman hung up with Dunait and waited for Baxter to return before going into Reginald's office with the information. Erman was not that fond of Baxter anyway, and he wanted the Security Director there when he told the General Manager what had happened. It would put Bob Baxter in a bad light, and Bob Baxter deserved what he got. After all, at one time he was a cop, and it would be other cops who presented obstacles to the success of the cell operation. It might be those other cops who ultimately threaten the lives of cell members and possibly his own. Cops might have to die, but for sure, one former cop most certainly would. Falco was going to make certain of that, it was in the plan.

Chapter Thirty-Two

The Floater

Ever since the American Embassy in Israel relayed information that they had received from General Abel Gollman to the State Department, the phones never stopped ringing. There was constant communication between the Embassy and the United States State Department. The main questions that came back to Ambassador Donald Richardson were: "Is the source a reliable one, and if so, why did it take so long for the Embassy to be notified?" Both good questions but not so easy to answer. Ambassador Richardson believed that

General Gollman was telling the truth about what limited information he had, but the obvious delay in notifying the Embassy was troublesome.

Gollman implied that if Israel would be able to turn over to the United States a completely thwarted terrorist attempt with the alleged terrorists in custody, America would be in Israel's debt and would support Israel more strongly with state-of-the-art military equipment and increased financial aid. However, things fell through, and now Israel put the United States in a very compromising position. What Israel did violated all agreed upon protocols. There would be ramifications as a result of this action, or in this case, the non-action.

Shortly after General Gollman's visit, he left the Embassy unannounced and hadn't been seen or heard from since; however, there were a number of visits from representatives of the Prime Minister's office. The Prime Minister knew that his military leaders had screwed up royally, and even though the Prime Minister knew exactly what had taken place, he denied any knowledge of the failed interrogation plan. He transferred all blame on the poor judgment and ineptness of his military hierarchy. In addition to the constant flow of representatives to the Embassy offering their "Mea Culpa," Israel's Prime Minister, on a secured line, spoke directly to the United States President, seeking his understanding and vindication for the "unauthorized" actions of his subordinates. The President listened and accepted the apologies of the Prime Minister, knowing for sure that any information regarding possible terrorism would not have been denied to the Prime Minister. The President also was certain that the interview and interrogation procedures that were conducted were done with the Minister's tacit approval.

It had only been a few hours since General Gollman, the Barbarian, had clandestinely left the American Embassy, when one of the marines assigned to the Embassy Security Detail knocked on Ambassador Richardson's door. The corporal interrupted one of the many meetings the Ambassador was having with representatives from the Israeli government: "Excuse me, Ambassador Richardson but can I speak with you in private?" Although this was out of the ordinary, the concerned look on the soldier's face told Richardson that he should excuse himself and meet with the marine.

"Please excuse the interruption, I will be right back." The Ambassador rose from his chair and exited through the door. "What is it corporal?" Without hesitation and very concerned with his message, the corporal answered: "We have recovered an unidentified body floating in the water behind the Embassy grounds. We have cordoned off the area until you can get to the scene. Only myself and two other marines are aware of the body." The Ambassador was shocked and concerned by what the ramifications could be, and he told the marine to stand by. He mentioned that he would accompany the soldier to the site as soon as he ended the meeting. He returned to the conference room and addressed the curious group: "I am very sorry, but something has come to my attention that has to be addressed immediately. I will ask my assistant to reschedule the meeting for a later date. I trust you will understand. The relationship between our two countries is of the utmost importance, but I cannot delay my response to a pressing event." The group nodded their understanding and rose as the Ambassador directly left the room. He addressed the corporal: "Okay corporal, lead on."

The Embassy grounds backed up to a small canal that was fed by the waters of the Mediterranean Sea. Ambassador Richardson and the corporal proceeded to the area at the rear of the property where the body was recovered. Because the area was surrounded by trees and bushes, it was somewhat secluded and hidden from any onlookers outside of the entrance gates. As the Ambassador approached, the marines who were guarding the site, opened ranks and allowed Richardson to get a close look at what had washed up on the Embassy shore line.

It was a horrific site, almost too disgusting to look at. The face was swollen but recognizable. The rest of the naked body was in a heavily deteriorated state which indicated to the Ambassador that what was left of a human being had been in the water for an extended period of time.

Ambassador Richardson had visited Jalecya prison on a number of occasions and had interacted with the commandant many times. One particular detail that Richardson remembered about seeing the Commandant was the noticeable scar in the form of an "X" that appeared above the Commandant's right eye. In fact, the Commandant had commented on it when he saw Richardson staring at it. Apparently, as a child playing on a rocky beach, he fell and landed face down on a large rock with jagged edges. Those jagged edges caused a lot of bleeding and pain and came close to affecting the sight in his right eye; but more significantly, they left their imprint on the Commandant's forehead for life. It was that same "X' that Ambassador Richardson saw on the floater lying before him. The missing Commandant, Major Berman Yithak, had been found.

Ambassador Richardson told the marines to transport the body to a secure location on the grounds while he went to notify the State Department of the development. The Ambassador would be guided by what they told him to do. The Secretary wanted to know all of the circumstances surrounding the find, and how the Ambassador identified the body. Richardson explained to the Secretary about the scar, and how it was still prominently displayed even though the rest of the body was severely deteriorated. The Secretary then told Ambassador Richardson that The State Department office would officially notify the Israeli government of the discovery. He also advised Richardson to photograph the body before he moved it.

Unfortunately, the Ambassador could no longer follow the direct order to "photograph- before-moving" since the body was already being moved. Only if he got to the marines quickly enough, could the body still be photographed as it laid on the shoreline. The Secretary also told the Ambassador to wait to hear from the Israeli authorities before he did anything. When they did contact him, Richardson was told to again contact the Secretary before he made any moves. Richardson understood and as soon as the Secretary disconnected, the Ambassador got on the line with the marine corporal in charge and told him that he wanted photographs before the body was moved. Fortunately, he reached them in time, and the corporal proceeded to photograph what looked like a scene from a monster movie.

Ambassador Richardson knew that everyone in the Israeli military hierarchy would be "saddened" by the loss of one of their outstanding loyal leaders. He also knew that the loss was, without a doubt, certainly caused by these same insincere mourners. As he thought about the circumstances surrounding the Major's demise, he wondered where General Abel Gollman might be. Would he also "accidentally" lose his life to some unforeseen circumstance, or would he be able to escape the unforgiving, murderous tentacles that reached out as a result of undesirable failure?

Richardson waited for contact from the Israeli government for two things: how they wanted to handle the transfer of Major Yithak's body, and the potential notification that General Gollman had been the victim of a tragic accident which sadly took his life. Within the hour, the Ambassador was contacted by Israeli authorities, and a contingent of six Israeli soldiers led by a lieutenant arrived at the front gate of the Embassy. They arrived in two military vans. One van carried the soldiers, and the other resembled a coroner's wagon that would be employed to carry the Major's body. Ambassador Richardson had the paperwork in hand that the Secretary had told him to create for the official transfer of the body. The Ambassador met the young lieutenant and directed him to the location where the body was being secured.

As the lieutenant approached the body, the Ambassador signaled to the marines guarding the body to remove the sheet that was covering the Major's face. The Israeli lieutenant looked at the face of the corpse, took a step back and saluted. He had served for a number of years under the Major and had no doubt that the body laid before him was the remains of Major Berman Yithak. The Lieutenant commented on the telltale "X" scar that marred the Major's forehead. The U.S. Marines took a step back and allowed the Israeli soldiers to lift the body onto a waiting gurney. They had to carefully take hold of the sheet on which the body had been placed so that no more damage was done to the remains.

Having secured the body on the gurney, the lieutenant gave the order to proceed to the van. He turned to the Ambassador and rendered a salute. Ambassador Richardson returned the salute and extended his hand for a more friendly handshake. The lieutenant seemed surprised but grasped the Ambassador's hand. He looked at the Ambassador and said: "America discovers failure and acts to correct that behavior. We discover failure and make certain that the individual will never fail again." He looked directly at Richardson, nodded and headed to the waiting vans. So ended the career of one Major Berman Yithak.

Chapter Thirty-Three

Temporary Headquarters

Ismul Rahej, the trusted senior security guard at the Shopping Center and full-blown Alliance member, had witnessed the incident where one of the custodians, after securing one of the explosive devices, had run from Detective Ossur. Ismul was aware of the fact that the custodian had reached the safe house and had surrendered the explosive device to the members there. He also knew that the device had been ultimately delivered back to the Facilities Director, Erman Falco.

Ismul was now on his way to the Facilities Director's office to pick up the explosive for re-location. He was the point person who originally set up the explosion locations. He would have no trouble in finding another suitable spot. The detectives in the jewelry store had thus far been a thorn in their side, so Falco recommended to Ismul that he find a location close to Best Jewelry so that if they had to trigger the device, it would take out the two detectives in addition to the planned destruction. They both chuckled at the thought of the detectives being blown apart.

Ismul had to be more careful now that additional detectives and uniformed personnel were assigned to the mall because of the alert and the additional information. In fact, now that the cell was down one custodian, Ismul might have to fill in. He would gladly do that and be an active participant in the grand plan for freedom. He was a diehard follower of Dunait and had the strongest allegiance to the success of the Alliance Cell.

As he left Falco's office, he began thinking of locations where the explosion would do the most harm and also eliminate the detectives. Although Erman Falco had suggested a location near or at the jewelry store, Ismul had an even better idea. Although his location would not injure or kill the jewelry store detectives, it might very well cause injuries and hopefully the demise of more than just two law enforcement officers.

He proceeded to the parking area adjacent to the mall that was reserved for first responder vehicles - police, fire, and emergency service. He was able to increase the capacity and explosive power of the device by adding additional elements to the already deadly device. When he got to the parking area, he was greeted by two uniformed officers who had just arrived for assignment. The officers, having been assigned to the mall on a number of occasions, knew Ismul and exchanged the usual "how's it going" platitudes.

Passing in front of Ismul, they proceeded to the Police Department's Temporary Headquarters Van. This is a van that is used to coordinate police activities at the scene of disasters, major community events and potential sites that would demand a large police presence. Since the NYPD had received what was thought to be reliable information regarding a potential terrorist threat, the Department deployed the Headquarters Vehicle in advance of any attack. All officers reporting for duty at the mall had to sign in at the van and were given their assignments, issued portable radios and received instructions and information about what might be occurring.

The sergeant at the desk in the van, also assigned meal breaks, partners, and equipment. The assigned posts included both inside and outside duties. Since the detectives had most of the inside covered, the majority of post assignments included adjacent streets to the mall and the outside parking areas.

Any bosses who arrived at the mall would first go to the Temporary Headquarters Van and sign in. They would then be brought up-to-date on what was going on. The Temporary Headquarters Van, a multi-million-dollar investment, was a miniature, mobile Police Headquarters. It had everything that was needed for any police action, and it communicated with all of the specialized units in the borough. It even came with a conference room, a bathroom and a room where the ranking officer in charge could catch a couple of "Z's," if needed. There was nothing left to chance; the boss had everything at his or her disposal.

Ismul watched for a while from a distance and saw many police officers as well as supervisors with a lot of gold on the brim of their hats, enter and exit the van. Falco wanted the jewelry store detectives eliminated, but imagine if Ismul could place a device at or so close to the van that a number of officers, including high ranking ones, could be put in jeopardy. He was sure that Falco would approve of his plan, so he waited patiently for the opportunity to put into effect. If he just kept standing around though, he would raise the suspicions of the officers assigned to the van area. So, he walked the entire block, and then went inside the mall and relocated to the space near the exit that led to the first responder parking area. Now, from his vantage point, he could observe the police movements at the van and not be so obvious. He just couldn't wait until Mr. Falco found out about his plan.

The weather had been overcast and within 30 minutes of Ismul assuming his surveillance post, a sudden downpour came, ushering the officers assigned to the outside van security, inside of the van to obtain their rain gear. As soon as they left, and after making sure there were no other officers in sight, Ismul ran to the rear of the van and scooted underneath, where he succeeded in attaching the enriched explosive device to the undercarriage of the Temporary Headquarters Vehicle. He came up and out from underneath just as the officers were stepping down from the van.

Ismul went across the street and on the other side of the van to make it look like he was assessing the parking condition in the outdoor parking lot. He had succeeded and had not raised anyone's suspicions. The deed was done. He left the outdoor parking lot and returned to the mall where he found a mall phone and dialed Erman Falco's office.

"Erman Falco speaking. Can I help You?"

"Hello Mr. Falco, it's Ismul. I just wanted you to know that I found the ideal location for the device." Falco interrupted: "Ismul, is there anyone in earshot of you?"

"No, Mr. Falco, I am alone in one of the employee corridors." Falco responded: "Okay, if you are sure. Tell where you located the device, and I hope it is close enough to the detectives that they won't be able to be recognized after the explosion." Ismul hesitated, but he was sure that Falco would be happy with the decision even though it was not what he originally wanted.

"Mr. Falco, when I left your office, I started thinking about where we could do the most damage, and I came up with a great idea. I walked to the area where the "first responder" parking is located, and I saw this big Police Department van with the words Temporary Headquarters painted on the side. I stayed out of sight and just observed for a while. There were a lot of officers and bosses going in and out of the van with a number of them remaining inside. The thought came to me that if I could attach the device to the van, the explosion would kill or injure a lot more than we anticipated. I also re-enforced the device so it is more powerful than before. When it started raining, I had my chance, and I got underneath the van and attached the explosive without any one being the wiser. When I finished, I came into the mall and called you."

Ismul was expecting congratulations, but all he got was dead silence. The pregnant pause was so long that Ismul said: "Hello, Mr. Falco. Are you still there?" Falco answered almost in a whispered but serious tone: "Is that where I told you to place the device?" Now louder: "Is It?"

Ismul, almost cowering and confused by the Director's response, voiced a humble "No." "That's right, Ismul. That is not what I told you to do." Ismul tried to respond: "But." "There are no 'buts.' You were supposed to place it in an area that would cause damage and take out the two detectives. That is not what you did. Instead, you risked the entire operation by putting the device on a police van that will probably be parked right behind the fake white police van that Dunait will be using to coordinate our attack. So, by blowing the Headquarters van, we could very well injure Dunait and damage the operations van. That's what you've done! Come back to the office so that we can figure something out. Do not go near the Headquarters Van. Can you follow that order?" Ismul whispered a "yes", and proceeded to the administrative offices, his tail between his legs and pondering what his fate might be. He knew it wouldn't be good, but they are down a man, so they can't afford to lose another - at least not right now!

Chapter Thirty-Four

The Reality

The operation start time was getting close, and as Ismul Rahej traveled through the mall on his way to Falco's office, he noticed some of his fellow cell members already assuming positions close to their assigned spots. He just observed without nodding or acknowledging anyone. The mall was extremely crowded, as was expected, and Rahej couldn't be more pleased. The threat of massive destruction and the loss of many lives would foster their cause. He was sure that their plan would be a success. However, now he had to face Erman Falco, who was not exactly pleased by what he had done. He would face the music, though, and suffer the consequences. He was too valuable an asset to be eliminated, and the lack of planned manpower helped him remain safe.

Dunait had been notified about the new location of the explosive device, and although he understood the thinking that more cops would be hurt or killed, he did not appreciate the close proximity to the van that he would occupy. Where the device was now located, most likely meant that it could not be used because of the potential collateral damage - Dunait himself.

As Ismul passed the jewelry store, both Marty and Tony saw him and motioned for him to come over to them. He slowly walked their way and as he arrived asked: "Hi, what can I do for you?" Tony answered: "We were just wondering who has access to the employee corridors, and if there are any locking devices on the doors." Without hesitation Ismul answered: "The main employee corridor doors are electronically locked and have card access. Only employees assigned to certain areas have access to those corridors. The smaller offshoot hallways are also electronically locked, and an employee must call the Facilities Director's office to be electronically buzzed in. The entrances are also under camera surveillance. Is there anything else I can help you with?" Ismul wanted to get out of there.

"No, Thanks." Ismul went on his way to Falco's office.

Both detectives were okay with the security of the employee entrances, and unless there was some inside help, the corridors would not be used in a potential attack. With all of the detectives and uniforms looking for those "suspicious" persons or "stand-outs," they still hadn't seen anything of significance. There was no sign of Alex or his companions, and the shopping center was blanketed with more uniforms, plainclothes officers and detectives than patrons at happy hour on St. Patrick's Day.

It was coming to the point that Ossur and Iniddor started to think that although the initial reports were that the source was a reliable one, something must have occurred that forced the potential attackers to call off whatever they were planning. Maybe, it was the enormous show of force by the NYPD, or maybe they miscalculated the amount of people in the mall or just maybe, it didn't feel right. Whatever it was, the consensus of opinion was that law enforcement had succeeded in thwarting a potential attack. That having been the case, however, no one let down their guard.

For lack of something better to do, Marty told Tony that he was going to call over to the Administration Building to see if they had seen or gotten any word from Alex Hassid. It was so crowded and noisy that Marty had to find a small corner of the corridor to call and be able to hear the person at the other end. The phone rang a number of times before Baxter answered: "Hello, Bob Baxter speaking." "Yeah Bob, it's Marty. Just wondering if you got anything on Alex yet?" Bob said that he had not seen or heard from Alex since the last time they spoke.

"Do you have any other information about what might be going on?" The detective said that he had nothing new, and that "no news was good news." Just as Detective Iniddor was about to hang up, he heard the other phone line ringing in the background, and Baxter told him to hold for a minute.

Iniddor heard Baxter answer the phone: "Hello, Bob Baxter speaking. Hello Alex, how are you doing? Good, what can I do for you? Sure, I understand. Why don't you come in, I'm sure we can find something for you to do. Okay see you in a little while." Baxter hung up with Alex and picked up the other line where Detective Iniddor had heard the whole conversation. Iniddor spoke: "I guess timing is everything. How long did Alex say he'd be before he got to your office?" Baxter answered: "He said he was going to catch a ride with some friends, and that he should be here in about forty-five minutes. He said that he was bored and wanted to keep himself busy, so he volunteered to help with whatever we needed." Marty emphasized to Baxter that he wanted to be notified as soon as Alex arrived. Bob Baxter agreed and the conversation concluded.

Marty headed back to the store and informed Tony that Alex was on his way back to the Administrative Building to presumably help with whatever. Marty wasn't sure that Alex's intentions were purely altruistic, but he could be wrong. He also wondered if he was going to show up with his two friends in tow, since at least one was wanted for the previous felonious assault in the mall.

Meeting with Alex would give Marty and Tony the opportunity to question Alex a little more about his strange attitude and disregard for information about Rachael's case. Alex, who originally had been quite direct with both detectives, and who looked them straight in the eyes wanting results immediately, now could not even make eye contact with them. Something was up, and Marty was determined to find out what it was.

The safe house phone rang, and Dunait was at the other end. He directed Alex to contact the Security Director and get himself inside of the Administrative Building. He told the other two cell members to accompany Alex there, but to stay out of sight as Alex attempted to gain entry into the building. They were to remain parked in the enclosed parking area until they received a signal from Alex that all was going according to plan. They would then take up their assigned positions inside of the mall and leave Alex to his assigned tasks. They confirmed to Dunait that they understood and told Alex that it was "time." Alex shuttered.

He was now going to become a part of an active terrorist attack. In fact, he was now a terrorist. It was a word that he thought would never apply directly to him, and he knew, no matter what happened, his life would never be the same.

Alex slowly rose out of his chair and reluctantly walked to the front entrance of the house - one cell member in front and one behind. There was still that air of mistrust that the other cell members harbored. There was absolutely no conversation on the way to the mall, and one could cut the intensity with a knife. When he got within about a mile from the mall, the cell member sitting next to Alex in the back seat, reached behind his back and came out with a fully loaded Glock 26, checked it and handed it over to Alex.

From previous meetings, Alex knew that he was going to be armed, but when it actually became a reality, he had all to do but to keep from dropping the weapon. The member then reached into another pocket in his pants and displayed an additional loaded magazine which he also handed to Alex with the words: "Make it count!" This alarmed Alex because according to everything he was told, weapons would only be used as a last resort. It was the threat of violence that would foster success, not the violence itself.

By the attitude and solemn composure of both his companions, Alex felt that there was no doubt in anyone's mind that the use of weapons was a certainty. He now had a fully loaded Glock and a stacked magazine. He was an armed terrorist and, in his mind, they expected him to use what he had, if necessary. Unfortunately, his thought was that it was going to be necessary. Would he be able to actually shoot someone? Could he kill another human being no matter what the cause? Could he play God and take a life? He hoped with all his heart that it didn't come to that.

Marty and Tony viewed the opportunity to speak and meet with Alex as a step in the right direction toward settling the uneasy feeling they both had about Alex's behavior. What they didn't realize was that Alex's appearance at the Administrative Building signaled the very beginning of the all-out assault on the Three Kings Shopping Center!

Chapter Thirty-Five

The Corpse

Ismul arrived at the administrative offices and was going directly to Erman Falco's office. When he passed Baxter's office, Bob was surprised to see him and called him in.

"How come you're back in the office? You should be overseeing the guard assignments inside the mall. I didn't call you in." Ismul answered: "The Facilities Director wanted to speak with me and asked me to come to his office. So, here I am." Baxter was a little perturbed over this since the Senior Security Guard reported directly to him. If Falco wanted to see Ismul, he should have told Baxter to reach out to him, and he should have told Baxter the reason why he wanted to see the guard. Again, there was no love lost between Baxter and Falco. They both were vying for the second-in-command position and the acknowledgement of operations control from General Manager Winsten.

Baxter let Ismul go, and told him to report back to him as soon as he finished with Falco. Ismul nodded and proceeded to the Facilities Director's office. Each of the management offices were large with state-of-the-art communications, public address capabilities and surveillance monitors. Through the miracle of technology and with the flip of a toggle switch, any and all cameras could be monitored wirelessly by police department personnel. An "information technology" agreement had been signed by both the management of the mall and the Commanding Officer of the Police Department's Information Technology Section that camera surveillance could be transmitted and monitored by NYPD personnel. The "toggle switch" arrangement allowed access to only those cameras that mall management wanted to permit at the time. So, although the police had monitoring capabilities, it was limited to the discretion of the shopping center management.

In addition to the high-tech equipment, the offices also housed large executive desks, ergonomic framed chairs and a large massage recliner that could be used as a single bed when necessary. When working long hours and mandated extended days that sometimes went into late evenings and possible overnight stays, it was not uncommon that a manager unwound and tried to get some shut-eye laying on his personal converted recliner.

Ismul knocked on Erman Falco's slightly ajar door and waited for the Director to tell him to come in. Following just a brief delay, Falco told Ismul Rahej to enter and to close the door behind him. Instead of sitting behind his desk, Ismul found him relaxing in the recliner. Falco's back was to Ismul and the door, and it seemed that Mr. Falco was studying the floorplan of the mall that was mounted on the wall in front of him. Ismul did not interrupt but waited for the Director to speak. Falco spun around in the recliner and stood up in front of the guard, and in a whispered but chastising tone said: "Do you realize what you have done? Dunait is not pleased with you, and he told me to do whatever I see fit. If things were different, I would not let you forget your mistake, but I have no choice. I still need your services, and it is much too close to our start time. Alex Hassid is coming to the office, and I want you to watch him closely."

Ismul breathed a sigh of relief. The operation took precedence, and he may have escaped the wrath of both Falco and Dunait, or at least delayed it. He listened carefully to what Mr. Falco was saying and told him that he would follow his orders to the letter. Ismul left Erman Falco's office and proceeded to Bob Baxter, as he had been told. He knocked on the side of the opened door and entered. He closed the door behind him. Baxter was glad to see that Ismul was keeping things confidential and secretive from Erman Falco.

Shortly after Ismul entered Bob Baxter's office, Alex Hassid arrived with his two companions at the parking area for the Administration Building. Alex looked at the two cell members one last time and tentatively exited the car. He walked with "cement" shoes to the entrance door and pressed for admittance. The electronic lock released, and Alex went inside.

It was close to 7:00pm, and the secretary and the clerical staff were already gone enjoying the Christmas Eve festivities. Alex quickly went to the window next to the secretary's desk and gave the "thumbs' up" signal to the two members who were still in the car. Alex saw the return signal and watched as they pulled away to take up their assigned positions. Things were moving along - maybe moving along much too quickly for Alex. He felt like it was an increasingly large snowball rolling down a steep incline and out of control. What would happen when that snowball collided with an immovable object and burst for everyone to see?

Alex had a hard time controlling his anxiety, and he was on edge with every move he took.

After a few unnerving moments at the window, Alex went to Bob Baxter's office to see what Bob had in store for him. He was curious as to what Baxter wanted to have him do. The Security Director's door was closed, so Alex gently knocked. There was no answer so he knocked again, but this time a little harder. Alex heard: "Come in." Alex stepped inside and closed the door, but was surprised to see Ismul Rahej behind the desk. Alex looked further and saw that Bob Baxter was lying on the recliner facing the wall. Alex looked at Ismul who gave him a finger to the lips indicating the "quiet" sign. Apparently, Bob Baxter, who had been working all kinds of late hours, was taking the opportunity to get some rest and catch up on some sleep. Alex acknowledged Ismul's sign and tiptoed over to the desk. Alex told Ismul about the conversation he had with Baxter, and that Baxter had told him to come in. Ismul nodded that he knew and asked Alex to sit down.

Before he got in any deeper and to the point of no return, it seemed like the perfect time for Alex to speak with Erman Falco and tell him about what happened to his son, Vin. He was hoping to see if Mr. Falco could be swayed to stop the madness and help Alex. Alex indicated to Ismul that he wanted to go to Mr. Falco's office and speak with the Facilities Director. Ismul shook his head and said in a whisper that the Director was very busy, and that Alex should wait 'till later. Alex could not wait 'till later, so without hesitation, he quickly rose from his chair and exited the office before Ismul could do anything to stop him.

He knocked heavily on Mr. Falco's door and, assuming that Ismul would be coming to stop him, entered without the customary "come in." Erman Falco was surprised and displeased that someone would just barge in and interrupt him. Alex heard Ismul's footsteps behind him and hurriedly blurted out: "Mr. Falco, I have to speak with you. It's urgent." Because of the urgency reflected on Alex's face, Erman Falco waved Ismul off and told him to return to Baxter's office. Alex went to the door and closed it. He turned to Mr. Falco and in a sympathetic tone said: "Mr. Falco, I have to tell you about Vin." Falco answered: "What about my son?" Alex responded: "We were all told that Vin's death was an accident, and that he was killed when a bullet missed its target and accidently hit him. No, Mr. Falco, that's not the case. Vin, your son, was the target."

Falco looked at Alex with alarm and disbelief. "What are you saying, Alex, that Dunait had my son killed? I can't believe that. Where did you get that information from? That's a very strong allegation to make, and there are consequences to lying." Alex did not back down: "I was told in confidence by the two cell members who were with me at the safe house. They knew. They had been privy to the plan to eliminate Vin. I am sorry to be the one to tell you, but I thought you should know the truth."

Still showing an air of disbelief, Erman responded: "Let me get this straight. You are telling me that my friend and compatriot for all these years ordered the death of my only son. If I find out that you have lied to me, I will make certain that you meet Allah before your scheduled time. However, if it is true, there are certain things that I have to do." Alex continued: "I have no reason to lie to you. Vin was a friend of mine. He shouldn't have lost his life that way." Alex took a brief pause and continued: "Mr. Falco I have concerns associating with and working for a group that would kill their own. As you are probably aware, I don't really want to be a part of an operation where innocent people may be killed, and our own cell members lost. I am asking for your help. Please stop this insanity, and for my family's sake, get me out of this madness."

Falco listened carefully, but until he could verify the truthfulness of Alex's statements, he was going to continue as the loyal follower he had always been. He looked directly at Alex and said: "I will find out the truth, but for now go into Baxter's office and relieve Ismul. Tell him I said to take his post in the mall."

Alex was confused and looked at the Director in a questioning manner. However, he just followed Falco's order and left. Why was he going to Bob Baxter's office to "relieve" Ismul when Baxter was there. He was sure that Bob Baxter didn't want Alex hanging out in his office while he was working; and if he was already awake, why would he want Ismul to stay in his office? Maybe Baxter could explain.

He, once again, knocked on Baxter's door, and this time Ismul opened it himself. Alex told Ismul what Falco had said, and without hesitation, Ismul took his belongings and exited the office, closing the door behind him. Alex was left alone with Bob Baxter who was still in the same reclined position as before. Alex remained quiet and really didn't know what he was supposed to be doing. Baxter was the one who was supposed to tell him where they needed help. However, with Baxter fast asleep, Alex was at a loss.

About five minutes into Alex's stay, Bob Baxter's office phone began ringing. In an effort to stop the noise and not wake Baxter, Alex ran to the phone and answered: "Hello, Bob Baxter's Office." Marty was on the other end wondering who was answering the phone. He was calling Baxter to see if Alex had arrived.

"This is Detective Iniddor, I'd like to know if Alex Hassid has arrived yet. Can I speak with Mr. Baxter, please?" Alex, thinking outside the box, responded: "Mr. Baxter just left the office on his way to see you. He should be there any minute." This was not the response that Marty was expecting. He wanted to speak with Alex. Why was Baxter coming to the store? Marty should be going to the office. Marty responded: "thank you," and ended the phone call. He was anxiously awaiting Baxter's arrival.

The ringing phone had apparently not awakened Baxter from his sound slumber. Alex was surprised that Baxter didn't even budge. His curiosity getting the better of him, he went over to the recliner to take a closer look. Baxter's eyes were bulging, his mouth wide open, and there was a petrified look on his face. Lying on his lap was a garrote, a metal collar that is used for strangulation.

Alex could not control the bile that rose in his stomach, reached his throat and rocketed from his mouth. He threw up everything that had been in his stomach and more. Alex could not go on. He ran to the door and grabbed the handle. It didn't turn. The door wasn't opening. It had been locked from the outside. Alex was imprisoned, but with one other who wouldn't care if the door was ever opened. Alex Hassid collapsed in fear!

Chapter Thirty-Six

The Body Count

The New York City Police Department Temporary Headquarters vehicle is a hub of constant activity with new officers coming in to get their assignment, and others leaving after being relieved. Additionally, Department bosses are stopping by to sign in that they were at the scene and monitoring the activities. One of the bosses who signed in and who remained on scene is the Chief of the Borough of Brooklyn and his special operations assistant, the captain who commands the Brooklyn Task force. After reviewing post assignments, personnel assets and the potential overall response plan, the chief, with the captain at his side, decided to do a walk-through and ultimately wind up at the Administrative Building to confer with the general manager of the shopping center. Being somewhat pompous and proud, the chief proceeded in full uniform to personally conduct an on-site review.

As the chief and the captain began their walking inspection, Marty was still awaiting Baxter's arrival. It had been close to twenty-five minutes, and there was no sign of the Security Director. Unfortunately, the unofficial code for a "boss-on-the-scene" came over the radio, so Marty really couldn't leave the area. He was annoyed that Baxter didn't show up, and even further annoyed that a high-ranking boss had decided to show up now.

It wasn't long before both Marty and Tony saw the familiar figure of the Borough Chief slowly making his way through the crowd. As the chief arrived at the jewelry store, both Tony and Marty respectively rendered a slight salute. The chief acknowledged, and then asked how things were in general. Marty, who knew both the chief and the captain, mentioned that everything seemed to be under control, and that he and Tony were following up on some possible leads. The chief was glad to see that they were productively dividing their time between the police responsibilities and the store responsibilities. It was the chief who had approved their original request for moonlighting, so he was well aware of what they were doing. Following the brief conversation, the chief and the captain continued through the mall enroute to the Administration Building. Their presence short circuited Marty's plan to go and find Baxter to see what was happening. The detectives definitely needed to talk to Alex.

As the bosses disappeared into the crowd, Tony's cell phone started ringing. They both thought that it was Baxter offering an excuse as to why he was so delayed. When Tony looked at the screen with Marty peering over his shoulder, the name Ralph Clemengas appeared. Ralph and the other remaining Brooklyn South Squad members who had been assigned to different shopping areas when the initial alert came, were now being re-assigned to the Three Kings Shopping Mall. This was a result of the additional information that the Department received.

Ralph, Ira, Frank and Angel were on their way to the Shopping Center. They were familiar with the area, and it was intelligent thinking to assume that they, more than others, would recognize something out of the ordinary. Since it was determined that the shopping center would be the likely target, why waste their expertise elsewhere? Marty and Tony welcomed the rest of the squad, and they notified the rest of the guys who were already assigned to the mall. They all felt better being able to work with a team that they already knew. Knowing the little idiosyncrasies of your teammates made life a lot easier.

Prior to the chief and the captain arriving at the Administration Building and after Erman Falco made a few phone calls, he left his office and went to Baxter's door to release the lock that he placed there. Alex heard the lock release and jumped up to try the handle. He opened the door, and Erman Falco was standing in front of him. He told Alex that, at the moment, nothing had changed, and he was waiting for certain confirmation. In the interim, Alex was to take his position in the General Manager's Office and guard Reginald Winsten at gunpoint. Knowing the ramifications of disobeying, Alex reached for the Glock to make sure it was still there and proceeded to the General Manager's office.

Mr. Winsten's door had been closed for quite a while; so, not wanting to give any type of warning, Alex knocked. Mr. Winsten answered quickly: "Who is it?" Alex said: "It's me, Mr. Winsten, Alex." Winsten responded: "Alex, I am quite busy right now. Can you come back later or see Mr. Baxter?" Bob Baxter's name sent a chill through Alex's whole body, but Alex, once again thinking outside the box, said that Detective Ossur gave him a message that the detective only wanted Winsten to hear.

Although the General Manager thought it odd, he got up from his desk and went to the door. He unlocked it and ushered Alex in: "Okay, Alex, what is this important message?" Alex reached behind his back and displayed the Glock, pointing it directly at the shocked manager.

"Alex, what is this?" Alex responded the best way he could: "Mr. Winsten, do as I say and you won't get hurt." He repeated himself and added: "I have no choice. Do not make me do something that I will regret." His serious tone and determination told Winsten that Alex might be capable of pulling the trigger, so the manager followed Alex's orders. He was not going to take any chances.

Alex directed Winsten to the chair behind the desk, and told Winsten to duct tape his left hand to the arm of the chair. That being done, Alex duct taped Winsten's right hand in the same manner. As he was told, Alex kept the Glock pointed at Winsten and left the door ajar. He told Winsten to keep quiet and warned him again not to do anything foolish. If Winsten did attempt something, could Alex actually pull the trigger? Just the thought of it nauseated Alex, but he maintained that determined terrorist look. In his mind was also the thought that he had to continue to deal with Erman Falco. Because of his lack of action, he didn't want Falco to feel that he had to resort to persuasively extreme measures to get Alex's cooperation.

It took a while before the chief and the captain arrived at the entrance to the Administration Building. The Facilities Director saw them approaching and knew that their arrival would only add to the tension that already existed in the building. Falco waited for the officers to press the buzzer, and then delayed granting their entrance. Falco was deciding on what he might have to do. The buzzer sounded again, and Falco released the electronic lock. The chief, who had been to the General Manager's office a number of times, walked right past the closed doors of both Bob Baxter's office and the Facilities Director's office. He went directly to Reginald Winsten's Executive Office. After all, he was the chief, and he was not going to speak to anyone but the man in charge, the General Manager.

The captain, walking alongside the chief, was the first to look into Winsten's office. He saw Alex Hassid with a gun in his hand pointing it at the General Manager. Instinct and training took over, and the captain reached for his sidearm. Two shots rang out, and everything seemed to go into slow motion. The task force captain fell to the floor with blood rushing out of his head and neck. Alex never moved from his frozen position, and the chief, having been removed from patrol activities for quite a while, was slow in reacting, which probably saved his life.

Erman Falco, who had quietly opened his office door as the officers passed, stood in the hallway with his gun pointed at the chief. He ordered the chief to carefully remove his weapon, place it on the floor and to face front. As the chief turned to the front, Falco came up behind him and used the butt of his gun to knock the chief unconscious. Both Reginald Winsten and Alex Hassid were in shock. To Winsten, who couldn't believe his trusted employee, Erman

Falco, was involved in such criminal behavior, it indicated that these apparent criminals were not above killing people, and to Alex it said: "One way or the other, I will not live past the night."

Falco tied up the unconscious chief and dragged him into Baxter's office where he stored the captain's body. As he arranged the bodies, living and dead, he wondered how high the body count would go. After locking Baxter's door, Falco quickly went to Alex. Knowing how fragile Alex's commitment was, he was shocked to find Alex still on guard and attentive to his assignment. Falco took Alex out of Winsten's office and out of earshot of the General Manager and asked how the young man was doing. Alex, reacting totally out of fear at this point, gave no reason for Erman Falco to suspect that his loyalty to the cause was in any way weakened. Falco knew better, but did not press the issue. Everything was still a go and the plan had not, thus far, been compromised.

It was obvious that in carrying out an operation of this magnitude, that there would be some snafu's and that was to be expected. As long as the stumbles were little ones, the plan would succeed. Falco told Alex that he was just waiting for the "go" from Dunait to put the plan into full forward gear. He said that it would probably come at any time. Falco went back to his office to await the signal.

Reginald Winsten saw the opportunity to speak with Alex. He started to speak but Alex boldly told him to "shut up." Reggie persisted: "You have not killed or injured anyone. Alex, you have your family to think about. You still have time to save yourself." Once again Alex repeated: "I told you to shut up. Now keep quiet." Winsten believed that it was a mixture of bravado and fear that influenced Alex's remarks. He tried again: "Look how much your family has been through. You have lost a father; a brother, and your sister has been injured. Do you want to just let the rest of the family fend for themselves while you're planted underground or languish in some decrepit jail cell. Stop now and help the cops. I'm sure there is a possibility that your cooperation will lessen any punishment that the courts might impose. Don't throw everything away."

This time Alex said nothing but thought about his family and the father and brother he would never see again. His only hope was for Erman Falco to get positive confirmation about how his son died. However, even with that, there was no guarantee that Falco would deviate from the plan that he had been working on for months. His son meant everything to him, but he had worked very long and hard to free his people. Vin Falco, however, would never again enjoy that freedom.

Chapter Thirty-Seven

The Public Address

Marty and Tony were patiently awaiting the return of the chief and also a response from Bob Baxter. It had been quite a while since they had heard anything. In discussing the situation with his partner, Marty noticed that Tony looked very tired and fatigued. He asked: "'Hey Tony, are you okay? You look like shit."

"I'm OK. It's just that I haven't been sleeping well at all. I have a lot on my mind and sleeping in a strange bed is not conducive to a good night's sleep." Marty was confused: "What do you mean that you're sleeping on the couch?"

Tony responded: "I haven't been back to Myrna's since the night of the party. I've been sleeping in some fleabag hotel downtown."

"Why didn't you tell me? You could have stayed with me." Tony just shook his head and said that he needed to be alone, and that he had a lot to sort out. Marty could understand that. In addition to working so many extended tours, fulfilling his moonlighting obligations, and being on alert for the impending potential terrorist attack, Tony had to turn himself in for the sexual assault charge right after the Christmas Holiday. It was a lot to carry, and he didn't carry it well. He looked terrible.

Just as they were finishing with their conversation, a coffee-toting Donna arrived on the scene. Once again, it was good to get that caffeine jolt, but for Tony, she was probably the last person he wanted to see. However, they both took the coffee, and once again, thanked her for her concern and generosity. She commented on how the crowd had somewhat decreased in number and mentioned that the weather had probably something to do with it. As the detectives looked out at the crowd, they estimated approximately 200 people still left in their area - the west wing. It had dwindled from approximately 400 earlier in the afternoon. The detectives welcomed the decrease in number, it made overall surveillance a lot easier.

At the same time, in the Administration Building, Erman Falco brought typewritten notes into Winsten's office. He told the General Manager that when he turned on the Public Address System, he was to read verbatim what was on the sheet of paper. Winsten's initial response was a firm: "Absolutely not. I am not going to help you take over my shopping center." That response did not go over well with Falco, and to show his displeasure and obtain the General Manager's cooperation, Falco viciously slapped Reginald Winsten across the face causing blood to seep from Winsten's mouth. Falco directed him again: "When I tell you, you will read what's on the paper!" The answer again was "No." Falco turned to Alex, who still had the gun trained on the General Manager, and said: "Shoot him!"

Alex just looked at Falco in disbelief. In a frustrated tirade, Falco took Alex's gun hand and pointed it at Winsten's leg and said: "Shoot." Still Alex couldn't muster enough courage to pull the trigger. Falco then put his hand around Alex's gun hand and forced Alex's trigger finger inside the trigger guard, applied finger pressure and the round discharged. Alex, with the unsolicited help from Erman Falco, had shot Reginald Winsten. Winsten was bleeding from his right leg and yelling out in pain. Falco approached Reggie again: "When I tell you, read from the paper." Winsten said nothing. Falco put the paperwork on the desk in front of Winsten and left the room. He was waiting for the final call from Dunait to start the ball rolling.

Winsten began pleading with Alex: "Alex, don't do this. You're not like them. They are killers. They don't care who gets hurt or killed. They are going to take you down with them. Nothing good can come from this. Stop them while you still can." Alex heard Winsten's plea but was still in shock from what he had just done. He saw the blood oozing through Winsten's pant leg and was nauseous. He couldn't stand the sight of the blood, but more so, he couldn't believe that he, with a little help, pulled the trigger.

Falco had left the room for two reasons: he wanted privacy when Dunait called, and secondly, he wanted to test Alex's commitment, knowing that Winsten would try to convince Alex to defect. Falco listened carefully to the conversation coming from Winsten's office. He heard Winsten's pleas but heard nothing in response from Alex. This was good and bad. It was good that Alex did not give in to bidding from Winsten, but bad in the fact that Falco did not hear a firm "No" to Winsten's badgering.

Falco was considering his next move when his cell phone rang and interrupted his thoughts. The ring was loud enough that Alex heard it from the next room. All Alex could think of was Dunait telling Erman Falco to begin. The operation would then forge ahead in all earnest. There would be no "getting out" now for Alex. The phone call seemed to last longer than it should have, and the tone that Alex heard from Falco was not one of total subservience and obedience but one of disbelief and sadness.

Alex heard Falco question the caller a number of times saying: "Are you sure? Are you Sure?" Erman Falco did not want to believe the remarks he heard at the other end. Then, there was silence. Alex thought he heard sobbing, but quickly dismissed such an absurd thought. He waited patiently for Falco to come into Winsten's office. When Falco came back into the office, his mood had changed. He still seemed determined to carry out his responsibilities, but the gusto seemed to have faded. He looked at Alex and said: "I am still waiting for the 'go-ahead.' When I get it, you have to convince your friend, looking at Winsten, that his cooperation is absolutely necessary."

He then pulled Alex aside and told him that if Reginald Winsten did not cooperate, they would have to go to plan "B", and plan "B" wasn't good for Winsten. Then Falco, looking quite pensive, put his hand on Alex's shoulder, and said that even if Dunait's plan was a total success, Dunait might not be able to revel in his achievement.

Alex didn't know what that meant, but he knew what Falco was saying about plan "B." If Alex couldn't convince the General Manager to cooperate, Winsten would be killed.

Alex had his work cut out for him. He went back into the office and found some clean rags with which he proceeded to tightly wrap around Winsten's leg to stop the bleeding. Just touching the area where the bullet had entered caused Winsten to grimace in pain. It seemed, however, that the round had passed right through the fleshy part of the leg without breaking any bones.

Having laid the Glock that he had been holding in his hand for what seemed like forever, on the desk, Alex began to explain to Reginald Winsten that there were no options left. When Falco received the signal from Dunait, Winsten would either cooperate or be killed. Alex emphasized to Winsten that he was sure that Falco would not hesitate to kill him. Alex was very convincing, even to the point of tearing up. Looking and listening to Alex, reality finally settled in with Reginald, and so, he reluctantly told Alex that when the time came, he would cooperate with his one-time trusted employee.

Alex was relieved and hoped that Mr. Winsten was being sincere with him - that when the time came, he would not change his mind. Alex had seen too much killing already and could not stand by and watch another person lose his life.

The waiting seemed forever but after approximately twenty minutes, Erman Falco's cell phone rang again. It was a quick conversation, something that Alex expected. Erman walked into Winsten's office, turned on the switch for the Public Address System and motioned for General Manager, Reginald Winsten, to speak. Winsten looked down at the typewritten paper and stared. However, he cleared his throat and started speaking when he felt the unmistakable pressure of a Glock semi-automatic handgun pressing up against his temple.

Chapter Thirty-Eight

The Negotiator

While keeping a sharp eye out for problems, Tony and Marty continued their conversation with Donna Uhrich. She now questioned them regarding the disposition of her case, and who was handling it, since Laura had passed and Paul was incapacitated. Ossur and Iniddor had accepted her coffee twice now, so they had to entertain some of her queries: "Have either of you heard anything about my investigation? I'm just wondering who is taking over since both Laura and Paul are out of the picture." Marty took the lead: "We really haven't heard anything new. We're not even sure who has taken the lead. The Sex Crimes Unit is very territorial when it comes to sharing information. They do it only on a need-to-know basis. We'll try to get some information for you." Donna started her reply but was interrupted by the attention-getting sound of the mall public address system, which is rarely used. Following the sound, a familiar voice to both Tony and Marty started speaking: "May I have your attention please? This is Reginald Winsten, General Manager of the Three Kings Shopping Center."

As if someone cast a spell over the shoppers, everyone seemed to stop moving just to listen to the voice coming over the public address system - something that most of them never experienced before. It had to be something very important for the General Manager to take the time to address the shoppers. Maybe, it's a Christmas Eve special sale, or maybe, it's a giveaway to a lucky shopper, or maybe, the hours of operation are being extended so that everyone can meet their shopping goals or just maybe, the General Manager decided to wish everyone a happy holiday season. Whatever it was, the use of the public address system is something that rarely occurs.

Just like all of the other people in the mall, Tony, Marty and Donna froze to listen. Winsten continued: "The west wing of the shopping mall is now under the control of the Alliance Cell, a group who are determined to fight against what they perceive as Israeli Tyranny." Winsten had drifted off script a bit by giving his opinion, and it earned him a sharp crack to the back of his head. Falco cut the public address system switch and warned Winsten: "Read only what's on the paper, if you value your life." Winsten gave a slight nod and continued: "The Alliance is making certain demands of Israel and while the United States, Israel and the Alliance negotiate, we on the west wing of the mall are being held hostage. If we all remain calm, and no one does anything foolish, we should be able to survive this without incident. I am asking for your total cooperation.

Please do not jeopardize the safety of others by acting foolish. The doors into the west wing have been electronically locked. Do not attempt to run to the exits. I have been told that members of the cell are in the west wing, and that they are armed with automatic weapons. They will not hesitate to use them if they have to. Once again, I am asking everyone to remain calm and follow directions so that we all can remain safe."

As was to be expected, shock, fear and disbelief circulated among the very vocal crowd of shoppers; however, this was quickly brought under control when certain cell members fired their automatic assault rifles in the air. At that point, you could hear a pin drop.

Winsten continued: "The Alliance is aware that there are law enforcement officers present in the west wing. You are to take your weapons to the fountain area in the middle of the walkway and drop them in the water. We know that there are four detectives and two police officers. Drop the weapons off now!"

The last thing that a police officer wants to do is to give up his weapon, so no one moved to the fountain area. Falco and Dunait knew that this would be the reaction of the law enforcement officers present, so they were prepared to deal with it. The shoppers had gravitated to each other and were now all huddled in the middle of the walkway. One of the cell members grabbed an elderly female out of the group and put a gun to her head.

Cameras showed exactly what was taking place, not only to those in the administrative offices but to the police supervisors in the Temporary Headquarters vehicle. So, Winsten pleaded: "If you don't get rid of your weapons, this woman will be killed." Speaking directly to the detectives, he continued: "You have automatic machine guns pointed at you, and they won't hesitate shooting you and killing the woman. Please, get rid of your guns."

Detectives Tony Ossur, Marty Iniddor, Juan Medina and Ralph Clemengas (Juan and Ralph had just been visiting Tony and Marty) and the two uniformed officers had no choice but to follow the directions of Winsten. They reluctantly deposited their weapons into the fountain. Winsten continued: "All of the stores on the west wing are to close their doors, and the proprietors are to join the shoppers in the middle of the walkway. Do it now!" Having witnessed the determination of the cell, the store owners did not hesitate in locking their stores and joining the group.

"Everyone stays in the middle of the walkway. The Alliance says that if anyone tries to escape, that person will be shot. If there is an attempt by the police to enter the west wing, the automatic weapons will be trained on the group, and the cell members will open fire. The demands of the Alliance will be shortly transmitted to the authorities. There will be no negotiations." The public address system went silent. The crowded shoppers didn't move but looked to the detectives for help.

With the cell members so close, it was difficult for Marty and Tony to discuss anything. Although Juan and Ralph were also there, they labored under the same restrictions. It was going to be nearly impossible to coordinate any kind of plan. For now, they would have to wait like everyone else.

Erman Falco had turned on the camera transmission switch so that the police bosses in the Temporary Headquarters Van could both see and hear what had transpired in the west wing of the mall. The severity and seriousness of what was occurring definitely set the responsibilities for solution to the police hierarchy, not necessarily present in the Headquarters Van. The major offices in the Department had to be notified up to and including the Office of the Police Commissioner. The situation at the shopping center was categorized as a "hostage situation," and therefore, the Police Department Hostage Negotiation Unit had to also be notified.

Sergeant Del, in addition to being the Squad Commander of the Brooklyn South Detective Squad, was also a qualified Department Hostage Negotiator. He was closest to the scene, so he responded and became the lead negotiator. He not only wanted to ensure the safety of the shoppers in the mall, but it was his team who were also involved. There were four of his detectives who were now at the mercy of a terrorist group known as the Alliance Cell.

When a negotiator arrived on the scene, it was the common practice to allow the negotiator to take control of the situation no matter what higher rank was present. Therefore, the Brooklyn South Detective Squad Commander was now the lead negotiator and in control.

As Sergeant Del prepared to contact the terrorist leader, notifications had to be made to other law enforcement agencies. This was an armed terrorist attack; so, the Federal Bureau of Investigation, the Central Intelligence Agency and the Alcohol, Tobacco and Firearms Departments had to be notified. Additionally, since the United States and Israel were both mentioned, the United States State Department had to be contacted. After conferring with the President, the State Department would be the agency which would issue any final dictates or agree to any negotiation.

Since there were so many agencies involved, the event comes under the auspices of the Incident Command Protocol. At present, the Incident Commander would come from the ranks of the New York City Police Department. This would be the highest-ranking NYPD officer on the scene. However, as mentioned, this boss would follow the parameters set by the lead negotiator. It was the negotiator who would dictate moves and strategies in an effort to talk the terrorists into a peaceful resolution.

Hostage negotiators are a special breed of cop. They go through many hours of vigorous training and have to possess a personality that lends itself to patience and tenacity. As one could imagine, negotiating with a hostage taker is a tremendously stressful task, and in this incident, the negotiator, in addition to trying to save approximately 200 innocent shoppers, had to deal with the fact that his detective team was also trapped – just a little added stress.

The voice at the other end of the public address system had said that there would be no negotiations; however, at this point, the authorities didn't even know the terrorists' demands. It was necessary, therefore, that contact be initiated. Sergeant Mario Dello dialed the number of the administrative offices.

Chapter Thirty-Nine

The President's Call

As things percolated in the Temporary Headquarters Van, other things behind the scenes went into motion. Even though there had not been any specific demands forwarded by the Alliance group, the President of the United States had already contacted the Prime Minister of Israel to give him a heads-up on a potentially catastrophic event. After inquiring as to the Prime Minister's knowledge of any particular protests or uprisings and having been informed that the Minister was unaware of anything brewing, the President disconnected with the promise to inform the Prime Minister on any developing information.

The President immediately contacted the Secretary of State and emphasized that he focus all attention on the developing incident at the Three Kings Shopping Center. The President needed more information on the Alliance group and what their demands might be. It was suggested that the Secretary contact the Director of the Central Intelligence Agency and the Ambassador in Israel to get some background on the terrorist cell.

With focused attention, the Secretary reached out for Ambassador Donald Richardson at the American Embassy in Jerusalem and Director Kenneth Blake of the Central Intelligence Agency. In turn, both the Ambassador and the Director extended their tentacled reach to the resources they both had. The Secretary had emphasized the urgency of the matter and demanded the collected information be in a ready-organized format to forward to the President for his next communication with the Israeli Prime Minister.

Ambassador Richardson conferred with his confidants and learned that the Alliance Cell was one of many such groups. He also learned that some of the self-appointed leaders of the group were vegetating in an Israeli prison, known as Jalecya. As he was told, there was a separate wing of the prison that housed political prisoners -

those individuals who led rebellion against the rule of the Israeli government. It was the members of this Alliance Cell that had caused damage to Israeli government facilities, and who had been responsible for the injuries and deaths of many Israeli soldiers.

The Israeli military leaders assigned to command the Jalecya facility were reputed to be heartless and cruel, and who could break the strongest rebel in the group. Richardson was aware of the commandants at the prison, and had met both of them – one now dead and the other fleeing for his life. The Ambassador connected the dots and put two and two together. The information that General Gollman had relayed to him was now part of an actual attack on a shopping center in Brooklyn, New York.

Central Intelligence Director Ken Blake reached out to his intelligence agents in the field who were homespun America-trained young men and women. The agents also included local Israeli operators who were close to the heartbeat of the community in which they resided. It was from these locals that Director Blake learned about Amir and Chail Hassid. He learned that Colonel Yithak had failed in obtaining certain information that the Israeli government wanted and had indirectly caused the death of Amir Hassid. He also found out that Yithak had been removed and replaced by one General Abel Gollman, known as the Barbarian. Gollman had arranged a clandestine operation and assigned Israeli agents to travel to the United States. However, the operation failed and as a result of this failure, General Gollman, fearing for his life, went to the United States Embassy and relayed information regarding a possible terrorist attack

Both Ambassador Richardson and Director Blake reacted in a laudable fashion and relayed whatever information they had obtained. They had completed their task in one hour's time. This was good for them, but even better for Secretary Walden who would now contact the President with the information. Walden knew that the President would not be happy with the fact that the United States, hearing it either through the Embassy or directly to the President, was not notified in a timely manner, especially when the information involved a potential terrorist strike threatening American lives. This sort of blunder could permanently hinder future relations between the two countries. And the harsh reality is the fact that the information would have even been further delayed or not received at all if the fearful General had not fled to the United States Embassy to save his life.

Secretary of State Daniel Walden placed a confidential call directly to the number the President had given him: "Hello, Mr. President, It's Dan Walden." "Okay Dan, what do you have for me?" Secretary Walden relayed all of the information gleaned from the reports forwarded by

Ambassador Richardson and Director Blake. To say the least, the President was livid when he learned that there was an intentional delay in forwarding the intelligence to the Embassy or directly to him. He had to calm down before he called the Israeli Prime Minister, because if he didn't, his remarks might serve to sever diplomatic relations, at least temporarily. If the result of the delay caused the deaths of American citizens, Israel would have the blood of those innocent people on its hands - hands that the President of the United States would be reluctant to ever shake again.

The President thanked Secretary Walden for his quick response and told his aid to get the Prime Minister of Israel on the line. It took more time than the President liked, but the Prime Minister was now on the phone.

"Hello, Mr. President. Were you able to get any specific details?" Although President Howard tried to control his tone and be as diplomatic as possible, the anger and the frustration influenced by deceit surfaced: "Yes, Mr. Prime Minister, I found out a number of things. I learned that there was a delay in notifying us of the possible terrorist attack, and I learned that there was an authorized clandestine operation that took place in New York involving alleged Israeli Agents."

Not giving the Prime Minister a chance to interrupt, the President continued without taking a break: "I also understand that if one of your generals had not come to the

American Embassy to relay the information to our Ambassador, that there might have been a more extended delay. It is also my understanding that Israel had prior knowledge of a group known as the Alliance Cell which had taken up residence in the United States. Mr. Prime Minister, I am not only disappointed but angered at the lack of cooperation and exchange of intelligence that could have possibly curtailed an incident that is now taking place in a shopping mall in Brooklyn, New York. Now, Mr. Prime Minister, could you explain why Israel has deviated from an agreement that has been in long standing between our two countries where the quick and open exchange of intelligence is necessary and agreed upon?"

There was a long pause before the Prime Minister spoke. He needed to collect his thoughts and displace some of the blame for what has been an unforgivable mistake. He, of course, employed the "plausible deniability" axiom as he spoke: "Mr. President, I am very concerned about what is going on in your country. I understand your frustration, but I have never had any intention of deceiving you or holding back any intelligence that could possibly negatively affect your country. If what you say is true, and my subordinates had information that they should have forwarded, I will make certain that they are duly punished, and that it never happens again. I will make them regret their actions or their lack of action."

These words further infuriated President Howard because he knew that the Prime Minister was aware that Major Yithak had been found floating in the Mediterranean Canal, and that General Gollman had fled and remained in hiding in fear of his life. However, President Howard swallowed his anger, assuming that down the road that he may need Israel's cooperation in resolving the shopping mall threat. He told the Prime Minister that when the Alliance Cell issued their demands, he would once again call on the Prime Minister for whatever cooperation was needed.

President Howard, in an unorthodox move, asked his assistant to contact the New York City Police Commissioner and the Federal Bureau of Investigation supervisor on the scene at the mall incident. It was the President's intention to speak directly to the designated hostage negotiator. Although all incidents of this kind are serious and demanding, he wanted to let whoever it was negotiating know that the results of this standoff could very well have national or even international ramifications. Not to say that there was already an inordinate amount of stress flowing through Sergeant Del's body, he was about to get another jolt of reality that for some would put them over the edge.

The Temporary Headquarters boss answered the hot line at the same time that the F.B.I. supervisor answered his phone. They both listened and simultaneously answered: "Yes, sir." The F.B.I. supervisor looked at the N.Y.P.D. boss and just shrugged. The hotline rang again, and the headquarters boss took the phone over to Sergeant Del who was preparing to speak with the terrorist leader in the administrative office. The boss presented the phone to Del and said: "It's for you."

Del was busy preparing: "Hey boss, I can't be bothered with every Tom, Dick and Harry asking how things are going or giving me suggestions on what to do. Please tell whoever it is that I'll call back later, if I can." The boss looked at him and in no uncertain terms said: "I think you better take this."

Seeing the look on the boss's face, he reluctantly took the phone and answered: "Hello this is Sergeant Del." The caller responded: "This is not Tom, Dick or Harry. It's Lawrence, Lawrence Howard." Shock masked Del's entire face. Unbeknownst to the Sergeant, in addition to the political and safety concerns that the President had to consider, he was also burdened with a personal dilemma - the welfare of his cousin, Miriam Howard. She was a friend and confidant his whole life. They grew up together and were still very close. In fact, it was she who ultimately convinced him to go into politics. The President continued: "I know you are busy, Sergeant, but I want you to know that I respect the NYPD negotiators, and you have whatever you need from me to help resolve the problem there. As you may know, no matter what the terrorists demand, a lot is riding on your ability and skills. I have total confidence in you. I'll closely follow your success, Sergeant Dello. Good luck and Godspeed."

The phone went dead, and Del looked up at everyone who had been watching and listening. He started to say that it was the President but was interrupted with a cacophony of "Yeah, we know!" If Del had been on edge before, he was now holding on by the tips of his fingers. The President of the United States told him that he would be watching.

Chapter Forty

The Cousins

Bay Ridge, Brooklyn is a blue-collar neighborhood that hosts various religious denominations, private and public schools, many one family homes, and borders a waterway known as the Narrows. It is in this relatively safe area where Mr. and Mrs. Jerome Howard settled and where they raised their son, Lawrence. They moved to this section of Brooklyn primarily because Jerome's brother, Matthew, was unrelenting in his attempt to persuade his brother to join him in this quiet, peaceful swath of suburbia. It is also the place where Matthew Howard decided to raise his daughter, Miriam.

Lawrence Howard could be described as a shy, loner-type of kid; so, having a cousin who he knew well and with whom he could share almost anything was a major asset for him. He and Miriam did everything together, including attending the same school and, at times, even being in the same class. It seemed that there was nothing that they couldn't tell each other, and nothing that they couldn't do together. It was this closeness, however, that prevented both of them from entering into any other relationships and possibly cultivating any other friendships. They had an exclusive friendship and only needed each other. Lawrence was shy, and Miriam was definitely an introvert, so their relationship neatly benefitted both of them. They needed no one else, and they didn't want anyone else.

Miriam was an excellent student and encouraged Lawrence to "study harder." With her constant influence, Lawrence became a good student and became interested in such topics as Government, Political Science, History and Geography. The same areas in which Miriam was excelling. As they grew older and experienced the teen years, there was increasing pressure for them to expand their social horizons and allow others into the private domain that had been theirs alone. Dating and socializing was relatively new for them, more so than for most, since their socialization process had been limited to the feelings, emotions, desires and experiences that they bounced off of each.

It was during this time period that they both met friends of the opposite sex. It was also during this time period that hormones began to race, and when teens began to see everything through the prism of sexual behavior. It was natural for a teenage girl or boy to have certain feelings for someone of the opposite sex, and so it was for both Lawrence and Miriam. This unique awakening began to create a schism between the two, and the bonds that held their private connection steadfastly together were starting to weaken.

It was unusual that they both found someone at approximately the same time, and for them, even more unusual that they were spending a lot more time with their new friend than with each other. It had never happened before, and although new and exciting, it just didn't feel right. They no longer could confide in each other like they used to; they no longer could totally depend on each other for emotional support that they might need, and they no longer could expect suggested solutions to the problems that life, in general, threw their way. Now, there was someone else who was there, who took up their time, who wanted to offer help, who wanted to be more than just friends.

For approximately two years, the relationship between Miriam and her cousin, Lawrence, remained lukewarm. The crutch that had been Lawrence and the tower of logic that had been Miriam were gone. In fact, whenever they were in each other's company, and that was not often, there was very little to say. While they were, at one time, able to speak for hours on end to each other, they were now at a loss for words.

Maybe out of guilt or sadness, they couldn't even discuss their relationships with each other. It seemed that they would never regain that private domain in which they had both existed. They both felt the same way, but neither would be the first now to openly discuss their feelings. However, though it wasn't openly apparent to either one of them, they both followed the other's life very closely.

The time came for high school graduation, and though they were both free from their previous relationships, the closeness that they had built in their younger years still seemed to be elusive. They were little more than cordial on graduation day and were shocked to hear that they were both going to the same college. At one time, this would have been the best news possible, but now, they were both unsure if it was what they really wanted. It might strain their weakened relationship even more. They would be meeting different people, and the socialization process might very well be more serious than either one of them wanted the other to know. They were cousins, however, and that should mean that if the need arose, they would be there for each other.

Much to their surprise, college life brought them closer than they had been in a while. They were not at the level of their original connection, but they were feeling much better than they had been. They found out that their majors were closely related: Miriam taking Political Science and Lawrence examining the potential in Governmental Administration. Once again, and not since their early days in education, they were in some of the same classes. They even began to socialize together, going out with the same groups of friends. Although both of them had opportunities to enter into a serious relationship, they shied away from the limitations and discipline needed to foster that relationship. They seemed to have reconciled their differences and started to, once again, rely on each other for support and comfort.

During her junior year, Miriam was awarded an internship in a local political office. In a very short time, she became an integral part of the operation in that office. She was well-liked by the politician and, more so, by the members of his staff. She worked in the office for her junior and senior years and was ultimately offered a permanent position on the staff. During this time, she became friendly with staff members working in other political offices and heard about an opening for an "aide" in the office of a local councilman. She immediately thought about Lawrence. Although he majored in Governmental Administration and did well, he was not enamored with the field of government relations. Miriam, who, once again, had gained his total trust, harassed him to the point that he at least applied for the position. He finally gave in.

Lawrence Howard applied for the position right out of college and started working as an aide to the councilman. As time went on, he was given more and more responsibilities and asked to resolve a number of challenges. He became an invaluable member of the councilman's team. He became so good that when an elected political position opened up in another district, his councilman strongly suggested that Lawrence campaign for the position.

He broached the subject with Miriam, and of course, she insisted that he start his campaign. Once again, he was not really sure that this was what he wanted. The conversation became hot and heavy between the two of them, and they found themselves nose to nose in heated discussion. Suddenly, they both stopped speaking and just stared at each other in disbelief. It was no longer a feeling of loyalty or support that surfaced, but one of romance and affection. The cousins were feeling the magnetic pull of love - not familial love but intimate love. They continued to stare but backed away from each other smiling. It was the smile of prohibition but also of understanding.

Miriam Howard remained his strongest supporter as he campaigned and ultimately won the election for "Councilman." He remained in that position for approximately four years, and it turned out to be the first step in his political career, as he went on to serve in a number of prominent political positions, ultimately leading to the President of the United States. One of his strongest advisers and leader of his campaign efforts was none other than Miriam Howard. Since she was single and remained single, she had plenty of time to devote to such things as campaigns. She remained very close to Lawrence, and it was he who loaned her the money to start a florist business - the florist shop in the Three Kings Shopping Center.

President Lawrence Howard also remained single and devoted his efforts and time to making the lives of Americans as successful, safe and secure as possible. However, he was presently dealing with a dilemma that threatened the lives of Americans and in particular one very special American - Miriam Howard.

Chapter Forty-One

The Demands

The unarmed four detectives and the two unarmed uniformed officers were now just part of a group being held hostage in the center walkway of the west wing of the Three Kings Shopping Center. There were other law enforcement officers in the mall, including two more Detectives from the Brooklyn South Squad, but they were all electronically "locked out." Erman Falco controlled access to the west wing and had electronically locked all access points. Tony and Marty assessed the situation and concluded that the probability of success, at this point, of taking down the armed cell members guarding them was close to zero. Even though the odds were against them, their detective's survival instincts were working overtime on an escape plan.

The cell members were armed with automatic machine guns and AR-15 Assault Rifles. Marty and Tony were armed with their experience and determination. The detectives were constantly surveying the situation looking for possible chinks in the defensive chain that the terrorists had constructed. The cell members did not maintain static positions but continuously moved around the petrified crowd of hostages. They were vigilant in ensuring that no one attempted to escape or cause the group to rebel against their captors.

The members of the Alliance Cell group, for the most part, were experienced and had worked closely together. However, because the cell had unexpectedly lost some of its members who were assigned to this operation, Dunait was forced to utilize some of the newer members. In fact, for one of the younger members, it was his first time actively participating in any action. Dunait, not totally trusting anyone, directed other team members to keep a close eye on the newest member, Seema.

Seema was never alone. He always had another cell member with him. This close companionship was employed for two reasons: it gave the new member confidence in not making a mistake, and it afforded other cell members the opportunity to keep a close eye on the new member who had not yet earned the trust of Dunait or other members of the group. After all, Seema was just inaugurated into the cell today, how could anyone really trust him? He was so new to the group that he wasn't even aware of the operation until this morning. As Seema circulated with his assigned partner on the fringe of the hostage group, he came upon the two detectives who he knew had been working in the jewelry store. Tony and Marty looked up and made eye contact with both of the terrorists and were surprised to see how young one of them was.

Seema was young and nervous and, probably because of his nerves, almost unintentionally smiled at the detectives. He looked directly at Marty, then looked at his hand that was wrapped tightly around the butt of the AR-15. Marty followed his gaze and as his eyes landed on Seema's hand, it slightly opened and displayed what Marty thought were the numbers 1013. It was fast, and the hand closed quickly as the two cell members continued on their patrol.

Marty got Tony's attention and relayed to him what had occurred. Although neither of them could be sure, the young cell member might have displayed the police radio call signal 10-13, "an officer needs help." If this was the case, and it was a very weak foundation to base any plan on, the detectives had an asset on the inside. Could they depend on what Marty thinks he saw, on what the numbers were and meant, and ultimately on the cooperation of an unknown entity, Seema? Before they did anything or let the other detectives know, both Tony and Marty wanted to be more certain that they actually had insider help. But how were they going to verify this new development?

Sergeant Dello, slowly recovering from the Presidential call, dialed the administrative office number of the Three Kings Shopping Center. The phone was answered after approximately seven rings. Reginald Winsten was on the phone.

"Hello this is Sergeant Dello from the New York City Police Department. Who am I speaking with?"

"Hello Sarge, this is Reginald Winsten, the General Manager of the mall."

"Hello Mr. Winsten. Is everyone okay there?" The phone call was on speaker so that both Alex and Erman Falco could hear the conversation. Winsten was about to tell the Sergeant about the slain captain, Bob Baxter and the chief, but a large hand landed on Winsten's shoulder and Falco nodded "No." Falco pointed to the typed paper that he had placed in front of Winsten and indicated that the General Manager read from it. Winsten disregarded the Sergeant's question regarding the status of the others in the office and started reading from the paper: "The following are the names of the political prisoners who the Alliance Cell wants released from Jalecya, the Israeli prison." The

Sergeant listened and recorded the twenty names that Winsten listed. The General Manager also informed the Sergeant that there will be no negotiations.

"If the Alliance does not get confirmation by midnight that the listed prisoners are released, hostages in the mall will be killed. Ten hostages would be killed every thirty minutes after midnight for as long as the prisoners remained incarcerated. The cell wants no contact until 10:00 pm when you will give me a progress report."

As the Sergeant was about to speak, the line went dead. He immediately attempted to reconnect, but the phone just continued to ring. Having failed to make contact, the lead negotiator hung up. Sergeant Del told one of the assisting police officers to continue trying to make contact with the terrorists. Del now had to inform all the agencies what the terrorists were demanding, and that the demands necessitated the potential involvement of two major countries - Israel and the United States.

Sergeant Dello turned to the Federal Agency representatives and told them what the terrorists were demanding. The looks on the faces of law enforcement officers told the whole story. The United States would have to garner the cooperation of Israel to release political prisoners who Israel considered a real danger to their State. The look said: "No way that this is going to happen." As was to be expected, each representative notified his/her respective agency and placed the decisions in the hands of the Directors, Ambassadors, Secretaries and ultimately the President.

Before Secretary of State Walden notified the President, he wanted to get the opinion of Ambassador Richardson in Israel. After relaying the message to Donald Richardson, Secretary Walden paused and waited for the Ambassador's opinion: "Well, Donald. What do you think?"

"Mr. Secretary, to tell you the truth, my initial thought was that the United States has a better chance of acquiring oil land in the Middle East than for Israel to give up its political prisoners. However, as I delved more deeply into the situation and the future of Israel, I came to the conclusion that Israel needs both our financial and military support as well as our expressed friendship on the world stage. With the possibility of one or all of these assets disappearing, Israel might be persuaded to cooperate. Of course, it is not a sure thing, but the potential for success is high." "Thanks, Donald. I wanted to get your take on things before I briefed the President. I am sure you will be hearing from me or the President very shortly." The Ambassador responded: "Yes sir. I will be waiting."

"Hello, Mr. President. The Alliance Cell has come down with its demands. It is mostly an attempt to free political prisoners who are being held in the Israeli prison at Jalecya. The Alliance forwarded a list of twenty such prisoners who they want released by midnight tonight." The President queried: "What happens if the prisoners are not released at all or not in the timely manner that is being dictated?" Secretary Walden reluctantly answered: "The terrorists are threatening to kill ten hostages every half hour that the prisoners remain in Israeli custody after midnight." The President took a deep breath and asked: "Dan, do you think that they are capable of carrying out such a threat? Do you think our negotiator would be able to broker a compromise to resolve the problem?"

"I am afraid, Mr. President, that the answers to both questions are disheartening. I believe that, from their reputation, they are quite capable of carrying out their threats, and 'no' I don't believe that the terrorists can be talked into a compromise. They do not even want to speak with the NYPD negotiator. He cannot make contact with them. They are expecting a 10:00 pm progress report on how the plans for the release are going."

In a very somber tone, the President thanked Secretary Walden for his report and mentioned that he would now contact the Prime Minister. The President also told Walden to let Ambassador Richardson know what was happening. Ultimately, if and when Israel agrees to capitulate to the demands of the terrorists, he wants Ambassador Richardson to witness the final release. The

Secretary told the President that he would contact Richardson immediately.

The conversation ended, and President Howard prepared himself for a very heated discussion regarding prisoner release. President Howard knew that as far as the Prime Minister was concerned, submitting to terrorists' demands would be something that smacked of an Israeli surrender to enemies of the State. At one time in his political career, President Howard had been Ambassador to Israel. His thinking on "prisoner exchange" and "hostage release" were somewhat more mellow than the practices and protocols that presently existed in the United States. He understood the problems, but he also understood the necessity for compromise, and in this particular case, Miriam Howard weighed heavy on his mind. It was apparent that she was a major influence in his thinking. After organizing his thoughts and mentally outlining his proposal, President Lawrence Howard got the Prime Minister of Israel on the line.

"Mr. Prime Minister, I have some news for you. News that you do not want to hear, I'm sure. The Alliance Cell has taken over the Three Kings Shopping Mall in Brooklyn, New York. They are holding approximately 200 innocent people as hostages and demanding the release of twenty political prisoners being held at the Jalecya prison in Netivot. The Alliance wants the prisoners released by midnight, tonight.

For every 30 minutes that the prisoners remain in Israeli custody after midnight, the cell is threatening to kill ten hostages. We cannot allow the slaughter of innocent people, and we are trying to negotiate with the terrorists. We have, thus far, been unsuccessful. In fact, they are refusing to even speak with the negotiator. A number of strategic attack plans have been developed, but they all come with the very real possibility of hostage casualties. I'm interested in your initial thinking, possible suggestions, and potential cooperation."

Prime Minister Aaron Sheroch paused before answering the President. It was a lot to think about and the release of political prisoners did not sit well with him.

"Mr. President, I share your concern regarding the safety of the hostages; however, before I can authorize the release of these prisoners, I have to present your request to the Knesset (the Knesset is the legislative ruling body in Israel). Only with their approval can I authorize such a potentially damaging act." By Minister Sheroch's tone, President Howard knew how the Prime Minister detested the possibility of submitting to the terrorists' demands, such demands that placed the political status of Israel in real jeopardy. These men were adamant in destroying the government control now in effect.

President Howard pushed: "Mr. Prime Minister, time is of the essence. By midnight, if there is no decision, innocent people may die." Pushing even harder, the President reminded Sheroch: "Need I bring to mind the fact that the United States possibly could have thwarted this action if it was not denied timely intelligence information. Israel's reluctance in divulging information on the planned attack has put us all in a compromising position. I cannot emphasize enough that we are fighting against a very real time limit. If we cannot implement a plan that guarantees a certain amount of safety for the hostages, Israel must seriously consider a release plan. The United States needs the unadulterated cooperation of its Mideast Ally. We would not look kindly on anything less."

President Howard laid the gauntlet down, and the Prime Minister knew it: "President Howard, I will call for an emergency meeting of the Knesset and present the possibility of a mass release. I will get back to you as quickly as I can and will be guided by their decision."

"Thank you, Mister Prime Minister, I await your swift and positive response." The President disconnected.

Chapter Forty-Two

The Turnaround

Marty couldn't get the idea out of his head that there might be someone who penetrated the terrorist shield and is working undercover. He's almost positive that when the young terrorist lowered his hand half-way down the handle, that he saw the numbers 1013 scrawled across the terrorist's hand. After seeing those numbers, Detective Iniddor quickly looked up at the gun-toting man and made eye contact. In Marty's head, that eye contact was confirmation that they were both on the same team. If this was the case, then there was potential for working out a positive plan for escape and possibly for stopping the attack all together. If Marty was wrong, his assumption could be disastrous.

While he carefully conversed with Tony, he noticed Donna, who was sitting on the other side of Tony, getting very fidgety. She apparently was very nervous over the situation and was probably still suffering from an elevated apprehension level as a result of her recent attack. Marty motioned to Tony on what he saw and encouraged Tony to calm Donna down. The terrorists emphasized the fact that anyone attempting to escape would be shot. If Tony could not stem her rising flow of nerves, and as Donna's condition grew, Marty could visualize Donna trying to get out from under the terrorists' glare and run anywhere in her attempt to escape the situation. She would be shot, because at present, there was no escape.

Juan Medina and Ralph Clemengas were close by, sitting about 5 feet from Marty and Tony. In an effort to get Marty's attention, Juan cleared his throat as loudly as he could. It had the desired effect. Marty turned his head and saw Juan hold open his hand and draw his index finger across the lower part of his palm. Marty believed that this was a sign that from Juan's vantage point, he had also seen what appeared to be the "1013." Marty acknowledged Juan's gesture with a slight positive nod and let Tony know the good news. Tony heard Marty, but his attention was drawn to the quick and erratic breathing coming from Donna. She was apparently hyperventilating. In many cases, this is the final stage before people take the next step and act out their apprehension. Tony couldn't allow that, so in an effort to bring her temperature down to a normal degree, he reached out and hugged her close to him. This allowed for two obvious results: it restrained Donna's movements and hampered any effort to get up and run, and secondly, it brought a warmth and confidence back into Donna that she had missed.

Unbeknownst to both Tony and Marty, Donna and her beer-bellied partner had split right after the sexual assault. Apparently, her partner could not deal with the fact that Donna "had allowed" someone to sexually assault her. It was that hackneyed adage that "you could have done something to stop it" or even better "did you enjoy being treated to rough sex?" His lack of understanding and empathy led Donna to call it quits. He remained in the apartment, and she went back temporarily to be with her parents. However, it was a permanent break, he did not want damaged goods, and she would never forgive him for his lack of understanding. Instead of being someone that she could lean on, he became a destructive force to her self-image.

It was over. So, Tony's hug was more welcome than Tony could know. She relaxed in the comfort of his strong hold, and the memory of how things used to be flooded her consciousness. She slowly calmed down, and Tony released the strong grip he had on her. She thanked him and looked affectionately into his eyes. Being burdened with the weight of his guilt, it was difficult for Tony to reciprocate. He just turned to Marty signaling that everything seemed to be back to normal. Now, the detectives had to come up with a plan on how they could utilize their newly found asset. Things were not great, but had gotten a lot better than they were a few minutes ago. They had an armed accomplice in a strategically advantageous position - the ranks of the terrorists.

Following the demands made by the Alliance and voiced by General Manager Winsten, Alex could not believe that Dunait would order the killing of hostages if the political prisoners were not released or not released on time. This was not what he signed up for. He wanted confirmation that the threat of killing people was, in fact, just that, a threat. He turned to Erman Falco who still had his weapon trained on the General Manager, and with an "I don't believe it face" wanted confirmation from Falco that the threat was unfounded. It did not come. Falco's face was stoic and unmoved and indicated that if it came down to having to use strict persuasion, people were going to die.

Alex was sick to his stomach, and it was then that he decided that he not only wouldn't help Dunait and his group, but that he would take any positive steps that he could to thwart the success of the attack. Alex turned to the General Manager, Reginald Winsten, who was so weak from the loss of blood that he began to unconsciously moan and sway in the chair. Alex, disregarding Director Falco, helped Mr. Winsten from the chair and laid him gently on the floor. He was very weak and somewhat delirious. The makeshift bandage that Alex had applied only temporarily stopped the bleeding. Winsten's pant leg was now soaked with his blood. Alex knew that if he continued to lose blood at the present rate, he would bleed out and die.

Alex, with his new found opposition determination, was not going to let Winsten die. No longer asking but rather in a dictating tone, Alex turned to Erman Falco and said: "I am going to get help for Mr. Winsten. If we don't, he will die." Falco answered: "And just how do you propose to do that?"

"I will call for an ambulance to come here, or I will get him outside and ask the police to help. One way or the other, I have to help him. Maybe we can have an emergency medical technician respond to the office." He was offering anything that came to his mind in an effort to save Winsten's life and convince Falco that something had to be done. Falco was not convinced. He did not want to weaken the hold that the Alliance now had. Falco told Alex to apply a tourniquet to the wound to stop further bleeding, but Alex told the Director that it was too late for that.

Alex insisted on getting help. The gun that had been trained on General Manager Winsten was now aimed at Alex. In no uncertain terms, Falco told Alex that things were going to remain as they were, and if Reginald Winsten died, so be it. When Alex rose quickly from his squatting position, Falco interpreted it as a threatening move. Falco swiped the butt of his weapon across Alex's face and dazed the surprised boy. Recovering from the hit, Alex now saw the barrel of Falco's Glock pointed directly at his head: "Alex, we will succeed with or without you. Do not push me to the point where my only option is to remove another obstacle that stands in our way. Live, by following our lead, or die, trying to dissent. It's your choice."

Alex had made his choice. He was no longer a cooperative member of a group that would kill innocent people. That group now became worse than the tyrannical government that they were rebelling against. As Alex bent down again to tend to Mr. Winsten, he reached into his waistband and pulled out the weapon that he had previously stashed there. It was a daring move, and one that he did reluctantly, but he had to stop this madman and the catastrophe that was about to follow. Alex was certain that Israel would not, at least at first, meet the demands made by the Alliance. That would mean the Alliance would show their determination and begin the slaughter of innocent people. He would have to stop it before it got to that point. And it started here and now by stopping Erman Falco.

Alex, gun in hand, twisted around and fired at Falco who was only about 5 feet away from him. Alex did not want to kill him, but wherever the rounds landed, as Falco had said, "So be it." Alex had pulled the trigger on a surprised Falco. He pulled it twice, and he heard the disappointing sound of "click, click." The gun malfunctioned, and now Alex was at the mercy of a man who knew that Alex meant to harm him and was to be considered the enemy.

Falco did not fire but looked at Alex shaking his head in disapproval: "Alex, we have never been sure of you or your loyalties, so do you think that I would allow you to have a loaded weapon while you were here. I unloaded my Glock and replaced it with yours, and then laid my weapon down where yours had been. So, you now carried my unloaded weapon. I am sorry that it turned out this way, but I can't allow you to throw a monkey wrench into our plans. I won't kill you now, but give me one reason to blow you away, and I will. I will not tell Dunait because he will order you killed. I appreciate your telling me the truth about Vin's death. That is the only reason you are still alive. Falco duct taped Alex and kept him in the room next to a now unconscious Reginald Winsten.

The bodies were building up. Some dead, some unconscious and some just tied up. It was not going as smoothly as anticipated, but there was nothing, at this point, that dictated to Dunait to call it off. Furthermore, they had already gone too far. They were at the point of no return.

As Falco was preparing for his next move and the notification from Dunait, his son's killer, he heard noise emanating from Baxter's office. The police chief had regained consciousness and was trying to break free from the duct tape binding. Falco went into the room and addressed the chief: "Welcome back. Don't do anything stupid, and I won't have to knock you unconscious again." The Chief responded: "You can still get out of this with your life. I heard your demands, and you will not succeed. Stop this while you still can." Erman Falco snickered: "Let me get this straight. We have already killed your captain, shot the General Manager of the mall, kidnapped and assaulted a police chief, and now kidnapped and assaulted a young kid who decided to change teams midstream. With all that, you say that I can still get out of this with my life, and that I should stop it while I still can. Maybe the shot on your head did more damage than meets the eye."

Falco continued: "We are taking over the mall and are going to free political prisoners held in Israel. We will kill hostages if we have to, and we will show the world the tyranny that exists in Israel. You should know, chief, that we are working closely with your department. In fact, we will shortly be getting an update on the progress of our demands from your befuddled negotiator. I know he will be trying to ultimately negotiate the release of at least some of the hostages as a "show of good faith" on my part, but I have no intention of showing good faith. Unfortunately, your poor negotiator is working under the additional stress of knowing that you are one of the hostages that he has to save.

Our leader is not especially fond of police, so there is a good possibility that you may be in the first round of expendable hostages. If that remains a strong possibility, we will make sure that your people know that you will be the first to be executed."

Chapter Forty-Three

The Undercover

During his past tenure as U.S. Ambassador to Israel, Lawrence Howard came to fully understand the political workings in Israel and the thinking of the representatives in the Knesset. He knew that there would be representatives who would be all for cooperating with the requests of the United States; representatives who would vote against a "no strings attached" commitment to approving such a drastic move; and he knew that the final decision would be influenced by the representatives who were undecided. President Howard had to depend on the effectiveness of the presentation that Prime Minister Sheroch would give to the entire legislative body. Unfortunately, the President wasn't sure how committed the Prime Minister himself was. It all depended on Sheroch.

The President had been patiently waiting for the Prime Minister to call with a decision; however, almost two hours had passed, and there was no communication from Minister Sheroch. Knowing that time was of the essence, President Howard told his aide to get the Prime Minister on the line. The aide handed the phone to the President as the Prime Minister got on the line: "Hello, Mr. President. I just arrived back from the emergency meeting and am awaiting a call from the majority leader as to their decision. I mentioned that we were up against a time constraint, and they said that they would get back to me as soon as possible. It should be any time now."

The President, holding back his frustration, said: "Prime Minister Sheroch, I hope they realize, and I assume that you emphasized that there are innocent lives at stake. As you know, the longer they take, the closer we get to an uncontrollable disaster. Also, I am sure that you reminded the body that the United States supports Israel in many ways, and that the absence of that support could be detrimental to the well-being of Israel and its people."

The Prime Minister, understanding the implied threat answered: "There is no doubt in any of the minds of the representatives that Israel depends on the support of its most important ally; however, what you are asking goes against the grain and thinking of a secure Israel. We are opening Pandora's box when it comes to an affirmative decision to submit to terrorists' demands. How do we combat something of this nature in the future?" The President, his balls twisted, answered: "Without the constant support of the United States, there may not be a future for Israel. Are you and the faint-hearted legislators in the Knesset willing to take that chance?"

"Mr. President, I assure you that I have done my best in presenting your case to the members of the Knesset. I have emphasized that the two nations have to continue to work together, and that only through total cooperation can a strong bond be maintained and survive. I will place another call to the majority leader in an attempt to expedite their decision." The President prodded: "Minister Sheroch, we don't have much time. Their lack of urgency is pushing us closer and closer to an unavoidable tragedy. Please get back to me as soon as possible."

"I will, Mr. President." The line went dead.

Sergeant Del, without success, had been continuously attempting to contact the terrorists in the administrative offices. The phone, however, just kept ringing. Del was getting worried as a significant amount of time had passed, and the progress report was almost due.

He would definitely be speaking with the leader then. Again, there was nothing positive, at this point, that the Sergeant could relate to whomever was in charge.

That would not go over well, and Del was worried that the Alliance would want to show how determined they really are and do something to demonstrate that determination. That something would, most likely, involve the safety of another human being.

The Temporary Headquarters phone rang, and the Secretary of State, Daniel Walden was on the other line. He spoke with the federal boss who was on the scene, present in the van. Following a brief conversation where all anyone heard was: "Yes Sir, I understand. Yes Sir," the Fed turned to the rest of the officers present in the van. He directed his comments mostly to Sergeant Dello, the NYPD hostage negotiator: "The President has advised Secretary of State Walden that Israel will only agree to the release of five prisoners of their choosing. It is their thinking that it remains too much of a retreat to totally submit to the demands of an insignificant rebel group. Israel is certain that the Alliance will agree to the compromise of five, counting the release as a victory."

Sergeant Del looked doubtful that the Alliance would settle for the release of just five of their countrymen; however, it might be a good place to start for a compromise agreement. With that as a foundation, the Sergeant dialed the number for the administrative offices. Falco answered: "What progress have you made on the release of the twenty political prisoners?" Del responded: "We have contacted the authorities in Israel, and they have brought your demands to the Knesset. The legislative body, in conjunction with the Prime Minister, is willing to release five prisoners of their choosing in return for the immediate cessation of your takeover, and the arrest of those who participated in the planning and implementation of the attack." All Sergeant Dello heard was the bang of the phone as the line went dead. It was apparent that the Alliance was playing "hardball," and, at this point, would accept nothing less than Israel's compliance to the stated demands. As soon as Del heard the disconnect, and as routine procedure in hostage negotiations, he attempted to reconnect with the speaker. The phone just rang and rang as if there was no one available to answer. Del, once again, told the police officer assistant to continue trying to reconnect.

All the onlookers realized what had happened and were at a loss to offer any positive suggestions. It was then that the fed boss addressed Sergeant Dello again. He told Del that he was instructed to relay the disposition of the Knesset to him, and in turn wait for the response of the cell group after they were told about the decision. He further told Del that if the compromise was not accepted by the group, that he was instructed to reveal a significant development.

Sergeant Dello looked at him in disbelief: "What are we playing games here? I need to know everything that is going on, if I am to succeed in saving lives. Do not parcel out information. If you have something to relate to me, do it now and make sure it is everything."

Sergeant Mario Dello was livid, and rightly so. The fed went on to say: "It was at the dictates of the Israeli government that I only reveal the following information if the compromise failed." Del lost it: "What the fuck do you have to tell me? My men and approximately two hundred innocent people are being held hostage at gunpoint, and you are playing 'guess my line.' Are you a fucking asshole?"

The Fed Boss couldn't take anymore and lunged at the Sergeant yelling: "Who the fuck are you calling an asshole?" Before it got any further, the group stepped between the two and separated them. When things finally got a little cooler, Del spoke up: "I'm still waiting for the information we should have had a while ago." Looking directly at Del, he said: "Well, if you shut your mouth for a minute, maybe I'll get a chance to speak." "I'm listening," said Del.

"The President relayed confidential information to the Secretary of State that he had received from the Prime Minister. Apparently, one of Israel's undercover agents penetrated the ranks of the Alliance and is acting as one of the terrorists in the mall. It is the belief of the Secretary that the agent will attempt to make contact with the detectives being held hostage." Del responded: "So, instead of us trying to find out a way that the agent could make contact with our guys, we sat here all this while with our fingers up our asses. That's just great! Is there anything else that you may have forgotten to relate or that you've been instructed to hide from the hostage negotiator on the scene?" It was more of a rhetorical question, so there was no answer offered and none expected.

Even though the news of an undercover agent was a positive factor, it did not erase the immediate problem of reconnecting with the terrorists. The negotiator had to find a way to let his men know that there was a human asset available to them. Hopefully, they had already made some kind of contact and were formulating a plan.

The fact still remained, though, that they were outnumbered, out-weaponed and lacked the ability to easily communicate. Nothing was impossible, but the probability of success was slim.

Chapter Forty-Four

The Shot

There was constant movement in and out of the Police Department's Temporary Headquarters Vehicle. Specialized units like: Emergency Service, the Sniper Unit, the Intelligence Division, the Hostage Negotiation Unit, the Detective Division, and others who were making their presence known, became part of the continuous flow of law enforcement. In addition to these specialized police units, Federal and State law enforcement were also present. With all of these agencies contributing to the organized chaos, no one even acknowledged the presence of the small white "police" van parked just a few yards in front of the Temporary Headquarters vehicle. One could say that the white van and Dunait were "hiding in plain sight."

Although Dunait had freedom of movement in the van, he had to be careful not to draw attention to any of his efforts. He was viewing all of the action inside the mall on the monitors that Erman Falco had installed. He saw and heard how distraught and how on edge the cowering hostages had become. In an effort to emphasize the determined control that the terrorists had over the hostages and the situation, Dunait, through Erman Falco, ordered the armed terrorists to fire their automatic weapons in the air and dictate that the hostages remain quiet and attentive.

The burst of gunfire not only brought the hostages under control but caught the attention of the police units who were positioned all around the mall. Hurried communications were exchanged between headquarters and the units in an attempt to explain the report of gunfire. Snipers focused their attention on any potential targets, Emergency Service cops took a stronger hold on the battering ram, and all officers came to the ready position with hands on their weapons. This distraction was a positive for Marty who immediately looked at the young terrorist he believed to be an asset. They both made eye contact, and this time, there was a confirmed nod that cemented Marty's assumption. The detectives now knew for sure that they had an ally who could help with an escape plan.

Erman Falco had notified Dunait about the compromise plan that Israel relayed to the United States. To Falco's surprise, Dunait was not shocked by the poor compromise offer. He knew that Israel had to start at the lowest point in order to negotiate a palatable deal. What Israel and the United States didn't realize was the fact that in Dunait's plan, there was no compromise. He wanted all twenty prisoners released or both nations would pay the price - the deaths of their fellow human beings.

It was Dunait's strong feeling that the Alliance would have to demonstrate their determination and sacrifice a few of the hostages in advance. He had no problem in doing this, but a number of his fellow terrorists were young and somewhat inexperienced. He wondered how they would react to the outright killing of others. It was a risk, but one that Dunait felt he would have to take. However, he would make the "killing" decision as the time for final compliance ran out. It was not beyond Dunait's thinking to truly carry out the initial threat of killing ten hostages for every 30 minutes past midnight - the release time of the twenty prisoners.

Dunait decided that just prior to the midnight deadline, he would order the death of one of the hostages. And it would have to be a hostage of note. He thought about one of the detectives, but then, an even better choice came to mind. During an Indian attack, if the chief of the tribe is killed, the rest of the Indians retreat until another chief is named. Dunait applied this strategic axiom to the present situation. The Alliance had captured a significant hostage - the New York City Police Department Chief of Brooklyn South, the chief of the tribe. His sacrificial death would surely send a message, but even more so, if his death was at the hands of young Alex Hassid, the action would serve to also cement Alex's involvement in the Alliance.

Dunait's evil mind was working on overdrive. He was salivating with the thought of shocking the other side into reluctant compliance with their demands. He and the Alliance will have won! It was his hope that the live recorded demonstration of raw emotionless killing would be the only indiscriminate killing that would have to take place.

Erman Falco shuttered at the thought of telling Dunait that the person he wanted to designate as the executioner was now duct taped and lying on the floor. Falco decided to mention this fact to Dunait later. He didn't want to rain on the enthusiasm he heard in Dunait's voice or incur the wrath of Dunait's angered disappointment. So, he just agreed with the leader and said that he would carry out the plan when ordered. Dunait was feeling more and more empowered by the developments that were taking place, and he felt totally safe working within the confines of his van, parked right under the noses of law enforcement.

The burst of gunfire sought to meter out an air of even more control. It did, and to some, it indicated again the seriousness and the danger of their situation. One of those feeling the pressure and stress of self-preservation was none other than Tony's sitting partner, Donna. Tony had been able to calm her before, but now her mental state was even more distressed. This time it wasn't physically apparent to anyone looking at her, but inside she was a mental mess. She could no longer patiently wait to see if she would be sacrificed at the hands of these armed and dangerous terrorists. She had to do something to ensure her future existence.

So many thoughts were rushing through Donna's mind that indecision was running rampant. She finally decided that she would act the next time the two armed men passed on their circular patrol. She would wait until they had their backs turned, and then she would quickly get up and run to the employee corridor entrance and find a way out from there. Donna would have liked some moral and physical support, but she knew that if she confided in Tony, he would, for her own sake, try to stop her. So, she said nothing and waited for the patrol to come her way. As if Tony surmised her plan, he turned to her and asked how she was doing. She quietly and meekly said that she was okay, forcing the words and the calm tone from her mouth.

All four of the detectives, as well as the two uniformed cops, were now aware of the undercover Israeli agent, Seema, and his desire to help. With the newly acquired jolt of confidence, the detectives of the Brooklyn South Squad were determined to develop a plan of escape with the absolute minimum of collateral damage. The detectives were the experienced ones, they were the ones who were forced to react in stressful situations, and they were the ones who always came out on top. They were up against armed terrorists who were young, inexperienced and probably just as nervous and frightened as the hostages they were guarding.

The detectives' first move would be the most important one, and it would dictate the final result of their action. As difficult as it was to communicate freely, they were finding a way to get their thoughts across to each other. The fact that the four detectives had worked together for a long time served as a definite advantage when it came to taking action. They knew each other's moves.

The patrols were completing their tour of the hostage circle. There were two teams of two who were closest to the detectives. Marty, Tony, Juan and Ralph would make their move at the same time that the uniformed offices attacked their closest team. If all went well, the cops would surprise and immobilize the three teams, and then arm themselves with the confiscated automatic weapons. The other terrorists would have to divert their attention away from the hostages and focus on the apparent new threat. With the training and expertise gained from many mandated visits to the police range, the detectives and the police officers would surely overwhelm and eliminate their captors. The timing and the accuracy of that first move would be the deciding factor.

They waited for their opportunity, but unbeknownst to them, someone else was also waiting for the right moment for her opportunity to escape. The armed men were just passing, and Donna saw her chance. She rose and started running as planned. Tony was surprised but reacted quickly in an effort to stop her from getting shot in an escape attempt. "Shooting" was something that the terrorist warned would happen if an escape attempt was made.

As the terrorist team saw what was happening, they turned and fired. Tony ran and leaped onto Donna to get her down and out of the path of the oncoming rounds. Seema's partner was the first to fire, but in an effort to show his determination, Seema "accidentally" nudged his partner out of the way and opened fire with a long and direct attack. After that extended barrage of gunfire, no one would ever doubt Seema's loyalty to the Alliance and its cause. Seema's barrel, however, was intentionally aimed at an angle that just rose above the heads of the two fleeing hostages.

Both Tony and Donna were down on the floor. Tony had succeeded in saving Donna from what could have been a fatal attempt at escape, but as he tried to get up, he felt pain in his abdomen. As he put his hand over the painful area, he felt a sticky, wet, fluid flow over his fingers. He failed in his attempt to rise. Donna got up to her knees and reacted to Tony's moan. She turned him over and laid his head in her lap. He had saved Donna, but his survival was now in jeopardy. He had been hit by one of the rounds fired by Seema's partner and was now losing blood. Unfortunately, Donna's escape attempt had interfered with the plans of the detectives and the cops. They would have to retry at another time when the opportunity arose. Seema's actions had saved further damage to Tony and allowed Donna to remain unharmed.

Disregarding the shouted orders of the terrorists, Marty ran to Tony's aid. In an attempt to stop the bleeding, Marty ripped off his shirt, wrapped it around his hand and applied direct pressure to the wound. It is never a good thing to get shot, but a round to the abdomen very rarely resulted in a positive outcome. Marty knew this, and so did Tony. As Marty had run to Tony, Seema, once again, got in the way of his cell partner and blocked his line of sight, so no more damage could be inflicted. Seema's cooperation, thus far, had been invaluable, and it seemed that his cover was still protected. Donna, with tears flowing down her face and in a state of shock, just kept stroking Tony's face saying: "I'm sorry. I'm sorry." Tony looked up at her and weakly responded: "No, I'm the one who's sorry!" Tony passed out.

Chapter Forty-Five

The Plan

The police brass in the Temporary Headquarters Vehicle as well as the Alliance Leader, Dunait, in his fake police van, both viewed the attempted escape in the mall. They also saw one of the detectives stop a bullet which caused him to become immobile and lay on the mall floor. Dunait did not like the way things were going and decided that he might have to push up the deadline time, the time to show everyone that the Alliance meant business. The police were also of the same mind, as the Incident Commander put all units on high alert – the step before a tactical and strategic entry. Snipers were focused on the administrative offices as well as the mall entrances. Emergency Service Cops were primed to forge ahead through the entrance doors, and the NYPD Task Force-Special Weapons Division, was ready to follow-up with a guns-drawn entry.

Dunait realized that after the Law Enforcement Officials viewed the mall escape incident that they would be positioned and ready to employ an all-out assault. So, Dunait knew he needed to pre-empt any police assault plan. He decided to contact Erman Falco and put the New York City Police Department on notice. It was time to shock the authorities into reality. Dunait ordered Falco to prepare Alex for his executioner role. He was going to execute the police chief while the chief's fellow officers watched on their camera feeds. This would put the fear of Allah in them all, and it should be clear sailing from there on in.

Following the news of a New York City Police Detective being shot, President Howard's patience with the Israeli government's decision on the release of five prisoners began to weigh heavy on his mind. He knew all too well that it was Israel's first attempt at a compromise offer, but it seemed that this terrorist group was willing to immediately go to the extreme to get what they wanted. The Alliance had no compassion for human life. The innocents were going to be used as pawns to ultimately attain submission to the group's demands. The President of the

United States was not willing to risk the lives of American citizens. He needed Israel to understand that and to understand it right now.

The more he thought about the position that the Israeli Prime Minister had taken, the more determined the President became to get the full cooperation of the Knesset and Prime Minister Sheroch. President Howard was, once again, on the line waiting for the Prime Minister.

"Hello, President Howard. How are things going? Are there any new developments?" "Yes, Minister Sheroch, there has been a major development. One of the New York City Police Detectives, who is among the hostages, has been shot. He was trying to protect a female hostage who could not take the stress of being at the mercy of armed terrorists. Disregarding the warnings of the cell members, she bolted for an employee entrance. The detective saw the patrolling terrorist raise his weapon to stop the escape, and the detective threw himself at the female, tackling her in an attempt to get her out of the line of fire. He succeeded in saving her from harm but caught a round in the stomach for his efforts. He is now lying on the floor of the mall probably bleeding to death. We cannot allow anything else like this to happen.

It is my strong opinion that this group is not interested in negotiations or compromise. I feel that they will go to the extreme to obtain what they want. It is much too risky to think that we can barter with them. The deadline is much too close, and I'm afraid that they will carry out their threats of killing people. The United States needs your help. Don't play politics with American lives. Contact your legislators, get the Knesset to think outside of the Israeli political box. Mr. Prime Minister, do it now. I have this terrible feeling in the pit of my stomach, and it has never been wrong."

The Prime Minister listened without interruption and understood the compassion the President had for his fellow Americans. However, if Israel acquiesced so easily to the demands of the Alliance, they would surely have to face the turmoil that would be generated by such a decision. The people of Israel would have a hard time understanding the need to free political prisoners who were responsible for many deaths and the destruction of sacred buildings. The Prime Minister was in an unenviable position. He didn't want to free prisoners, but he didn't want to risk the death of innocent people and possible reduction in support from the United States.

He collected his thoughts and spoke to the President: "Mr. President, I truly understood your concerns and the precarious position in which you find yourself. I cannot guarantee that the Knesset will respond in the manner that you want, but I will strongly voice my opinion to support your request. Give me some time to reach out to certain legislators, and I will get back to you as soon as possible."

"Prime Minister Sheroch, let me remind you that time is not our friend. I need to know immediately. That is the only way that I can possibly ensure the safety of the two hundred hostages. And while you are pleading my case, emphasize that Israel has requested the "sky blanket defense system" that the United States has developed. I am sure that you and the members of the Knesset would agree that Israel would be a much safer place with the "sky blanket" in operation. It would be a serious misfortune if for some reason, the delivery of the defense system was delayed, or for that matter, even canceled. Neither you nor I would want that to happen. Bring my case to the Knesset and get back to me as soon as possible. I will be awaiting your call."

This time the Prime Minister didn't consider President Howard's words as a veiled threat, it was an out and out "if Israel does not fully cooperate with the United States, we will leave Israel to its own destiny" threat. Prime Minister Sheroch answered the President: "I will get right back to you. Stay by the phone, Mr. President."

Lawrence Howard finally felt that he had gotten through to his counterpart. Sheroch now had to quickly convince his fellow leaders of the imminent threat to the hostages, but more so, because of the President's words, the very serious threat to the safety and security of a stable Israel.

After a short time, Prime Minister Sheroch contacted President Howard. Sheroch told the President that the members of the Knesset voted to increase the number of prisoners that they are going to release; however, the number only increased to ten. President Howard's expected response was pointed and threatening: "You do realize that ten is not what the terrorists are demanding. You are playing with fire, and I will not be there to put out the flames.!"

Lawrence Howard did not parse his words, but before he could go on, Prime Minister Sheroch interrupted: "I and the Knesset were aware that this number would not satisfy the terrorists' demands nor your request; so, we have devised an alternate plan that should please the Alliance but also maintain the safety, security and dignity of Israel. It will also allow the hostages to remain safe." The President was fuming over the lack of cooperation that he was experiencing, but he kept an open mind and continued to listen: "Please tell me about this miraculous plan that you have."

"Mr. President, it might not be miraculous, but it is well thought out and could very possibly work." President Howard heard the word "possibly" and he exploded: "Did I hear you say 'possibly work?' You are playing with lives. We need something that will definitely work and secure the safety of the hostages." Sheroch responded: "Maybe, it was a poor choice of words, but let me finish. Through the ingenuity of our Information Technology people and sophisticated camera work, we will be able to show 'cut and pasted' images of the staged release of the twenty prisoners without ever opening one jail cell.

This release will be sent via satellite transmission for everyone to see, including the members of the Alliance. According to the Alliance, once the prisoners have been released, the hostages will no longer be in danger. It will show that we have fulfilled the terrorists' demands and diffused the situation. What you do with pursuing the remaining cell members is totally up to you, and you will have my full cooperation in tracking them down and arresting them. It is a plan that I'm sure will work."

President Howard listened without interruption but needed at least one question answered: "The terrorists seem to be somewhat organized and the leader possesses a fair amount of intelligence. What do you do if the Alliance has someone on the outside of the prison wanting to witness the actual release?"

"Because of the fact that this decision is one that the Israeli people do not favor, for the sake of safety and crowd control for the many expected protesters, we will secure the perimeter of Jalecya to a point where one cannot really see what is going on. By the time that the rebels realize that they have been duped, we will be in the clear, and your forces will have taken back the mall."

President Howard responded: "It seems that you have a lot more faith in the plan than I. There are so many variables that can negatively affect a successful outcome. You realize that, if in any way the rebels catch on to your scheme, you will have signed the death warrant for innocent people – my innocent people. I appreciate your trying to implement a counter plan to the demands of the terrorists, but I want you to know that the United States is not in full agreement with the decision and will hold Israel responsible for any negative results and for the lack of the requested cooperation."

"Understood, Mr. President. I will get back to the legislators and prepare for the implementation of the plan. I will contact you again when we are ready. Good-bye." The line went dead. Shaking his head in disbelief and concern, President Howard reached out for his Secretary of State.

"Hello, Mr. President. How can I help?" President Howard responded: "The first thing you could do is pray that the hostages will be safe. When you finish praying, I want you to contact Ambassador Richardson in Israel and have him keep a close eye on what's about to happen. Let me explain."

The President went on to explain the plan that Prime Minister Sheroch and the members of the Knesset were about to put into action. Howard also directed Secretary Walden to contact his lead at the scene of the "takeover" and advise him to inform the Headquarters personnel that Israel had submitted to the demands of the terrorists, not revealing the subterfuge. Everyone but the President, the Secretary of State and Ambassador Richardson would be kept in the dark regarding the staged release. The Secretary knew by the President's tone that he was not at all certain that such a plan would work, but being a loyal soldier, even though he shared the same concerns as the President, he followed the directives of his boss.

Secretary Walden advised the President that he would immediately notify his representative at the scene and Ambassador Richardson in Israel.

Ambassador Richardson, after speaking with Secretary Walden, informed the Secretary that the Embassy staff had done some research on the terrorist group. They were ruthless in their approach and would not hesitate in taking violent actions to reach a goal. This was not what the Secretary wanted to hear but praised the Ambassador and his staff for their initiative. Richardson would travel to Jalecya and personally eyeball the implementation of the Israeli "staged" prisoner release plan.

Secretary Walden then contacted the Temporary Headquarters Vehicle parked at the mall. He spoke to his aide who relayed the good news to all of the bosses present.

Sergeant Del was shocked that the diplomatic liaison to Israel was able to convince a very rigid government to submit to terrorists' demands. He didn't realize, first of all, that it wasn't a diplomat who was doing the convincing, but the President himself; and secondly, that the Israeli government did not submit to the terrorists' demands.

There was shock and surprise but also relief when the news was relayed. It was now up to Sergeant Dello to contact the Alliance leader and confirm with him that the demands had been met. Since Erman Falco was not answering the phone, Del sent a uniformed police officer with a megaphone and a sign to the administrative offices. With cameras everywhere, the cell member in the administrative offices would surely see the message. At that point, Del would initiate another call to the office in hope that now, the phone would be answered. The plan was in effect, and there was no turning back!

Chapter Forty-Six

The Miracle of Technology

Dunait was watching events unfold and became uneasy about waiting to demonstrate his determination in getting Israel to agree to the demands. He did not like the attempted escape and was disturbed that a detective had already been shot. He understood that law enforcement, in general, reacts differently when any one of their own is injured or killed. They were at that point. Their tactical advancement would be both swift and focused. Dunait had to use whatever he had available to delay police efforts. He had to divert their attention to something more heinous and personal to them. He called Erman Falco on his cell phone. The Director answered: "Hello."

"Falco, it is time to show the police and the world that we are determined in our efforts to free our countrymen. It is time to show that we will go to the extreme to get what we want. Is Alex ready to demonstrate his loyalty to the cause?" Falco responded without actually giving a direct answer to the question: "Alex is right here, Dunait." Alex was within earshot of the conversation and heard Falco refer to him. Falco had untied Alex and brought him into his office where the police chief was duct taped to a chair. The chair was positioned in front of a wired panel that identified the bomb locations in the mall and displayed the marked buttons that would wirelessly ignite the explosives.

Falco arranged the camera so that those viewing their monitors would only see the chief seated and immobile in a chair, and Alex standing just a few feet away from him with a gun in his hand. Falco had given Alex a Glock with one round chambered in the weapon. He told Alex that if he didn't do what he was ordered to do, then Falco would pull the trigger on his weapon that was pointed directly at Alex. Erman Falco was standing in the doorway of the office and was out of camera range, so those viewing the live execution would only see the chief and Alex. They would witness Alex pulling the trigger and the chief slumping into the grips of death.

Dunait knew that there could be two different reactions to this horrendous demonstration: one, it would instill fear showing that the terrorists are not afraid of killing the hostages who were in mortal danger if Israel and the United States did not come together and answer to the demands quickly; and two, it could have a negative effect and serve as a rallying point for law enforcement to tactically assault the west wing to prevent further slaughter. It was clear to Dunait, though, that law enforcement knew the risk they faced if they employed the second reaction. It was more than obvious that there would be additional collateral damage with hostages being executed and police officers being shot. So, he felt confident in telling Falco that the time had arrived for serious action.

Alex, feeling the weight of the gun straining in his hand, dropped the gun to his side. Falco immediately responded: "Raise the gun and point it at the chief." Alex did not respond. Falco, now in a loud and certain tone, ordered: "Alex, raise the gun. Do it now!" Alex turned to look at his one-time protector and saw the barrel of a semi-automatic weapon pointed directly at him. Alex had to do something because he knew that there was no way that he could become an executioner and end the chief's life. His options were limited, but he made up his mind to try to eliminate the man holding a gun on him. Dunait was still on the line waiting to hear the gunshot and see the completion of what would be a turning point event. Just before Alex was ready to turn on Erman Falco, the Director told Alex to wait.

Both Falco and Alex heard a voice coming from what sounded like outside of the front entrance of the Administrative Building. From his position in the doorway of the office, Falco leaned out and not only heard a voice amplified over a loudspeaker but saw a large sign being held by a uniformed police officer. The sign was a translation of the voiced message which said that Israel had agreed to the demands of the Alliance, and that all twenty political prisoners would be released. Neither Erman Falco or Alex Hassid could believe that the end was in sight. Falco addressed Dunait: "We have won. The police are telling me that our demands are being met. I am sure that this office phone will soon be ringing. I will let you know as soon as I am contacted." They disconnected.

Although Falco viewed this development as a sure win, Dunait would not celebrate until he actually saw the prisoners walking out of Jalecya and was notified by his allies that, in fact, his countrymen were free. He had learned from experience that Israel did not like to lose and would employ any tactic that they could to become a winner. The police chief, who was to be the sacrificial lamb, was grateful that an accord had been reached, but like Dunait, he didn't think things were exactly what they seemed. Fortunately though, if it meant that his life would be spared, he was glad that someone came up with something.

As Erman Falco expected, the office phone started ringing again. Falco secured Alex again, and answered the phone: "Yeah Hello."

"This is Sergeant Dello speaking. Who am I speaking to?"

"You can call me Falco." The Sergeant went on: "Well Falco, you must have seen and heard the message that your demands have been met. When can we secure the hostages and bring them out safely?"

"Sergeant, just because you say that the demands have been met, doesn't make it so. We need proof that our twenty countrymen are, in fact, free. Until we have positive proof that they have been released, things will remain as they are. These are the orders of my leader, and we will wait for proof. Then and only then will we discuss the freeing of the hostages and our unhindered escape."

Sergeant Del had no problem in assuring Erman Falco that he would see the prisoners being released from Jalecya. He explained that it would just take a little while longer. Falco answered: "We still have a deadline, and we are very close to the end of that timeline. You have until midnight to prove to us that the prisoners have been released. If they are not, you know what will begin to happen." Del could not negotiate any type of extension. The terrorists were holding to their original threat, and Del did not know where the State Department was with securing the prisoner release from Israel.

A call was placed to the Office of the Secretary of State to find out how long before the prisoners would be freed. Del was even under more pressure now. There was an agreement, but the deadline set by the Alliance leader was quickly approaching, and the safety of the hostages was still in jeopardy.

Secretary Dan Walden placed a call to the President who in turn, once again, contacted Prime Minister Sheroch. The Prime Minister assured President Howard that the recorded prisoner release would be ready before the deadline and through satellite technology, it would be broadcast so that everyone could witness the prisoners gaining their freedom. He said that the plan would go into effect momentarily. Prime Minister Sheroch advised President Howard to notify the negotiator at the scene. He could then alert the terrorists who would be able to view the release. Howard agreed and hung up. Sergeant Dello dialed the administrative office phone again. Falco, who was in constant touch with Dunait, answered: "Yes."

"Falco, this is Sergeant Dello again. I have been advised that the release of your countrymen will momentarily appear on your monitor there in the office" The Sergeant instructed Falco on how to gain the reception.

"We will wait and see. I will call you back on this number when we are satisfied. If we are not, the killing will begin." Del was certain that the siege would end as soon as the terrorists saw their countrymen on the way to freedom. However, he was not one of those who was privy to the fact that what the terrorists would be viewing was tantamount to a low-funded Hollywood production. It was a production that, if not believed to be genuine, would result in a catastrophic and deadly outcome.

Chapter Forty-Seven

When the Smoke Cleared

Erman Falco and Dunait waited patiently to see their fellow countrymen walk to freedom. Falco was able to send reception of the event directly to the monitor in Dunait's van. They waited for what they thought was an exceedingly long time; however, if they succeeded, the wait would be well worth it. Finally, after a lot of interference, the picture came into view. It was the twenty political prisoners, as promised. They marched out of the prison gates right into a waiting prison bus. Falco and Dunait witnessed the men board the bus, and then watched as the bus pulled away leaving for the agreed upon location. Both men were pleased by what they saw. Their plan had worked and with very little resistance. Dunait, not totally trusting his Israeli adversaries, waited for a visual confirmation from one of his allies on the ground in Israel before celebrating. The bus ride would only take approximately twenty minutes, so Dunait had to wait only a short time to get the confirmation for which he was eagerly awaiting. Falco, being confident that the Alliance had succeeded, prematurely congratulated Dunait for freeing the prisoners and executing a solid plan.

The drop-off location was secured with Israeli soldiers who were there to make certain that the prisoners would not be attacked by protesting crowds. Twenty minutes passed, and the bus still had not arrived. Approximately thirty minutes after the prisoners boarded the bus, and according to the Alliance spy on the ground, the bus finally arrived at the specified location. The spy notified Dunait that the bus had arrived, but that no one disembarked, and the windows were so heavily tinted that movement inside the bus was undetectable. Dunait understood that there might be some delay in finally allowing the prisoners to exit the bus; however, he was not expecting what was about to occur.

As Falco and Dunait awaited the release, the administrative office phone rang. Surprised at the sound of the phone, Falco apprehensively answered: "Yeah, who is this?"

"It's Sergeant Dello. As you know, the prisoners have left Jalecya and are on the bus at the location that you stipulated. However, before the authorities release the prisoners, they want a show of good faith." Falco, not liking the last-minute change, questioned the Sergeant: "What do you mean a show of good faith? What does Israel want?" Sergeant Del explained: "Before the prisoners are set free, you must free some of the hostages that you have in the mall. Preferably, women and children should be allowed to leave."

"That was not the agreement. There was no talk of letting anyone go before the prisoners were released. We did not agree to that and I, alone, cannot make that decision. I will get back to you, but the deadline has arrived, and it is not the time to start changing parameters. What happens from this point on is in your hands!" Falco hung up. He then immediately contacted Dunait, and to say the least, Dunait was not at all pleased to hear that the authorities were putting stumbling blocks in the way of the planned release. The leader was not in agreement with allowing all of the women and children to leave. He realized how close the Alliance was to success, so he knew he had to do something. He decided to equal the numbers. He would let twenty hostages go for the release of the twenty political prisoners on the bus. After much consternation, he relayed his decision to Falco who in turn contacted the negotiator. Although both Falco and Dunait thought it to be more than fair, it was not as well received as they thought it would be.

Sergeant Dello told them that he would discuss the terms further with the decision makers and get back to them. Falco again reminded the Sergeant that the deadline had passed, and if there were any more delays, the threat of killing hostages would become a reality. Falco also knew that Dunait was at the point where he would show everyone that he meant business. He would authorize the execution of innocent people. The United States and Israel were playing with fire. This was not a normal negotiation scenario. The two countries were not dealing with a "fair play" terrorist. Dunait was ready to do whatever it took to succeed without delay.

Sergeant Dello relayed Falco's remarks to the supervisors present in the Temporary Headquarters Van. They, in turn, got in touch with the heads of their respective agencies or departments. The negotiator, the Sergeant, emphasized to all of them that the leader of the Alliance was one small step away from carrying out his initial threat. This was not a time to test the terrorists' resolve. Dello also reminded the agency representatives that the threat deadline had passed and that they, law enforcement, were living on borrowed time.

Even with the emphatic warnings, the decision did not come about quickly. Finally, after what seemed like an eternity, Sergeant Dello was notified that the powers-to-be had accepted the one-for-one release compromise. However, the Sergeant was also told to stall for as much time as he could before implementing the compromise. He did not understand the logic behind stalling to get hostages to freedom. He was a good soldier and always followed orders, but this time, he was reluctant to automatically abide by the latest decision. He was the negotiator, and he knew just how far he could go with the terrorists. His judgment should be respected, and his guidelines and recommendations should be the ones that are accepted.

Sergeant Dello did not like or understand the ploy to stall for more time. He started to feel that he didn't know everything that was going on behind the scenes. He was the negotiator; he should know it all. Were there details that were not revealed to him? Was he not privy to all the information available? If that were the case, then he was not negotiating in good faith, and his effectiveness with the terrorists would be greatly diminished.

Sergeant Dello, knowing that the Alliance leaders would see right through any attempt at delay, contacted Erman Falco at the administrative offices. A harsh and obviously frustrated voice answered the phone: "Well, what is taking so long? You are gambling with the lives of the hostages. There will be no more delays! We are ready to release twenty hostages that we have chosen. They will be taken to the loading dock area of the west wing and exit through the connecting door. They will then walk into the back alley, unescorted by you, to the rear gate area where you will meet them. Is that understood?"

"Yes, I got it." Falco Continued: "The gate is under camera surveillance so we will see when you collect the twenty people. As soon as that is completed, we will look at our monitors and will want to see the prison bus doors open, and our countrymen step from the bus. Until the bus pulls away, and we see the twenty men standing free, the threat remains in effect. Do you understand?" Sergeant Dello, unaware of any possible snare, agreed to the terms and waited for the hostages to be escorted to the loading dock area. Uniformed officers were alerted to meet the hostages and take them into protective custody.

Since there were cameras monitoring the event, the bosses in the Temporary Headquarters Vehicle, Dunait in his van, and Falco in the administrative offices all watched as the hostages marched to freedom. As planned, they walked down the rear alley to the loading gate and were met by approximately a dozen heavily armed officers. The transfer was completed without a hitch, and there was a feeling of relief in the Temporary Headquarters Vehicle. Now, Sergeant Dello, once again, advised the agency representatives to contact their respective bosses to initiate the release of the prisoners without delay.

The clatter of the bus doors opening was a welcomed sound. The bus stayed for a very short time, and then drove away in a cloud of smoke that was thicker than any fog that ever appeared in that area. The man-made smoky fog remained anchored to the ground. It was near impossible for anyone to see the twenty men who had been released. Therefore, an absolute confirmation on the prisoner release could not be given.

Dunait waited for the call from his spy on the ground confirming the release. He waited and waited, but the call never came either confirming or denying what had occurred. Unbeknownst to him, Dunait's spy had been arrested as part of a summary arrest plan initiated by the Israeli police at the site of the proposed release. Almost everyone there was taken into custody even before the bus allegedly unloaded and drove away. So, the only evidence that Dunait could rely on now was the video of the men getting on the bus outside of the prison. This was not enough for Falco and definitely not enough for Dunait. Still not trusting the sincerity of the Israeli Government, the Alliance leader wanted more proof of the release or the carnage would begin.

Chapter Forty-Eight

The Sniper

A large number of protesters and onlookers at the release site were taken into custody by the Israeli police. This accomplished two things: one, it most likely eliminated anyone in the crowd from reporting back to Dunait and the terrorists; and two, it prevented an escalation by the protesters, further securing the safety of the twenty political prisoners. As Dunait was trying to figure out how he could get a firm confirmation that his countrymen were set free, his cell phone rang with a number that was not familiar to him. He let it ring a number of times before he answered: "Hello, who is calling, please?"

"It is an old friend who worked with you when you were part of the Israeli military." Dunait was confused; he hadn't been part of the military for many years. However, he had worked as a soldier for over five years before he became disenchanted with the military goals and the policies that they supported. It was then that he vocalized his discontent and decided to actively oppose the regime by joining the Alliance Cell in Israel. So, the caller had to be someone who he knew over twenty years ago. Why would someone who he knew that far in his past be contacting him now?

Dunait spoke: "You have me at a disadvantage, but presently I cannot play a guessing game. I am involved in serious business that demands my strict attention." By the tone of Dunait's voice, the caller realized that Dunait was about to disconnect and terminate the conversation. Although Dunait was curious as to the identification of the caller and the reason for the call, he had more demanding things to think about. The caller interrupted Dunait's thinking process by saying: "For your information, I was at the designated release site for the twenty prisoners. Although the majority of the people there were arrested, I was able to take cover and evade the efforts of the soldiers. I saw the entire event."

The caller now had the attention of Dunait. If the caller was able to confirm the release, then the plan could proceed as scheduled; but before Dunait could place any truth in the information that would be revealed to him, he had to know the caller's name and his reputation for speaking the truth. Dunait got right to the point: "Before I listen to anything you have to say, I want to know who you are and why you want to ally yourself with me." The caller responded: "You knew me as 'Goldie', or as 'Corporal Gollman'; however, I am now former General Abel Gollman of the Israeli Army." Dunait could not believe his ears. He was speaking to one of the most feared military leaders in Israel, "The Barbarian."

Dunait took a deep breath as he mentally digested what was taking place: "I have not seen or spoken to you in over twenty years, and you have been one of the most trusted leaders in the Israeli hierarchy. You have been a formidable adversary, and your focus was to destroy any dissenting factions. Why are you now contacting me?"

"Apparently, in the eyes of my superiors, I have failed, and you know how the military deals with failures. My predecessor was found floating in a canal behind the American Embassy. I do not want to end up like that! I have been on the run for days now, but I learned of the prison release location. I was there when the prison bus pulled up. I was lucky to have escaped the lock-up, but I must be quick because there are still soldiers in the area." Dunait, satisfied with the level of veracity, listened carefully: "Okay General, what do you have to tell me?"

Gollman related the entire procedure up until the smoke condition. He then said: "When the smoke cleared, there was no sign of the prisoners. No prisoners stepped off of the bus and, in my opinion, there were never any prisoners on the bus." Dunait argued that he actually saw the twenty men board the bus. Gollman said: "You might have seen the images of the twenty men boarding the bus, but in reality, the prisoners never left their cells. You've been duped by an imaging process that was developed not so long ago. I know you might think that I have a goal of revenge in telling you this, but ask yourself, why then did the soldiers clear everyone from the site? Let me answer. They did it so that a spy who you may have planted could not report back to you. I believe it worked. I was able to secure good cover, and thus far, I have been lucky, but my luck can quickly run out."

As Gollman finished his sentence, Dunait heard a voice in the background yelling: "Hey you. Stop or I will fire. Stop!" Dunait then heard the faint sound of gunfire. The phone disconnected and Gollman joined his predecessor. His luck had just run out!

Dunait witnessed what he believed was Abel Gollman's last moments on earth; and Dunait was more convinced that Gollman was telling the truth. That meant that the twenty prisoners were still incarcerated, and that Israel had, once again, lied. He was not going to let them win again. He contacted Falco, and told him to order the execution of ten hostages, and to make certain that it was on camera so that everyone could see. Erman Falco did not understand why the order was given since the prisoner exchange went so well. He questioned Dunait: "I don't understand. We have won. Ordering hostages killed will only make our safe escape more difficult. Why are we doing this?"

"You know better than to question my decisions. We did not win. Israel and the United States have tricked us into believing that the prisoners were released. What we witnessed was a fake video image of the men. They are still in their cells in Jalecya. Now, do as I tell you. Begin the executions!" Falco was taken aback by the news and didn't understand how they were able to see the prisoner release that didn't occur. He answered Dunait: "Do you want me to start with the police chief?"

"That is an excellent idea. I want everyone to see that their leaders are just as vulnerable as anyone else. When you finish with the chief, tell our men to pick nine others, and they should include at least one of the detectives. When that is done, contact Sergeant Dello and tell him that the original threat of ten hostages killed for every thirty-minute delay in freeing our countrymen is in effect. Erman, if we have to kill all two hundred people to win, we will, and the police have to believe that we will do it. Apparently, this is the only way to convince them."

Falco got off the phone and knew what his marching orders were. However, he still had to get Alex to pull the trigger. Since the conversation with Dunait was anything but a whisper, Alex heard the general context of the call. He, once again, would be put in the position of executioner. This time, however, Erman Falco would be on his guard for any deception. It was going to be a lot harder for Alex to escape the task.

Falco untied Alex and got him to his feet. The Director again rearranged the camera so that only the chief, tied to a chair, and Alex, with gun in hand, would be seen on the screen. Alex, because of his reluctance to cooperate, earned a punch in the kidneys. He fell to the floor in pain but was immediately lifted up and put in the firing position again. He was ordered to raise the gun and fire. Alex refused and went down again with a sharp blow to the head. He was beside himself. He had run out of options. If he didn't shoot the chief, he would be shot. He didn't want to kill anyone, but he had an obligation to his family to remain alive and take care of them.

Finally, when Alex was given the order for the third time, he raised his gun and pointed it at the bound sacrifice.

Just like the last time, Falco moved to the doorway to remove himself from the camera range; however, he pointed his weapon directly at Alex. Seeing what was about to happen, Sergeant Dello kept ringing the administrative office in an effort to stop what amounted to the murder of the Chief of Brooklyn South. Erman Falco paid no attention to the ringing and urged Alex to fire.

The NYPD sniper team had been in position for the duration of the "takeover" and were just waiting for the "clear-to-fire" signal to employ their expertise. When Erman Falco moved to the doorway and out of camera range, he came within range of the sniper's scope. The special unit officer focused on the target, Erman Falco, and notified headquarters that he had a clear shot at the terrorist. He awaited the "good-to-go" signal to come over the radio. Something had to be done to save the chief's life, and because Falco had his weapon pointed at Alex, it was assumed that Alex did not want to play executioner.

With Erman Falco being eliminated, the thinking was that the chief would be out of danger. At the constant and demanding urging of Erman Falco, Alex slowly exerted pressure on the trigger. As Alex began his journey into murderous oblivion, the police sniper was alerted to the "good-to-go" signal on the radio. The sniper's rifle sent a round through the secretary's window that Alex had used to give the "Okay" sign to his two comrades who had waited in the car on the trip back from the safe house. The round found its target, and Erman Falco went down. The shot sent shock waves through Alex, and he dropped the gun to the floor. He raised his hands in surrender and hoped that he would not be the next target. When Alex dropped his gun, Dunait immediately got on the phone wanting to know what happened. However, Erman Falco was unable to answer his cell phone. With Falco not responding, Dunait had to resort to the violence of plan "B". The slaughter was about to begin.

Chapter Forty-Nine

The Explosion

With the Sniper firing at Falco, all of the other police units were given the "go" signal. This occurred simultaneously with an order that was given by Dunait to the armed terrorists inside the west wing. Fortunately, the specialized police units reacted more quickly than the terrorists. Emergency Service experts dropped through the skylights, accurately firing their weapons as they descended. Other officers broke through the electronically locked entrance doors with canine officers leading the way. The Emergency Service Officers were locating and firing at any armed individuals. Seema, the undercover Israeli agent, was one of those armed individuals. Marty, Donna and Tony, still lying in Donna's lap, had been previously dragged back to the edge of the group of cowering hostages.

Marty knew that Seema would be seen as an armed adversary, so he tackled Seema to the ground, disarming him and potentially saving his life. As Seema went down due to Marty's quick thinking, Seema's cell partner also went down. He had been fatally wounded by an Emergency Service Police Officer. Seeing their fellow cell members being shot by the advancing police units, the remaining members laid down their weapons and tried to disappear into the large crowd of former hostages that they were guarding. However, the hostages gave up the cell members to the approaching police officers. All of the Alliance members in the west wing had either been killed, wounded or arrested – all but one.

Ismul Rahej, the Senior Security Guard, had successfully convinced the police and the fearful hostages that he too had suffered at the hands of the terrorists. In fact, the police employed Ismul to use his access card and allow them entry into the administrative offices which had been under siege. When the police gained entry and proceeded to the offices, they found Erman Falco fatally wounded and near death, Alex Hassid, still in the state of shock, and the

Brooklyn Borough Chief, who was still bound to his death chair.

The first order of business, of course, was to release the chief while securing the other offices. When they entered Bob Baxter's Office, they found Bob and the Task Force Captain who accompanied the chief, lying dead on the floor. When they entered Reginald Winsten's office, they saw that he had bled out and was propped up, still in a sitting position, against the far wall. Alex Hassid was hand-cuffed and taken into custody, and the Emergency Medical Technicians were called for Erman Falco.

Ismul was able to move a little closer to Falco and gain a line-of-sight position with him. Falco was able to nod toward the electronics board that was directly above him and put up two fingers for Ismul to see. Knowing that by his next action he would give up his guise as a victim of the terrorists, Ismul, the loyal exponent of the cause, lunged at the toggle switch labeled number two and pushed it. The Borough Chief saw Ismul and realized that the toggle switch was labeled "Police Van". He pushed Ismul out of the way, ordered his arrest and took an officer's radio: "This is Chief Jansen. Evacuate the Headquarters Vehicle immediately. There is a bomb. Evacuate! Evacuate!"

Lucky for the law enforcement members in the van, the bomb had been wired with a delay so that the resident of the fake white "Police" van, parked right in front of the

Temporary Headquarters Van, would have time to escape from possible harm. The police officers and federal agents inside of the Headquarters Van, hearing Chief Jansen's direct order, reacted quickly and exited without delay. When the last person out, Sergeant Mario Dello, was about twenty-five feet away from the van, the group witnessed an explosion that was deafening as well as totally devastating. Luckily, no one in the group was injured.

Dunait, the original reason why there was a delay on the timing trigger of the bomb, did not have access to a police radio; so, he did not hear Chief Jansen give the order to evacuate. However, since the area around the van was being monitored by Falco's handy camera work, Dunait saw the police personnel running out of their van and running from the vehicle. He hesitated but decided that it was better to be safe than sorry. He saw what was happening in the west wing, and he knew that his members were being killed or captured. His plan had failed, but he wanted to live another day, develop another plan and continue to fight against the perceived unjust rule of Israel.

As he slid open his van door, the Temporary Headquarters Vehicle exploded sending pieces of metal everywhere. The concussion of the explosion sent Dunait careening back into the van and landing on the floor. As he attempted to get up and escape, he heard a clang, a piece of metal from the Temporary Headquarters Van crashing into his vehicle. Unfortunately for him, a metal piece penetrated the gas tank, and the red-hot metal ignited the fuel that was in the tank. The police officers witnessed a second massive explosion, one which eliminated any chance of Dunait formulating another plan against the Government of Israel. There would be no plan, there would be no Dunait.

Back in the administrative offices, both explosions were seen and heard on the monitor. Across Falco's face, Ismul and the chief saw what they believed to be the beginnings of a smile - a smile from a dying man. As the Emergency Medical Technicians attempted to save Falco, he whispered loud enough so that all could hear: "He killed my son!" His smile grew wide, and then he died.

Ismul confessed to the locations of the explosives and gas pellets. The siege, however, was far from over. According to police procedures, every one of the hostages had to be interviewed, and the remaining cell members had to be processed and charged. Additionally, the members of the Alliance would be interrogated as to information on additional chapters or plans. These interrogations would be initiated by both local and federal authorities. Unlike what Israel had done, the United States would invite Israeli Intelligence to assist in the interrogations since much of what occurred was focused on the actions in Israel.

In addition to everything else, there would be a formal inquiry into the delay that Israel created in notifying the United States of what was a plausible terrorist attack. Ambassador Richarson would have his work cut out for him. He would be the lead investigation into the lack of intelligence sharing. The relationship between him and his counterpart would never be the same.

As for the Secretary of State, Daniel Walden, his pointed warning to Israel came with a guaranteed reduction in both financial and material support. It was the strong leaning of both Dan Walden and President Lawrence Howard that the trust they once shared with the Government of Israel had been diminished. Additional United States support would have to be earned over time. Unfortunately for Israel, irreparable damage might have been done, and the United States has a long memory.

On the floor of the west wing at the Three Kings Shopping Center, Emergency Medical Technicians were tending to the wounds of Detective Tony Ossur. He was very weak and had lost a lot of blood. He laid with Donna who was holding his head in her lap. At one point, he held up his hand and forced the EMT's to stop. He motioned to Marty to come close so that he could whisper into his ear. As Marty bent down to listen, Tony said: "I told you I'd never go to prison. Please, take care of her." Marty, who usually always had a retort, could say nothing.

Tony turned toward Donna and motioned her to come closer. She bent her head down so she could hear, and Tony whispered: "I am so sorry." Donna, through her tears, was able to say: "I know." Tony looked from Donna to Marty, smiled and closed his eyes. Detective Tony Ossur took his final breath. Marty could hold back the tears no longer as his face glistened with a stream of water. Donna, who was also awash in tears, turned and hugged Marty as she sobbed with grief. They were closer now than they had ever been before. Anthony (Tony) Ossur died on Christmas Day - his birthday.

Chapter Fifty

An Inspector's Funeral

There was a line of uniformed officers that seemed like it extended for miles. They were all at attention and in rank. If one looked closely, he could see that the patch on their uniforms was different for a lot of the officers, which meant that many different departments were represented, different cities, different states, and in some instances, different countries. One could also see the traditional bagpipe section of the New York City Police Department ceremonial unit. It is the Ceremonial Unit of the New York City Police Department that handles all of the arrangements for an "Inspector's Funeral", one of the highest honors a deceased member of the Police Department can receive. It is rendered to a deceased member who died in the line of duty. Unfortunately, these events happen all too often.

In the past two weeks, the Ceremonial Unit had to make arrangements to schedule four of these funerals. The scheduling included notifications to the Mayor's Office, the Bishops Office, City and State Legislators, and a country-wide advisement to all law enforcement agencies. The Patrolmen's Benevolent Association, the Detectives' Endowment Association and the other fraternal organizations also play a large role in organizing and notifying different constituents. They are also the ones who take care of the arrangements for the family of the deceased. The family is escorted by the association to which the deceased member belonged. From the pick up to the drive home, the Association never leaves the family. It is explained to the family that they will always be a part of the Association.

The first Inspector's Funeral was arranged for Detective Sergeant Laura Noldir. The Sergeant's Benevolent Association escorted Laura's wife and mother to the Sacred Heart Church where the Funeral Mass was being celebrated. Laura's wife was carrying their young, adopted daughter who was only 14 months old.

Laura had been raised in Queens County, and the streets of Queens were filled with grieving onlookers. The church was filled with police personnel from the Police Commissioner on down. There was very little space in the church for other than police officers, and that is the way it should be. Outside of her immediate family, the officers were the people who would miss her the most. These were her co-workers, her trusted friends, her confidants and her other family.

Following the Holy Mass, some of the police officers who were closest to the Detective Sergeant, were allowed to make comments about Laura. The most pointed speech was delivered by Laura Noldir's Commanding Officer. He emphasized the Sergeant's dedication to her job, and how she approached each assignment with the steadfast determination that was needed to offer a valued solution to whatever problem she faced. Her partners in the Sex Crimes Unit offered their personal insight into how Laura treated them, and they emphasized that she was the best supervisor they had ever had. It was her kind and concerned approach that they would sorely miss. It was a feeling that did not need to be expressed as tear-filled eyes reflected their affection for Detective Sergeant Laura Noldir.

Three days later, the streets were once again filled with uniformed officers. This time, the parish of St. Martin of Tours in Seaford, Long Island, hosted the Inspector's

Funeral for Task Force Captain Bret Lauder. He had accompanied the Brooklyn Borough Chief to the scene of the terrorist takeover. Although there may have been different police representatives present for this funeral, the number was approximately the same, and the streets were lined with uniforms for as far as the eye could see. Again, the hierarchy of the New York City Police Department was present, but this time, since St. Martin's was a large structure, many of the community people were able to attend the service. Even though there was additional space, the Church was bursting at the seams with the number of occupants. The speeches were similar, but had, as expected, different speakers.

Captain Lauder had been on the force for over twenty years and had supervised many officers. He made many friends and was lauded for his leadership under pressure. The task force is utilized to supplement the officers in the local precinct. The officers in the task force had more riot training, and crowd control training than the average precinct officer; so, the task force was called upon to respond to such events as protests and riots. How the police reacted in these circumstances was mostly dependent upon the leadership of the ranking officers, and Captain Bret Lauder was excellent under pressure. The Police Commissioner, who personally knew the Captain, praised him for his tact and calming approach in situations where others might tend to escalate the problem. The bagpipes pumped again as the hearse pulled away from the church and proceeded, as was the custom, to drive through the neighborhood where the Captain and his family resided. His family remained strong, which only added to the solemness of the very sad situation. His youngest son, also a member of the New York City Police Department, comforted his family, but remained with the uniformed force and saluted his father as the coffin passed by in the hearse.

An exception to the requirements needed to have an Inspector's Funeral, one of which is to have been an active member of the Department who died in the line of duty, was one given to retired Sergeant Bob Baxter. Sergeant Baxter was one of the casualties of the terrorist takeover, and because of that, and the fact that he was a relatively new retiree, was given an Inspector's Funeral. This was rare, but it was the opinion of the police brass that he had earned this show of respect. He had worked closely with the Police Department and added to the ease with which police and detectives could perform their duties. Again, the house of worship, St Matthews Catholic Church in Bayport, Long Island, was filled to the hilt. The fact that participants were attending an Inspector's Funeral for Bob Baxter added little comfort to the overall grief felt by everyone there.

This Holy Mass was somewhat unique since one of the celebrants was a young priest who had been ordained just one year ago, Bob Baxter's young son. His eulogy was different as it combined the grief he felt with the joy of his father reaping his final reward with God in heaven. It was the company line of the Catholic Church, but hard for many people to displace the grief with the joy of knowing their deceased relative was now in a better place. However, Father Baxter was somewhat effective in soothing the loss that his sister, brother and mother were now feeling.

The final Inspector's Funeral was in honor of Detective Anthony (Tony) Ossur. Marty had attended all the funerals so far, but this one, as expected, was the most difficult. Marty had been asked by the Ceremonial Unit if he wanted to be one of the pole bearers. It was an honor that Marty was not expecting, but unfortunately one that he could not readily accept. He could not bear the fact that he was carrying his partner, his friend, to his final resting place. It was hard enough just looking at the coffin that contained his partner, let alone carrying him away. Marty was in civilian clothes positioned with the rest of the detectives who attended the funeral. The Brooklyn South Squad, with Sergeant Mario Dello leading, lined the steps of St. Francis of Assisi, forming the honor guard for Tony's casket. Marty entered the church with Myrna and escorted her to the area reserved for "family."

He then went outside and met with Donna and escorted her into another section of the church. Once again,

St. Francis was a large facility, so many of the community people were allowed into the service. This was an advantage for Marty since the odds of the two women bumping into each other were remote. It seemed that even in death, Tony placed Marty in a compromising position. Marty just had to be sure that at the conclusion of the Mass, the women left from different exits.

Marty was asked if he wanted to speak, eulogizing his partner, Tony. Again, although he wanted to relate many things about his partner, he knew that he would not be able to finish, so he bowed out. He was also in turmoil regarding the recent incidents in which Tony was involved. It was hard to barter hypocrisy with veracity. Marty would not speak. Marty had enough problems to work out in keeping two of Tony's paramours from colliding.

Detective Tony Ossur had been a very active investigator and had a great reputation for "closing" cases. There were many accolades and interesting stories regarding Tony's journey through his twenty-three years in the Department. The Brooklyn streets were lined with an infinite number of uniforms but an even greater number of civilian on-lookers. Tony had been a son of Brooklyn, and they loved him. The service came to an end with the bagpipes leading the way out of the church. Marty kept an eye on both Myrna and Donna. Things seemed to be going well as they started to leave via the exit closest to them. This forced them to walk in opposite directions. Marty breathed a sigh of relief and mentally confirmed to Tony that things were "okay."

As Marty finally got to the back door, he gazed over the swelling crowd and couldn't believe his eyes. He saw people hugging and consoling each other, but he noticed two particular people hugging and comforting each other. Myrna and Donna were entangled in each other's arms. They were crying and sharing their moment of grief, and it seemed that it was a relief for them to actually come out of the shadows. Marty was shocked but displayed a small smile of comfort and disbelief. They knew all along. Tony had fooled no one!

Chapter Fifty-One

Four Years Later

A lot can happen in four years, and it has. The Hassid family was once again reunited after Alex served his three years in a Federal Penitentiary. He was released on "good behavior." Alex had cooperated with federal authorities and testified against the remaining members of the Alliance. As a result of his cooperation, he was handed down a minimum sentence. However, it was advised that the family be given protection by the United States Federal Marshals. This meant that Alex would no longer see his family who would be moved to an undisclosed location.

Although this would be difficult for everyone, it was decided that to better ensure the safety of his mother and sister, the family should take the offer that the Marshal Service put on the table. They were now residents in the witness protection program.

The threat of retaliation against Alex and his family was real. Alex's testimony facilitated the prosecution of several individuals who ultimately received long term prison sentences. So, Alex was constantly looking over his shoulder. His mother remained sullen and did not like the arrangements that she was forced to live under; but for her safety and that of her daughter, Rachael, she reluctantly accepted her fate. Rachael had fully recovered from her ordeal and, under an assumed name and with the help of the Marshall Service, was in her senior year of college. Her degree in Criminal Science was the first step toward her goal toward becoming a Criminal Psychologist.

Through the offerings at the Federal Penitentiary, Alex was able to finish College and earn a degree in Education. While incarcerated, he started a program for other inmates to increase their knowledge of the English language and build upon whatever writing skills they possessed. Again, with the help of the Federal Marshal Service, he was now employed as an instructor at a halfway house supported by the Federal Government. He lived with the dread that he could never see his family, but with the comfort that their safety was somewhat ensured; and maybe, down the road, there would be some way to safely meet with his family, even for just a few moments.

Ambassador Donald Richardson worked long and hard to re-develop a trusted working relationship with Israel. He was successful in formulating a document that was signed by representatives from both the United States and Israel. This document guaranteed, under penalty of permanently reduced support, the timely and accurate exchange of intelligence information and any other information deemed to be necessary for either country to know.

As a result of his efforts, he was promoted to a position in the re-elected President's Cabinet. President Lawrence Howard was reelected to pilot the "U.S.S. United States" for another four years. Much of the credit for ensuring the safety of the hostages went to the President as he was the one responsible for gaining whatever cooperation people felt Israel gave. President Howard also re-appointed Dan Walden as the Secretary of State. Dan had done a good job in directing his subordinates in a time of crisis. Dan was cool and calm under pressure and always made sure that the President was kept up to date on any important or developing situations. He was an asset that the President strongly relied upon.

The President also continued the appointment of the Director of the Central Intelligence Agency and the Director of the Federal Bureau of Investigation. They had both played an integral role in relaying information and making informed judgment calls throughout the crisis. Howard also made arrangements for undercover Israeli agent, Seema Jacobs, to receive the highest civilian award that the United States could offer, the Medal of Freedom. As a result of Seema's quick actions, he saved the lives of a number of hostages. President Howard presented this award to Seema in front of Congress at the State of the Union Address.

The New York City Police Department's Chief of Brooklyn South, Barry Jansen, went on extended leave before resuming his challenging responsibilities. After becoming a hostage and his life just seconds away from being snuffed out by a young man who was being pressured to pull the trigger, Jansen reluctantly assumed his position as Chief of the very busy borough of Brooklyn. However, he just wasn't the same individual, and his reluctance was noticed by the upper echelon of the Department. Chief Barry Jansen was a valued asset for the Department, and the Police Commissioner was not ready to let such talent go by the wayside.

Timing is everything, and the Chief of Personnel had just submitted his retirement papers. Therefore, the Chief of

Personnel position was soon to be open for appointment. This would be a perfect transfer position for the Chief of Brooklyn South. The change would be good and the reduction in stress level would help Jansen get back to his old ways. Against the advice of some of the Headquarters' Chiefs, the three-and four-star vintage, the Police Commissioner made up his mind. If Barry Jansen were transferred to the Chief of Personnel position, it would result in a promotion since the new position would raise him from a two-star Chief to a three-star Chief.

Police politics being what they are, the existing Chiefs had their own ideas as to who should be promoted and get the coveted third star. Their recommendations and suggestions were welcomed, but the Commissioner had already decided. He wasn't going to lose an intelligent leader, and one who earned the promotion. Borough Chief Barry Jansen was now Chief of Personnel Barry Jansen.

What happened to the personnel who were assigned to the Brooklyn South Detective Squad? Sergeant Mario Dello, who had taken the Lieutenant's Civil Service Promotion test, was notified that Civil Service had reached his number for promotion. The Sergeant was promoted to Lieutenant and, because of his prior training and experience, was appointed as the Commanding Officer of the Police Department Hostage Negotiation Unit. This was a position that was well respected by the entire Department.

Many Lieutenants would have liked the position, but Lieutenant Mario Dello earned it. His promotion and appointment as Commanding Officer left a vacancy for another line negotiator.

One of those officers who applied for the position of "negotiator" was Detective Gary Glasser from the Brooklyn South Detective Squad. Sergeant Dello had seen Detective Glasser in action a number of times and was impressed with his patience and calmness under pressure. Del had seen Glasser mediate intense arguments right in the squad room. Detective Gary Glasser would be the ideal candidate for the position, and with some technical training that he would have to complete, Glasser might become the best negotiator the Brooklyn South Hostage Negotiating team might have.

With Sergeant Dello being promoted, a vacancy existed for the position of Commanding Officer of the Brooklyn South Detective Squad. This was also a position that many bosses would like and to which many applied. The appointment to this position involved several variables. After much discussion and consideration, the Chief of Detectives Office in conjunction with the Police Commissioner's Office, and input from some very influential political leaders, a Sergeant who had been in the rank for only a short time, but had an outstanding record was being considered. The Sergeant, who had suffered a significant loss as a result of distinguished police action, was officially appointed. Sergeant Robert Lauder was now the Commanding Officer of the Brooklyn South Detective Squad. This was a surprise to many, but no one argued the fact that having lost his father to an executioner should surely weigh heavily on a final decision for appointment.

Having been in command for only a short period of time and still learning the "ins and outs" of Detective Squad work, Sergeant Lauder was called to the scene of an apparent homicide. It was the holiday season, once again, and the streets were filled with shoppers. The Three Kings Shopping Mall was also bustling as usual with last-minute gift-getters. Sergeant Lauder responded to the rear alley of the west wing of the shopping mall. The apparently tortured body of a young male lay in a dumpster just inside of the loading gate. The scene was gruesome and something that the Sergeant was not used to seeing. Feeling the bile rise in his throat, he quickly turned away and avoided the embarrassment of heaving in front of his detectives.

Lying in the half-full dumpster was a male approximately twenty-five years of age. His eyes had been plucked out and attached with toothpicks to his chest. Both ears had large nails protruding from them – nails that surely were hammered directly through the eardrum right into the brain. His tongue had been cut out of his mouth and stapled across his glued lips. To say that this homicide was meant to send a message was an understatement. Alex Hassid no longer had to look over his shoulder, in fact, he couldn't. Alex had taken a calculated risk in cooperating with the authorities, and, at least, for a short time benefited from it. He knew that sooner or later his time might run out. That time was now.

Also at the scene was the new Director of Security for the Three Kings Shopping Center. The homicide involved mall property and therefore, management had to know some of the specifics. The Director approached Sergeant Lauder: "Excuse me, Sarge. Let me introduce myself. I'm Martin Iniddor, the Director of Security for the shopping mall." The Sergeant knew the name and knew that Iniddor had, at one time not so long ago, been a member of the Squad that he now commanded. Sergeant Lauder shared whatever information he could with the Director, but Marty knew that a message had been sent when it came to the work of the terrorists: "You do not see anything, you do not hear anything, and you never say anything."

Following the terrorist incident, and shortly after his return to work, Marty realized that things would never be the same without his partner. He struggled with his feelings every day. Following up on a case in the mall, Marty had to interview the new General Manager. As he introduced himself to the manager, who, of course, was aware of what had recently occurred there, the General Manager acknowledged the fact that Detective Iniddor had been intricately involved in the final resolution of the horrific event.

After answering all of the questions posed by Detective Iniddor, the manager asked the detective how long he planned to remain with the Police Department. This question hit home with Marty because he had been thinking about packing it in. What ensued was a long conversation about the aspects of the security position in the mall. The conversation actually evolved into an employment interview and before he knew it, Detective Marty Iniddor had accepted the position of the Director of Security for the Three Kings Shopping Center. Approximately two weeks later and having turned in his retirement papers, former Brooklyn South Detective Martin Iniddor was sitting behind the desk that was once occupied by retired Police Sergeant Bob Baxter. Marty thought about his future and hoped it would not end up the same way as Bob's had.

As Detective Iniddor was leaving on the day of the informal interview, a familiar face was approaching the entrance to the administrative offices. A detective from the Sex Crimes Unit was coming into the office to interview the General Manager on the complaint of a female worker. Both men stopped in recognition and surprise. Detective Paul Staffio had never fully physically recovered from the serious injuries he had incurred in the vehicle accident that killed Detective Sergeant Laura Noldir. Because of his physical disability, Staffio was mostly assigned to paperwork for which the Sex Crime Unit was responsible. However, in this case, he was assisting the assigned investigator with routine interviews. Marty stopped and acknowledged Staffio: "Hey Paul, how are you doing? I heard that you were transferred to the Sex Crimes Unit. How do you like it?"

"I'm doing well, Marty, Thanks. I'm never going to be one hundred percent, but I can hold my own, and the Sex Crimes Unit is the right place for me. The guys have been great, and we've really been getting along." Marty responded: "That's good to hear. By the way, did anyone make any progress on the hit and run that got you and Laura?"

Paul was surprised that Marty had not heard: "I thought you guys knew. Shortly after the accident, we were able to identify the driver, but by the time we were able to respond for the arrest, the driver had met with a fatal accident. He was working under a car when the hydraulic lift gave way, and the car landed on top of him, instantly killing him. The lift was inspected and found to be in proper working order; so, we are looking at the possibility that someone intentionally released the lift." For some reason, Marty's thoughts immediately went to his partner. He thought: "Tony, you didn't?"

Paul interrupted Marty's quick thought and said: "Well, it was good to see you, and I was very sorry to hear about your partner."

"Thanks, Paul. Well, I should be on my way. Take care." Marty left and Paul attended to his business. As Marty headed for his police ride, he knew his decision to leave the public sector and become a member of the private sector would thrill his wife, Lisa. Things had been somewhat strained since his ordeal at the mall. There would be less pressure and more time for them to spend together. He was anxious to let his wife know and to see her reaction. He knew it would be a good one. She would hear the words she was hoping to hear for a long time: "I'm retiring."

The Brooklyn South Detective Squad had been decimated by transfers, promotions, retirements, and death. Mario Dello was now a Lieutenant and Commanding Officer of the Hostage Negotiating Team. Detective Gary Glasser joined Del's team and was in training to become a Police Department Hostage Negotiator. Detective Jim Jones, who had just over fifteen years on the job, decided to retire early and become a partner with his brother-in-law in a talent agency. Jim knew nothing about the business, but his brother-in-law knew everything. The business had grown so much that it was becoming impossible to manage for one individual; but Dave, Jim's relative, trusted no one except his brother-in-law, Jim. There was plenty of money to be made and many interesting people to meet. Jim Jones fit in really well and became a successful partner in the business.

Detective Frank Austin, the other black Detective assigned to the Squad, only had about 2 to 3 years left before full retirement, and he could do that standing on his head. He was content staying in the Squad and waiting for his retirement date.

It was rumored that Detective Juan Medina, who also took early retirement – 15 years, was the manager of a brothel on the east side of the upper Bronx. It was also rumored that the brothel was patronized by many important people, but the reputation the brothel had for confidentiality was second to none, so the clientele were relatively comfortable returning time and time again as steady customers to pay for the unusual favors that the ladies offered. Juan had utilized many of the contacts he had made when he worked in Vice, and the workers were more than happy to come on board. The profits were outstanding for both the workers and for Juan. The only thing he had to worry about was the occasional visit from Public Morals Officers, but that was well taken care of.

Detective Angel Torres was still determined to help the Puerto Rican Community in any way that he could. He met with families, advised youths on their potential, and became a one-man recruiter for the New York City Police Department. This was all done in addition to solving cases.

He had become a fixture in the Brooklyn South Squad and was going nowhere else.

Since no one really ever pushed Detective Ralph Clemengas, he was happy to remain the lazy non-productive cop he had always been. However, with the new Commanding Officer, Sergeant Lauder, he was being looked at more carefully and was being held to a higher standard than before. If things got to the point that it became uncomfortable for him, Clemengas would put in a transfer to his old stomping grounds, the youth gang task force. He was there as a cop, and he was sure that with all of his street connections, they would welcome him back as a detective. However, for now he was okay with things and would bide his time.

Detective Ira Jacobs, who was influential in getting Gary Glasser transferred to the Squad, was never really happy being an investigator. He yearned for the days when he was out of the limelight and responsible for nothing but answering office phones and scheduling meetings for the chaplain. That was when he was a cop. His promotion to detective necessitated a transfer and thus his assignment to the Brooklyn South Detective Squad. However, since his first day in the Squad, he was looking for a way to get back to the Chaplain's Office. He was very good friends with the Jewish Chaplain who originally tried to keep him in the office, but the politics, at the time, did not allow for such an obvious "contract."

Things had changed, however, and a detective assigned to the Chaplain's Office could also be utilized as a liaison to the Jewish Community. It was with this introduction to the Police Commissioner that the transfer of Detective Ira Jacobs was approved. Ira did not like the street, and it was rumored that he feared it. As a result of his present transfer, Detective Ira Jacobs would never have to worry about the street or Detective Nick Possidos again.

One could say that Nick Possidos was actually happy to see Ira Jacobs go. They never saw eye-to-eye. Nick felt that Ira was always looking over his shoulder to correct a mistake the Greek had made or to clarify the pronunciation of an English word that had been influenced with a strong Greek accent. It seemed that Ira was always looking for the opportunity to embarrass Nick, and in a couple of instances, this perceived attitude brought the two Detectives to yelling matches and very close to physical involvement.

No one knows why it continued because Nick towered over Ira and would have destroyed him if they entered into combat. If it wasn't for the rest of the Squad always being on high alert to separate the combatants whenever the two were working the same shift, Ira Jacobs would have had a continuous residency at Inter-County

General Hospital. Maybe, that was what Ira really wanted, to retire on three quarters pay; however, it was a risky and painful way to acquire a tax-free pension. So, to say the least, Detective Nick Possidos was more than happy to see Ira Jacobs leave. It made Nick's stay in the squad all the more pleasant because he was not planning on going anywhere.

Lastly, the desk that had once held the ideas, suggestions, resolutions, paperwork, confidential files and a daffodil of one of the most experienced, streetwise detectives on the force was now being occupied by a young, inexperienced, wet-behind-the-ears poor excuse for an investigator. His name is Billy Jansen, yes that's right, the same last name as the former Brooklyn South Borough Chief and now the three Star Chief of Personnel, Barry Jansen. Now, no one is saying that it's an impossibility that after four years on the job, one can't earn a detective's gold shield, but in four years on the job, the probability of one earning a coveted detective's position, especially one in the Brooklyn South Squad, is very unlikely. So, it was correctly assumed that his father played a significant role in the decision to appoint Billy Jansen to the position of "detective."

It was especially difficult for Marty to look across his desk at the one directly opposite his and see it vacant. It was even more difficult to see it occupied by someone else, not his partner, a stranger. The vacancy and then the ultimate recent appointment played a significant role in Marty's final decision to leave. Although founded on nothing but emotion, Marty could not accept the reality that his partner was not there, and that someone else was sitting where Tony should be. In fact, it was even difficult for Marty to be face-to-face with the newcomer. It was not because of Marty's evaluation of Jansen's experience or capabilities. It had nothing to do with that. It was just that Detective Billy Jansen could never be and would never be Detective Anthony (Tony) Ossur. He would never earn the title or position of "partner." Unfortunately, as far as Marty was concerned, no one would. Yeah, a lot can happen in four years, and it has!

Chapter Fifty-Two

Epilogue

It's that time of the year again. It never fails to bring out the best in most people but the worst in some. The holiday season is unique in its dressings and obvious with the infusion of the sometimes bitterly cold weather that accompanies it. However, that cold weather supports the joyful anticipation of a possible white Christmas. Four years have passed since that horrible Holiday season that some will never forget, and that others hope will fade from their memory. People still arrive by the carloads to the mall, but if you look closely, many are apprehensive and shop with the idea of making a hasty exit as quickly as possible from the one-time scene of chaos and tragedy.

For the Director of Security at the Three Kings Shopping Center, the season is filled with new challenges, but more so with the sad memory of the loss of someone very dear to him. The season also brought those solemn times flooding back into Donna's consciousness. She still worked at the Compass Travel Agency but now was charged with the responsibilities of the Agency Manager. Whenever she could, she would go to Starbucks and order her caffeine shot with the intention of always dropping one off for Marty. In some small way, it made her feelings of remorse and longing less severe, and it gave her time to enter into some small conversation that always took her mind off of the obvious, sad, elephant in the room.

Marty welcomed her visits and had gotten a lot closer to that person who had never really appealed to him. In fact, Marty had tried to convince Tony a number of times that Donna wasn't the one for him; but his condemnations of their relationship always fell on deaf ears. Now, Marty wasn't so sure that he was correct in his judgment call. He came to see a different side of Donna, and it overshadowed the negativity he once felt toward her.

In addition to the routine that Donna had developed including Marty every time she visited that high-end coffee solarium, they had both developed a custom, for lack of a better word, regarding visits to Tony on his Christmas Birthday. Neither one had missed a year that they didn't pay their respects to the memory of a partner and lover.

At first, they both went separately and had happened to meet at the gravesite during their visit. However, after the second year, they decided to go together since they would usually meet up there anyway. Marty's wife, Lisa, had no problem with this arrangement and, in fact, encouraged the joint effort. It seemed that Marty came back home from the cemetery better in dealing with the sad circumstances. It was easier when he had someone who was also involved with Tony. They could relish in some happy memories and recall the good times. Marty's wife, Lisa, was not going to become a third wheel when it had to do with two people who were so passionately affected by the existence of another human being.

The journey of Marty and Diane started in Brooklyn, but ultimately led to a small cemetery located in Staten Island. Their visit was always scheduled for Christmas Day. This had two advantages: they were able to wish Tony a "Happy Birthday," and, in a strange way, wish him the best of the holiday season. It brought him back to life in their minds in spite of that Christmas day not so long ago.

This particular Christmas was a bitterly cold one with heavy flurries of that white stuff sticking to everything. It seemed that the car ride was taking forever. The Belt

Parkway was jammed, as usual, and the bad weather added more drama to the already stop-and-go parade. The usual forty-five-minute journey took approximately one hour and twenty minutes. That's a long time to be in traffic, and during these trips, conversation was always at a minimum as both Marty and Donna each dwelled upon their own private memories.

On Christmas Day, the cemetery can be crowded or desolate according to the weather conditions that day. The weather conditions being miserable, it seemed that Marty and Donna had the whole cemetery to themselves. This was not a bonus; however, it just made the whole effort more solemn, more sad.

They left the car and started to walk the short distance to Tony's final resting place, but this visit was different from all the rest. Marty and Donna, always the lone travelers to the cemetery every Christmas Day, were not alone this time. Attached to Donna and walking gleefully along with her was Donna's four-year-old son - a four-year old son whose existence totally surprised Marty. Iniddor had no knowledge of any son and never even knew Donna had been pregnant. It was apparent that Marty had not seen her during her pregnancy.

At first, Marty thought this new addition to be an unwelcome intrusion, but the little guy soon won Marty over. He was a cute kid and really didn't upset any of the usual routines. What the child's presence did do, however, by necessity, was shorten the length of the visit, which maybe wasn't a bad thing.

They stayed for a shorter time than usual because they were both worried about the cold weather and how it affected the child's health. All of the time that they stayed at the gravesite, Donna's son was holding two flowers in his hand. When it was time to leave, and as Marty and Donna bid their silent farewells, Donna's son asked: "Now, Mommy?" Donna nodded a "yes" to her son, and he took one of the flowers from his hand and placed it gently on the grave. He kept the other flower tightly enveloped in his grasp. Marty said nothing but watched tearfully as the young boy placed a daffodil carefully on Tony's grave. As they turned to go, Marty had to ask: "Donna, why does he keep holding the other flower in his hand?"

"You know Marty, for some reason, he likes flowers, and daffodils are his favorite ones. As a matter of fact, he keeps one in his room because he says it makes him feel good. He likes to always have one around." Marty stopped in his tracks as Donna ushered her son along: "Come on, Anthony, let's hurry so your daffodil doesn't die."

Author's Bio:

Martin J. Roddini is a twenty-three-year veteran of the New York City Police Department who served as a Police Officer, Detective and Deputy Chief on loan to the Traffic Department. His expertise led him to the position of Chief of Police with various departments in both New York and New Jersey. He is still active in the law enforcement arena by utilizing his time to conduct survival training for Active Shooter events and creating vulnerability studies for schools and businesses. He has been the Director of Security at a number of Higher Education Facilities and served as a Security Consultant. Martin lives with his family in Nassau County, Long Island and is now devoting his time to his new passion of writing novels.

ACKNOWLEDGEMENTS

I want to thank my son, Marty, and my wife, Lisa, for suggesting that I pick up where I left off many years ago and complete the novel. Without their insistence, it would still remain an incomplete endeavor. Lisa, Marty, and his wife, Ariana, Donna and Bobby have devoted a lot of time proofreading my work, allowing me to produce a more polished creation, thank you. Special thanks to Marty for his perseverance and keen eye in spotting errors and areas of concern. Thank you to my grandson, Christopher, for his computer expertise and unfailing patience with my lack of electronic knowledge. Thanks to both Lauryn and Jenna who also assisted with their computer savvy. I want to thank Dave Manzolillo for the generous amount of time he devoted to creating a cover design that allows the novel to visually come alive. Thanks to Boulevard Books, Avi Gvili, and Aliyah Manuel who took a chance on publishing the work of a brand-new author in the world of creative writing. Many thanks to my friend and author, Anthony Celano, who helped guide me through this first attempt at writing and who never fails in supporting me. Finally, to my former partner, Anthony (Tony) Russo, whose friendship inspired me to write this fictional account of some of the possible experiences that exist in a detective squad, thank you.